Cover design by
www.catherineclarkedesign.co.uk
some design images obtained from Adobe stock

9781915887603

Williams & Whiting (Publishers)
15 Chestnut Grove, Hurstpierpoint,
West Sussex, BN6 9SS

Also by Marilyn Pemberton
from Williams & Whiting

The Jewel Garden
Sold For A Song

The Grandmothers' Footsteps Series:
A Teller of Tales
A Keeper of Tales
A Seeker of Tales

Also by Marilyn Pemberton

Out of the Shadows: the life and works of Mary De Morgan

Under The Eye

by

Marilyn Pemberton

WILLIAMS & WHITING

In loving memory of my mother, Ines Maria Michelina Hammond (née Ellul) (1917 – 2003)

Born Al Qahirah (Cairo), Egypt

Chapter 1

Beattie

Egyptian Museum of Antiquities, Cairo – Monday, January 20th 1936.

There was nothing in the packing case, Mr Sayed assured us, which should be leaking or smelling of excrement.

'I packed the artefacts myself. It contains only small solid objects, nothing that would leak or smell so, so ......'

'Maybe a rat or a cat got inside unnoticed. Marcus, for goodness' sake, stop what you're doing!' My warning came out shriller than intended but it had the desired effect. Marcus, who had been prising the nails that fixed the lid, stopped and looked at me in surprise.

'Whatever is the matter, Beattie? We need to see what's in there.'

'If whatever's in there isn't dead, it's likely to be extremely frightened and probably angry. It might well leap out and bite you. You could catch something horrid. Don't rats carry the bubonic plague?'

'Rats?' Mr Sayed looked horrified. 'Surely not!'

I am always happy to pass on anything my expensive education had taught me. 'There are more rats underground in London than there are people above ground. It would be quite easy for a rat to infiltrate the lower rooms of the British Museum. Where did you pack this case?'

Mr Sayed was short and rotund of torso and face, the latter of which was shiny with perspiration that trickled down his cheeks, by-passing his rather magnificent moustache, over his double chin and disappeared into his white, starched collar. It never ceased to amaze me that middle and upper-class Egyptian men now chose to wear European attire rather than the far cooler and more comfortable *gallebaya*, the long, voluminous

1

robes worn by the *fellahin*, the working-class men. He mopped his face with a pristinely white handkerchief and looked relieved. 'It was on the ground floor. So, it is not likely to be a rat. But Miss Trevethan is right, Mr Dunwoody. You need to take great care when removing the lid.'

Marcus had had an equally expensive though far more useful education. 'The last plague in England was in the seventeenth century. But you're right, we need to be careful. I'll get one of the boys to open it.'

He left the work room, leaving Mr Sayed and me to breathe the fetid air and try and quell our active imaginations. It was a smallish room with white-washed walls, lined with bookshelves sagging under the weight of tomes on the history of ancient Egypt, how to read hieroglyphics, the art of mummification, the Who's Who of pharaonic dynasties and whatever else Marcus and his fellow archaeologists needed to know in order to study and record the artefacts they had dug up in the desert. Unfortunately most of them would be taken to one of the underground rooms here in the Egyptian Museum of Antiquities, Cairo, where they would probably never see the light of day again. The wooden packing case, which Mr Sayed and I were eyeing suspiciously, was about two feet wide by three feet long by three feet deep. It should have contained items that had been loaned to the British Museum and that Mr Sayed, on behalf of the Director of the Department of Antiquities, had been tasked with bringing back home. Due to the value of the contents Mr Sayed had been allowed to take the case onto the aeroplane as luggage, rather than risk putting it in the hold of a ship that would take weeks to journey from England to Egypt.

'Did you have a good trip, Mr Sayed?' I'm a diplomat's daughter; I know how to make polite conversation.

'It was long and tiring and I have a great distrust of aeroplanes. I am not a stupid man, but I do not know how they

2

stay in the air, and this makes me very nervous.' He took one step nearer to the offending case but still far enough away not to be fully overcome by the quite awful smell that was wafting thickly through the small gaps in the wood. 'I've had it with me all the way from the British Museum and it has not been opened until now.'

'Didn't customs open it at Alexandria?'

He shook his head but before he could explain Marcus returned with one of the young Arab boys who did all the work at the excavations and took none of the glory; one, apparently, he was willing to sacrifice. Marcus handed him the crowbar and indicated that he should remove the remaining nails. The boy didn't seem upset by the smell; no doubt it was one he was familiar with where he lived. I had once walked through the old quarter of Cairo where the majority of the working-class Egyptians lived and my lasting impression was of the stench that hung heavily in the air, leaching from the walls that leaned in towards me as I brushed past and rising from the ground at each step.

The boy removed the last nail and with a nod from Marcus threw off the lid. Even he stepped back as the smell gleefully escaped from its confines and enjoyed the luxury of spreading itself into the four corners of the room, assaulting our noses and making us gag. None of us was close enough to see inside although we all tried to peer in.

No crazed animal leapt out.

We all took a tentative step forward, then another. The crate was full to the top with wood shavings that covered whatever it was that I sincerely hoped was now dead. Marcus cautiously took a handful of sawdust and threw it onto the floor. Mr Sayed and I mirrored his action and the boy swept up after us, putting the debris into a sack. We continued emptying the packing case finding nothing until the crate was half empty. Only then did we begin to see the artefacts wrapped in brown paper, which we took out and placed unopened on the side – and a patch of dark blue woollen material. Marcus and I looked enquiringly at Mr Sayed, who shook his head in puzzlement.

Marcus cautiously prodded the material, but we were none the wiser as to what it was.

We carried on throwing more handfuls of shavings onto the floor for the boy to clear up and putting the wrapped artefacts onto the side, thus opening a space around the unknown object. I decided to take a risk and dug my fingers deeper into the thin curls of wood until I felt something cold and soft. I managed to grasp whatever it was and lifted it up, screamed and threw it back down. 'It's a hand! A hand!'

It had all happened so quickly no one else had seen it. 'Are you sure?' Marcus sounded sceptical, which annoyed me no end.

'Of course I'm sure! Not just a hand. It was attached. That's a body. There's a body in the packing case. Oh my God! A body in the packing case!'

I glared accusingly at Mr Sayed, but he looked as horrified as I felt. Marcus, still looking sceptical, put his own hand into the box, felt around and lifted up a smaller version attached to an arm sleeved in the same dark blue material. I felt the need to scream again but managed to keep it inside my mouth, until it dissolved and came out as just an unladylike grunt. 'It's a very small hand.'

Marcus nodded in agreement. 'We need to get it out. To see if it's, well, you know, dead or alive.'

I didn't feel inclined to find out, nor apparently did Mr Sayed, so we stepped back whilst Marcus put on a pair of rubber gloves as the shavings were now wet and stained with faeces. I noticed his nose wrinkle each time he took a handful and put them straight into the sack that the boy held open for him.

I watched with increasing surprise and consternation as the body of a small girl was revealed. She was curled in the foetal position, but I could see that she wore a dark blue coat, frayed round the collar and cuffs, and a similarly coloured pleated skirt, which had lifted up, revealing her soiled knickers. I felt embarrassed for her and pulled the skirt down over her legs. She lay on her side and her face was covered by straight, black shiny hair. I brushed it aside and gasped at the coldness of her cheek and the blueness of her skin. 'Is she dead?' My voice came out as a hoarse whisper.

'She must be. How long has she been in there, Mr Sayed?

Mr Sayed seemed to be finding it difficult to swallow. 'If she went in at the British Museum, which I suppose she must have done, then she's been in there for three days. She must be dead, surely?'

One of the other odd things that I had gleaned from my school days was that a person can survive for a week or more without water and even longer without food. Whether this applied to a young girl stuffed into a packing case and transported halfway across the world on an Imperial Airways aeroplane, I didn't know. 'She could still be alive. She may just be unconscious. Check her pulse.'

Marcus seemed nervous of touching her. He had no trouble touching the mummified bodies of people who had been dead for thousands of years, but he seemed hesitant to touch this child. I tutted impatiently and put my three middle fingers on the inside of her wrist and tried to feel for a pulse.

Nothing.

I was still holding her wrist when Mr Sayed came back into the room – I hadn't even noticed he had left – followed by a man looking to be in his mid-twenties and wearing a uniform, topped with the habitual red, plumed tarbush.

'This is my sister's son, Darius Karim. He's a police officer. I knew he had a meeting with the Director so I went and fetched him. This whole thing needs to be handled by the police.'

I opened my mouth to chastise Mr Sayed on referring to the girl as a thing, but Marcus gave me a warning look that, in this instance, I decided to pay heed to.

The nephew looked nothing like his uncle, being taller, slimmer, and showing no signs of distress. In fact, he looked cool and collected. He similarly sported a moustache, which bristled over the thin line of his unsmiling lips, and he had only one chin. His eyes, black as Pontefract cakes, looked Marcus and me up and down and then strode across the room to the edge of the crate and peered in. He pulled a face at the smell and poked at the girl's arm.

This made me inordinately angry and before Marcus could stop me with a glance I blurted out, 'Stop it! She's just a child, don't prod her like that.'

The policeman looked at me stone-faced and turned to Marcus, for I, being female, was of no account. 'Is she dead? Who is she? What is she doing in the box? How did she get in there? Who are you and what are you doing here?'

Marcus, obviously annoyed at the policeman's attitude and evident belief that he, Marcus, was somehow to blame, answered equally curtly. 'We're not sure if she's dead. We don't know who she is. We don't know what she is doing in the box. We don't know how she got here. I am Mr Marcus Dunwoody. I am an archaeologist and I work for the Egyptian Museum of Antiquity. I was here today to help Mr Sayed, your uncle, unpack this case of artefacts that was on loan to the British Museum and which he has brought back to put in their rightful place.'

The policeman did not seem impressed by Marcus's role in repatriating some of his country's treasures; he merely raised one dark, beautifully curved eyebrow and said, still turned towards Marcus, 'And who is she?'

I felt my face flush with anger, and I shot Marcus a look that made him close his mouth. 'I am quite capable of speaking for myself, constable. I am Miss Beatrice Trevethan, daughter of Sir Gryffyn Trevethan, adviser to the Minister of the Interior, who, as I am sure you are aware, is your ultimate boss.' I expected some reaction but other than a twitch of his left eye his disdainful expression didn't change one iota.

'And why are you here? It is hardly the place for a diplomat's daughter.'

I don't think I imagined the sneer in his voice. He was just a constable, how dare he be so rude to me? I am, however, politeness personified, and I answered his question quite calmly.

'Mr Dunwoody and I are – well we are friends and I often come and help him when he is at the museum.'

'She has a very neat hand and writes the labels and updates the catalogue.' Thank you, Marcus. Not for nothing my very expensive education at a private girls' school in Bath followed by a year at a finishing school in Berne.

'We know nothing about this girl, constable, but I know this, if she is alive, she needs to be taken to a hospital. Only she can answer all your questions and only if she is alive.' He looked at me appraisingly and turned to another policeman I hadn't noticed who was standing in the doorway and spoke to him in Arabic, a language I had never been able to master. He turned to Marcus. 'Go now. And take her with you.'

This was beyond the pale! I strode over to him, stretched myself to my full height, only a few inches shorter than him and glared. 'Please do me the courtesy of talking to me directly and calling me by my name, which is, just to remind you, Miss Trevethan. Hadn't you better write that in your little book?'

His eyes never left mine as he slowly took a small notebook and pencil from his trouser pocket, licked the lead and painstakingly wrote my name in capital letters, circled it and put a question mark. He raised an eyebrow as if to say, 'Satisfied?' and put the pad and pencil back in his pocket.

'What are you going to do with the girl? She's probably English. You need to notify the British Consul.'

A flash of anger momentarily crossed his face. 'I know what I need to do, thank you Miss Trevethan. I may be an Egyptian, but I am not incompetent. Now, please leave this room.'

He watched as I was finally dragged out of the room by an apologetic and embarrassed Marcus. As we left the building, we passed two men carrying a stretcher. At my insistence, Marcus asked them which hospital they belonged to.

Chapter 2

Effie

What language did angels speak? It certainly wasn't English. Whatever it was, I found the words whispered in my ear very soothing, just as I did the cool sheets that covered my body and the soft mattress that bore it. That they were angels I had no doubt, for didn't they have wide, white wings behind their heads that curled up so that their tips pointed to heaven's ceiling?

If I was in heaven, I must have died.

I didn't remember dying. How had it happened? Had I been run over by a motor car? That would have been a quick death. Ma Foster always told us that if we ever got tired of life we should just stand in front of one of them new-fangled motorobiles. That's what she called them, motorobiles. Had I been killed by a motorobile? Wouldn't I remember something of it if I had?

All this thinking made my head hurt. I closed my ears and eyes and drifted off to a world where a gold statuette in my hand grew to a giant size and shouted at me in a language I didn't understand; a jewelled amulet I wore on my wrist slithered up my arm, its forked tongue darting in and out as its fangs pierced my skin, the beads of blood dripping to the floor and shattering into a thousand crimson pieces; thousands of scarabs swarmed towards me in a shimmering river, those whose progress I obstructed scuttled up my legs and body until I was totally covered. I wanted to scream but dare not open my mouth. I could feel them trying to get in, but I clamped my lips together as tight as I could and flung my arms about to try and rid myself of my unwanted glistening robe.

I found I could no longer breathe through my nose, and I was eventually forced to open my mouth. I shuddered with revulsion as a scarab sidled its way in. I could feel the hardness of its shell on my tongue. I gagged and tried not to swallow but in the end I had to and was surprised to find that I was swallowing soup.

I risked opening my eyes enough to make out the dim shape of an angel slowly putting a spoon into a bowl and then into my mouth. All the while she was murmuring in the angel language. I managed a few spoonfuls before it all came back up, landing in the angel's lap. Her voice wasn't so soothing now.

The next time I woke there was a man sitting by my bed. He wore a khaki uniform and a funny red hat on his head. He looked more like a soldier than an angel. I suppose soldiers must go to heaven as well. When he saw that I was awake he leaned forward and smiled, his teeth looked brilliantly white under his thick, black moustache and brown face.

'Do you speak English?' Of course I did but something, I don't know what, made me keep my mouth shut. I frowned at him, so he thought I didn't understand.

'*Parlez-vous francais*?' I had no idea what he was saying.

'*hal tatahadath alearabiatu*?' That sounded like the angel language.

I closed my eyes, pretending to go back to sleep. He sighed. When I opened them again, he had gone.

It was dark but there was sufficient light from bulbs strung across the ceiling for me to see. I began to have serious doubts that I was in heaven; it looked to me as if I was in some sort of dormitory. There must have been twenty beds, ten along each wall and every bed had a person in it, all in various stages of sleep. There were the night-time noises I remembered from my time in Saint Augustus's Orphanage, fondly, or not so fondly, known as Saint Gussy's: the snores, snuffles, sighs and farts. But I couldn't be back there; it had closed down in the early 1930s after some sort of scandal. I never knew the details and the place was never mentioned by Ma or Pa Foster, who had taken me in along with a few of the others. They'd said it would only be for a short while, but that had been over three years ago.

I turned my head on the pillow and saw a low wooden table next to my bed, which held a jug of water and a beaker. I suddenly felt thirsty but couldn't find the strength to turn on my side and reach out. I wouldn't feel thirsty if I was in heaven, would I? I lay still when I heard footsteps and an angel walked down the corridor between the beds. I could see now that it wasn't wings she had on her back but a large, white hat on her head. She wore a blue dress and a white apron and looked just like a nurse.

Hospital. I was in hospital. For a few moments I felt quite disappointed that I wasn't in heaven but soon cheered up when I realised that it also meant I couldn't be dead. Had I been run over by one of Ma Foster's motorobiles after all, just not been killed? I looked at my arms then used a hand to feel my face and body but couldn't detect any wounds of any sort although it hurt when I tried to straighten my legs. I looked around again and noticed my satchel hanging from the back of a chair. Had I been on the way to school? Oh, I wish I could remember, but try as I might, I couldn't recall what I had been doing that morning that might have resulted in me having to be in hospital, especially as I didn't seem to have any injuries.

The next time I woke the man in the uniform was there again. He was standing at the bottom of the bed talking to a fat nurse. They spoke in what I still thought of as the angel language and they both kept glancing at me. The nurse shook her head a number of times, her hat wobbling dangerously on her head, and seemed to be telling the man in uniform off. She saw that I was awake and came and lifted me into a sitting position with thick, warm arms that I wished would hold me for much longer. As I was shifted up the bed I couldn't help crying out as pain shot up both my bent legs, which I still couldn't straighten. She made reassuring shushing noises and spoke harshly, or so it seemed to me, to the man in uniform. She stuck a thermometer into my mouth and put her fingertips on the inside of my wrist. Her hands were warm and dry, and she smiled at me. I smiled back. A smile is a smile in any language. Her skin was darker than the man in uniform's, almost as dark as Ma Foster's sideboard where she kept her best crockery. I realised that actually every nurse I could see had a face far darker than I was used to seeing on the streets of London, hatted and scarfed against the January cold.

How very odd.

The nurse lifted a glass of water to my lips and despite its warmth I began to gulp it down, but she quickly pulled the glass away and put her hand up like one of the policemen at Oxford Circus stopping the traffic. She took a little sip herself and indicated that I should do the same. When the glass was empty, she rubbed her stomach and raised her eyebrows. Was I hungry? Not half! I nodded and, having said a few words to the man in uniform she padded down the ward.

'So May Bloom, are you going to speak to me?'

I couldn't stop the gasp escaping from my lips. How did he know that name? Who was he? Where was I? Why couldn't I remember?

'Ah, so you do understand me.' Ignoring the frowns of the nurses and patients he dragged the chair noisily across the tiled floor so that he was sitting just inches from me. 'I know you must be very frightened, but there is no need to be scared of me.'

'Isn't there?' We were both startled at the voice that was hurled across the bed. It came from a woman who looked like a film star. She wore a belted pale blue summer frock and carried a wide-brimmed straw hat in one hand and swung a white parasol in the other. Even in my confusion I wondered why she was wearing such an outfit in January. She had short curly hair, a darker ginger than Billy's, but ginger all the same, and she looked furious. Her cheeks were bright red, and I could see her green eyes bright with anger. Hovering behind her was a man who looked as if he didn't want to be there.

'You can't possibly mean to interrogate the poor child when she's in her hospital bed? Look at her! She's barely conscious.'

The man in uniform glanced at me as if to check then stood and very politely I thought, bowed to the angry lady. 'How nice to see you again so soon, Miss Trevethan. And you Mr Dunwoody. I see that you have used your superior intelligence to track down where we have put the girl to recover from her ordeal.' He was smiling at the angry lady, but it didn't seem real; he showed a lot of teeth but the skin round his eyes didn't crinkle.

'It wasn't hard to find her. I spoke to my father yesterday and he agreed that I should act as the girl's ...' she put her head to the side as if thinking, 'as her champion. Did you not get the message?'

What was a champion and why did I need one? The man in uniform had stood up, indicating that the angry lady should sit. 'Yes, Miss Trevethan, I received the message, I just didn't expect you to arrive so early.'

'Well, an early bird catches the worm.' The man in uniform looked as confused as I felt. What on earth was she talking about? 'It's an English saying, Constable Karim.' She didn't explain any further and I stored the phrase away so that I could ask Ma Foster what it meant. Where was Ma Foster, anyway? Why wasn't she here instead of these strangers? Maybe she didn't know I had had an accident. Wouldn't she have missed me at breakfast and when she waved everyone off to school? She wasn't my real Ma of course, but even so, she was the only Ma I had, and I had thought that she liked me well enough. I felt a pang of disappointment, and something hot ran down my cheek.

13

The man in uniform was standing at the bottom of the bed. 'It is possibly a good thing that you are willing to act as her, er, champion. She may talk to you, you being a female. I know her name, it is May Bloom.'

'How do you know that if she hasn't spoken to you?'

'I found this in her bag.' He handed her a piece of card that I could see was a library card for a book I had borrowed months ago. I'd wondered where it had gone. The lady, who wasn't angry anymore, squinted at the card and shook her head, which made her curls shiver. She reached into her bag and brought out a pair of glasses. When she had put them on, she looked more like a teacher than a film star.

'This will interest you, Marcus. It's a borrower's card for a book about Tutenkhamun by an Ernest Budge. Ah, and it was lent to a May Bloom last August. So your assumption is that this girl is May Bloom, which does seem to be a reasonable one.'

The man she called Marcus was brown but a different colour brown to the man in uniform and the nurses – more of a golden brown. He ran his fingers through his hair, something he must have done often as it looked just like our Dick's when he had just got up, all spiky and sticky up.

'Ernest Wallis Budge was Keeper of Egyptian and Syrian Antiquities at the British Museum for many years. He died a year or so ago.'

The man in uniform didn't look the slightest bit interested at this piece of information that the other man correctly explained. 'So, it seems that not returning library books must be added to her many other crimes.'

The lady looked angry again. 'To what crimes are you referring?'

Yes, indeed! What crimes? I remembered that she'd called him Constable Karim. Was he a copper then? He didn't look like one.

14

'Apart from travelling with no ticket and entering Egypt without valid papers?'

Egypt? What on earth is he talking about? I've never gone anywhere outside of London in my whole life.

But then I saw what the man in uniform had in his hand; it was a gold statuette of the God Anubis. 'She is most likely also a thief.'

And that's when I remembered.

Chapter 3

Beattie

The girl went rigid at the sight of the statuette, and she started to quake. Not a gentle shiver but an all-consuming judder as if her whole body was being violently shaken by an invisible demon. Her huge, black eyes in a face the colour of my parasol darted every which way, and her mouth was open wide, but she made no noise.

We three stood frozen not knowing what to do until a large Nubian nurse came bustling over carrying a bowl of what looked like porridge. She unceremoniously shooed us out of the way. The beds in this hospital for native women and children had no curtains around them, privacy not being of paramount importance it seemed, so we were able to watch as she put her trunk-like arms around the skinny child and held her tight against her ample bosom, rocking and cooing to her. The girl clung to the nurse as a drowning man would to an overhanging branch. She made incoherent mewling noises that I eventually realised were a medley of words, only some of which I could recognise: 'No,' 'where,' 'how,' 'help.'

Her distress was contagious, and I felt my heartbeat and breathing quicken and my stomach churn. I felt a trickle of sweat meander its way down my spine, and I wish I'd remembered to bring my fan. I glanced at Marcus, who was chewing his top lip, a sure sign he was anxious. I thought that Constable Karim betrayed a flicker of emotion but when he noticed me looking at him his expression stiffened into one of cold detachment.

Eventually the girl's shudders reduced to shivers then to hiccups and the nurse gently lay her back down onto the pillow. The girl's eyes were still flitting between the three of us, the nurse, the other beds, the ceiling and the statuette, which Constable Karim was still holding in his hand, until she finally just shut them. It was obvious she wasn't asleep, but I suppose she hoped that if she couldn't see us, we didn't exist.

The nurse spoke harshly to the policeman, who spoke harshly back, then she sat on the side of the bed and started to spoon the porridge into the girl's mouth. I can't imagine it was very tasty, but she ate it eagerly, still with her eyes closed, and I wondered when in fact she had last eaten a proper meal. I felt a surge of anger course through my veins at what the poor child must have suffered and what she was likely to suffer, and I turned on the policeman meaning to give him what for. 'You really must ...' but I stopped as I saw Marcus give his head a small shake. He knew me too well and he was right. An Egyptian man, whatever his job, would never accept being told what to do from a woman, especially an English one. I let Marcus take over.

'May I suggest, Officer Karim, that you and I leave this female zone and go to your office?' I liked that Marcus had called him Officer rather than Constable, making him sound far more important than he was. 'I can give you my statement of what happened yesterday, and you can tell me how you are going to proceed.' Well done, Marcus, for speaking to him as if he is leading this investigation. 'Miss Trevethan can stay here a while and see if she can get any information out of Miss Bloom. If she does, I'll make sure she writes it all down and gets it to you immediately. Does that sound acceptable to you?'

Constable Karim listened to Marcus whilst all the while looking at me. I felt his eyes bore into my skin, leaving hot pin pricks all over my face. When Marcus had finished his little speech the policeman nodded once, turned and strode down the ward looking neither right nor left. Marcus raised his eyebrows at me and strode equally manfully after him. When the sound of their footsteps had quite disappeared, the girl opened her eyes. When she realised I was still there she started to look distressed

17

again so I went to her side and crouched down so that I didn't tower over her.

'It's all right, May. Can I call you that? I'm here to help you. Please don't be frightened of me. I just want to talk to you so that I can understand what has happened to you and to get you home. Your parents must be worried sick. Please, will you let me stay a while?'

Her face, framed by straight, black hair cut into a medium-length bob, had regained its colour, which was what people call dusky; not brown like an Egyptian's but not white like mine either. I wondered if either her mother or father was from England and the other from these parts, or perhaps India. She looked at me with her wide eyes and nodded slightly. The nurse had finished feeding her and she held an open hand in front of my face. '*Cinq minutes.*' I held up two open hands. '*Dix minutes.*' She pursed her lips, gave a nod and waddled away.

My knees were beginning to ache, so I stood up and sat on the side of the bed, still indented and warm from the nurse's generous behind. Nine minutes left but I didn't want to rush the child. 'May's a pretty name. Is that the month you were born in?'

She frowned and whispered something that I couldn't hear. I leant closer and asked her to say it again. 'I'm called Effie.'

'Effie? Your name's Effie?' She nodded. 'Who's May Bloom then? Did you borrow her library card?' Effie wriggled restlessly and started looking around her as if searching for an answer. 'It's all right, Effie, there's nothing wrong with having someone else's library card. We just need to find out who you are. So, your name's Effie. What's your surname?'

She stared unblinkingly at me for what seemed like minutes. Her eyes roamed over my hair, followed the contours of my face and peered into my eyes. Whatever she saw seemed to reassure her for she gave an imperceptible nod and started to speak. 'My name *is* May Bloom, but everyone calls me Effie.

18

It's short for ....' She looked embarrassed and looked down as she needlessly smoothed the sheet that covered her.

I waited but she didn't say what it was short for, and I was running out of time. 'Well, Effie, we need to get in touch with your parents. Can you tell me where you live? We can contact the police in England, and someone will go round and tell them you're here.'

'Where's here?'

'We found you in a packing case that was transported from the British Museum in London to a museum in Cairo. Cairo is ...'

'I know where Cairo is. It's the capital of Egypt although it hasn't always been. There have been lots of them: Memphis, Thebes, Alexandria and, well, lots more. Cairo's only been the capital for less than one thousand years.' Her face and voice had become quite animated, and she grinned proudly at me.

'Well, you are obviously an intelligent girl and very knowledgeable about Egypt. You'll get on splendidly with my friend Mr Dunwoody. He's an archaeologist.' Effie's eyes lit up then dulled as she saw the nurse coming down the ward towards us. My ten minutes was up. 'Quickly, Effie, what's your address? Your Mother and Father must be beside themselves with worry.' I took a pad of paper and pencil out of my bag and looked at her enquiringly. She seemed reluctant to tell me. Was she in some sort of trouble at home? Had she run away and was frightened of going back there? 'Come on, Effie. They have to be told. They won't care what you did; they'll just want you home.'

'I didn't do nothing! Anyway, it's Sekforde Street. Number sixteen.'

By now the nurse was standing over me, tapping her foot impatiently. I may have been Sir Gryffyn Trevethan's daughter but in here, where the doctors were gods and the nurses their hand maidens, I was a nobody. '*Je serai de retour demain. J'ai besoin d'en savoir plus sur elle.*' I stood up and gave Effie a peck on her cheek. 'I'll be back tomorrow morning. We'll have a good chat and see if you're well enough to get you out of here.' Though goodness knows where she'd go. Effie rubbed her cheek as if caressing the kiss or perhaps rubbing it off. When I looked back, she smiled at me, a proper grin, and gave a little wave before giving a yelp of pain as the nurse massaged her legs, trying to ease them from an L-shape into an I-shape. As I walked out of the ward a young policeman passed me, accompanied by a nurse. I turned and watched them go to Effie's bed. The policeman sat on a chair, back ramrod straight, feet firmly on the ground and parallel to each other, hands resting on his knees, eyes fixed on Effie. He looked like one of the statues of the Pharaohs that stood in the Museum. How ridiculous! They were putting a guard on her as if she were a dangerous criminal. Did they really think she was going to run away? Where on earth would she go?

Lateef was sitting in the car, in exactly the same position as we had left him when he had dropped Marcus and me at the hospital an hour earlier. Lateef was officially my father's driver, guide and guard but if Daddy didn't need him he was available to me. I couldn't remember a time when he wasn't there and I was fond of him and, I think, he of me, despite the fact that he knew very little English, and I had bothered to learn only the most basic French. Daddy spoke Arabic with him, of course, but it had never been on the curriculum of any of my schools. He was of indeterminate age; his face was deeply lined and the texture of old leather, all moisture sucked out by the relentless Egyptian heat, but his body, what could be seen of it under his robe, was that of a young man, lithe and strong. I knew nothing of his life; each night, having made sure he could be of no further service to us, he walked away to a life we had no knowledge of.

'*Le bureau du télégraphe, s'il vous plait*, Lateef.' He started the car and I relaxed onto the comfortable, slightly shabby leather rear seat and fanned myself with my hat. It wasn't scorchingly hot, it being January, but the air inside the car was unpleasantly warm, even with the windows open. I closed my eyes and let the sounds of the trams, cars, horse-drawn carriages, donkeys and people tell their story. Each was an instrument in an orchestra that played an unmelodic symphony that filled the air and rebounded off the walls of the buildings bordering the wide streets. I knew these to be department stores, hotels, restaurants, European bars and cafés, Embassies, offices and upper-class residences. The poor native shops, cafés and dwellings were out of sight and sound.

Lateef pulled up outside the Eastern Telegraph Company, opened the door for me and walked in front of me into a square office, where there were rows of tables, each supporting a telegraph machine, behind which sat men, mostly European by the looks of them, and in front of which were seats for the customers. I headed for an empty seat and sat down, Lateef standing close behind me to protect me from marauding Bedouins.

'I'd like to send a telegraph to England.'

'Of course, ma'am. Could you complete this form please?' He had a French accent but spoke perfect English. I filled in the name – Mr and Mrs Bloom - and the address Effie had given me, then the message, 'EFFIE SAFE AND WELL IN CAIRO. POLICE WILL CONTACT.' Was that enough? Was it even true? It would have to do; all I wanted to do was to let them know that their daughter hadn't been abducted or murdered. I handed the man the paper and the one hundred *millièmes* he requested – triple the normal cost for an urgent telegraph – and left him tap, tap, tapping away. I didn't really understand how it happened; all I knew was that those taps would somehow translate back into words typed onto a piece of paper that would soon be delivered to Mr and Mrs Bloom.

Back in the car, I asked Lateef to take me to the Museum. I assumed that Marcus's *tête-à-tête* with Constable Karim wouldn't have lasted long and that he would now be back in his cubby hole, drooling over the artefacts Mr Sayed had brought back. As we drove, I noticed that there were more and more people on the streets. They were swarming out of the side streets, out of buildings, jumping off buses and trams; young men in gangs, arms linked, voices raised in anger. Some held banners with Arabic writing, one was crudely painted with a huge eye of Horus watching over the crowd. The car began to slow down, and I had closed the rear windows before Lateef had finished commanding, *'Fermez les fenêtres!'* The disparate shouts had united into a primal ululation that throbbed in the air. I knew, without understanding any words that they demanded that I and all my kind leave their country. A group of men, all young, all wearing blue shirts, saw me huddled in the back of the car and ran over and pressed their distorted, angry faces against the windows; they knocked on the glass harder and harder until I was sure they'd smash it, and then what? Would they drag me out and tear me from limb to limb as a warning to other Brits?

'Get us out of here!'

Lateef pressed on the horn and accelerated slowly; the men moved aside just enough to avoid the wheels, but they grasped any part of the car they could get their fingers round and started to rock it.

I screamed.

Lateef reached into the glove compartment.

A volley of shots was fired.

The men fled.

Their frenzied shouts were replaced by the thunder of hooves as a line of mounted police walked purposefully along the street towards us, the tassels on the policemen's tarbushes swaying in perfect harmony. One still had his arm in the air from firing a gun over the heads of the protesters.

By the time the line passed us there was no sign of the demonstration other than a couple of banners trampled underfoot, their insistent words torn to shreds, the eye of Horus staring unblinkingly up into the blue sky.

I realised that I was perched on the edge of my seat and was holding my breath. I let it out with a long sigh and sat back in the seat. My heart was still hammering, and I re-opened the window with shaking hands. Lateef surreptitiously replaced the revolver into the glove compartment and looked back at me.

'*Bien?*'

'*Oui, bien, merci.*' I even managed a smile of sorts.

We arrived at the Museum with no further interruptions. Lateef didn't accompany me inside and I told him to go back to the Embassy; Marcus would take me home. As I walked through the galleries to get to the workroom I felt calmed by the stillness, the quiet and the presence of the immortalised pharaohs and their gods who had lived in a world I couldn't imagine and who stared impassively into a world they could never have imagined.

The workroom door was shut, so I tapped on it and walked in without waiting for a reply. Marcus was caressing a scarab, although there was no evidence that he was drooling. He looked up at the interruption, but the beginnings of a scowl changed to a smile when he saw it was me. He put the beetle on the palm of his hand to show me, but I wasn't interested in ancient artefacts. I wanted to feel his arms around me; I wanted him to kiss me; I wanted him to tell me he loved me and that everything would be all right.

'Oh, Marcus.' I couldn't say any more as the words were drowned by my sobs and washed away by my tears. He stood stock still, his hand still extended as if offering me a gift, then

23

he strode over to me and wrapped his arms around me, hugging me tightly.

'What's happened? Are you hurt? Is it your Father? Tell me'

I savoured the warmth of him; the smell of him; the sound of him. He hadn't kissed me or said the words I so longed to hear but I'd already waited a long time and could wait a bit longer. I told him about the demonstration and how frightened I'd been.

He had to release me from his hug so that I could speak without his shirt muffling me, but he kept his hands on my shoulders and looked at me with a suitably worried expression on his face.

'Things are getting dangerous again. You say the men who threatened you wore blue shirts?'

I nodded and shivered at the memory. 'They were like a swarm of angry hornets attacking – whatever it is hornets attack.'

'They'll attack a beehive. You were the queen bee.' I hoped he would kiss me, but he just squeezed my shoulders. 'The Blue Shirts are a Fascist youth group. Very anti-British.'

'Why are they demonstrating now? They got their independence years ago.'

He took his hands off my shoulders leaving them feeling cold and exposed. 'In name only; that's what Pater says anyway. They want us all out of their country so they can run it how they want. Can't blame them, to be honest. I've often wondered how I'd feel if the Egyptians occupied England and declared it a protectorate and ran the country by their rules.'

'Killing me wouldn't have helped their cause.'

'You weren't in any real danger, were you? Lateef was there, wasn't he?'

I felt my face flush with resentment at his dismissal of the danger and my voice rose an octave. 'Lateef was one man against a pack of ferocious, starving wolves that saw me as their dinner.'

'When did they transform from hornets into wolves?'

I stared at him in amazement. How could he joke? I looked into his kind, blue eyes and I giggled like a stupid schoolgirl that I hadn't been for six years.

'Idiot! Show me what you were looking at when I came in.'

He held out his hand, the scarab nestled in his cupped palm. Many such artefacts lose their sheen over time but not this one. The carved wings of the beetle were still a beautiful iridescent green, outlined in a glittering gold. Marcus turned it over and there was a clearly carved cartouche. 'I'm not sure who that is yet, but isn't it glorious?'

'Can I hold it?' Marcus placed it right way up on my open hand; it almost filled my palm. It was heavy and I imagined it coming to life and scurrying up my arm. I shivered and handed it back. 'I don't like beetles.'

'Did you find out anything from the girl?'

I'd almost forgotten about her. I was about to tell him what I'd discovered when one of the other English archaeologists flung open the door and rushed into the room.

'He's dead! He's dead!'

'Who's dead?' Marcus and I asked in unison.

'The King. King George is dead.'

Chapter 4

Effie

There was a different policeman sitting by my bed this morning. The one yesterday had been on the plump side; this one was skinny. Otherwise they looked identical: the same beige uniform with shiny brass buttons; the same black boots that needed a good spit and polish; the same funny red hat perched on top of their short, shiny black hair; the same dark eyes that were fixed on me; the same black moustache – yesterday's was a bit ragged but today's was bushy; the same silent mouth that never spoke or smiled, not at me, anyway.

I had a lot to think about yesterday and apart from a short and painful walk around the ward I had spent most of the day dozing and remembering. I was looking forward to the pretty lady coming again; I was ready to tell her what had happened.

I was eating some toast when she came, her heels clicking on the tiles as she walked down the ward. I wanted to be like her when I grew up: tall, slim, confident and bossy. Today she was wearing a pale green cotton dress with buttons down the front and a full skirt with two enormous bulging pockets at the front. She carried the same hat as she had yesterday.

'*Laissez nous!*'

She stood right in front of the policeman and glowered at him. At first he shook his head and straightened his back even more. But he seemed to wilt under her glare and after just a few minutes he got up and shuffled to the entrance to the ward, where he could still keep an eye on me. Did he really think I was going to run away? Where to? Didn't he know I was an uninvited stranger in his city, in his country?

The lady pulled the chair nearer so that she was by my head. She clasped the nearest hand in both of hers and held on to it. 'How are you, Effie?'

I'm glad she remembered my name, even if I couldn't remember hers.

'I'm fine, Miss.'

She smiled. 'Of course you won't remember but my name is Miss Trevethan. You said yesterday that your name is really May, but you are called Effie. Can you tell me why?'

Could I? Would she laugh at me? There was only one way to find out.

'It's short for Nefertiti.'

She looked surprised but didn't laugh – not out loud, anyway. She seemed to be studying me and then she gave a nod. 'I expect Nefertiti looked just like you when she was, what, nine?'

'I'm ten years and eight months! When I was little one of the nuns at the orphanage found me looking at a picture of Nefertiti in a book about Egypt and she said that I looked just like her. Because of my hair and skin, you know?'

Miss Trevethan looked puzzled for a moment. 'You were in an orphanage?'

'I was left on the steps of Saint Augustus's Orphanage in Bloomsbury in July. They thought I was a few months old so that's why the nuns called me May Bloom. But they started calling me Effie when I tore the picture of Nefertiti out of the book and carried it with me everywhere.'

She frowned and gave her head a little shake. 'So, don't you live at Sekforde Street then?'

'Oh, yes. The Orphanage closed down ages ago and Ma and Pa Foster took a few of us in. There was me, Billy, Dora and Dick, Cyril and Betty. Billy has hair the same colour as yours; we call him Carrots.'

Miss Trevethan laughed and touched her curls. 'Someone only ever calls me that once.' She raised her fist in pretend anger, making me giggle.

'Anyway, we six have been there for ages apart from Betty; she wasn't there for long because she was young and pretty and someone took her away. The rest of us are too old and ugly to be adopted now.'

Miss Trevethan gasped and squeezed my hand. 'That's a dreadful thing to say.'

'True though. Who wants someone like me when you can have someone young and pretty?'

Miss Trevethan sat up as if she had remembered something. 'Ma and Pa Foster. So, they're not Mr and Mrs Bloom.' It wasn't a question, so I didn't bother answering. 'Bother! Oh well, hopefully they'll still understand the message I sent.'

'You sent a message to England from Cairo? How?'

She gave a proper smile this time and her eyes lit up. 'Yes. It's called a telegraph and you tell a man, I expect he's called a telegrapher, what words you want to say, he taps the message into a machine and somehow the message goes along wires under the land and sea until it gets to another machine in England and the taps are converted to words again that are typed onto a card, which is then delivered to the people at the other end.'

'Crikey. I never know'd they could do that. What did you say in the message?'

'Well, I didn't know much so I just said you were safe in Cairo.'

I couldn't help spluttering with laughter at the thought of Ma and Pa's faces when they received the message. 'They'll have a real shock when they read that!'

'They will indeed. Almost as big a shock as when we opened the packing case and found you curled up inside. We thought you were dead. Do you remember how you got there?'

I had thought of nothing else yesterday, so I was able to explain it. 'I always go to the British Museum every Saturday. Me and Dora help with the cleaning in the morning then Ma

Foster gives us some pennies. Dora buys sweets but I always spend mine on bus fare to the British Museum. I like to draw some of the things there. I'm trying to learn as much as I can about Egypt so that .... Well, just because.' I sneaked a look at Miss Trevethan, and she nodded her head as if she understood why, but she couldn't do. She told me to carry on. 'I didn't finish some drawings I'd started on the Saturday, and I found out they were taking them away the following Saturday so I ...'

'You what?'

'Well, I bunked off school on the Friday and went to the Museum instead. I got some pennies saved up for Ma Foster's birthday, but I used some of them for the bus. We never learn much on a Friday, anyway.'

Miss Trevethan didn't shout at me but just cocked her head, a bit like a pigeon, 'Today's Wednesday, so that was five days ago.'

I felt a shock ripple through my body. 'Five days? I've been away for five days?'

'Yes, which is why I wanted to tell your parents, well, Ma and Pa Foster as you call them, that you're all right. The whole of the London police force must be looking for you!'

'Would they bother? I mean, I ain't anyone special.'

'Of course you are and of course they'll be looking for you. Carry on with your story.'

'It ain't a story, it's the truth. Anyway, this time I went along a corridor I'd never been before. There's usually a chain across it and a notice saying 'Keep Out' but it wasn't there so I reckoned it was all right to go there. There were closed doors on either side except for one so I went in.' I could feel my cheeks flush and my heart thud as I remembered what I had seen in that room. 'It was like Aladdin's cave! You know the story?' Miss Trevethan nodded. 'There were all sorts of things spread out on the surfaces. I walked along the counters just looking and touching them. I even sketched a few of them.

Then I heard voices getting nearer and nearer and I suppose I knew I shouldn't really be there. I thought they'd think I was a thief or summat and I panicked. There was a box right by me with the lid laid on top but not fixed on. It was full of bits of wood, like when Cyril whittles a stick.'

Miss Trevethan nodded her understanding. 'So I climbed in and pulled the lid over me. There were hard things in there that I kept lying on but in the end I managed to bury myself in the wood. I thought I'd just stay there until they went out again, but someone came right over and hammered the lid on. I was right scared, I can tell you.'

Miss Trevethan sat back in the chair and shook her head in wonderment. 'Why didn't you say something, shout out so they'd know you were there?'

'But I shouldn't have been there, should I? I was frightened what they'd do to me; maybe stop me going to the British Museum ever again. I was just terrified, and I didn't know what to do, so I just lay there. It was bloomin' uncomfortable I can tell you, all them things sticking in me.' A wave of tiredness came over me and I lay back on my pillow and closed my eyes.

'Do you want me to go? I can come back tomorrow.'

'No, I want to tell you everything now. That policeman thinks I'm a thief. Well, I ain't, Miss, I really ain't.'

'I believe you, Effie, honestly, I do. Here, have a drink of water, your throat must be dry.'

I drank gratefully then resumed my tale.

'I think they put me, well the box, in a car or a bus or something. That's what it felt like, all bouncing around. Then I don't know, somewhere very noisy. There were lots of men shouting and I was bumped here there and everywhere. At one time I wasn't moving for quite a while, and it wasn't so noisy so I tried to push off the lid, but I couldn't. That's when I began to get really scared.' I didn't tell her that that was when I wet myself for the first time. 'I had my bag with me, and I managed to get to it. I had an apple and a sandwich in there, so I ate that. Then I dozed and when I woke, I didn't know where I was. I mean, I knew I was inside a box, but I didn't know where the box was. It was shaking and there was a steady noise, a bit like an engine.'

'That's when you must have been in the aeroplane. You must have been terrified!'

'Well, I didn't know I was in an aeroplane. All I knew was that I was cold, and I felt bruised all over. My head hurt and I was hungry, but I didn't have anything else to eat. And it was pitch black.' I didn't tell her that that was when I thought I was back in the coal cellar at the orphanage where I had been put because I'd wet the bed again; I didn't tell her that I did what I'd done all them other times and shit myself. 'I must have fallen asleep 'cos the next thing I know I'm in here in the hospital.' It wasn't quite like that but I didn't feel like telling her about how I was convinced I was going to die of cold; how I was terrified of the dark, how I kept hearing the voices of the nuns telling me I was dirty and God didn't love me; how I dreamt I was lying bare in a cold bath with someone holding my head under water; how I saw a lady in white beckon to me; how I couldn't move; how I felt as if someone was sticking knives into me. No, she didn't need to know all that.

'You have had quite an adventure, Miss Bloom.'

Miss Trevethan and I swung our heads towards the voice. It was the horrid policeman from yesterday morning, who had called me a thief.

He turned to Miss Trevethan 'Condolences on your loss, Miss Trevethan. "The King is dead, long live the King." Isn't that what you English say?'

It was only then that I noticed she wore a black armband. 'Who's died?'

She turned to me, her face relaxing from a scowl; she obviously disliked the policeman as much as I did. 'Our King

31

George died a few days ago. The new King is his eldest son, Edward.' She did her pigeon impression. 'He'll be Edward the seventh, no, eighth.'

I wondered if I should feel sad, but I'd never met the man, nor wasn't likely to, so why pretend? The policeman was still standing at the bottom of my bed, studying me. I felt uncomfortable under his stare and felt my cheeks go hot. I felt guilty but I don't know what of; I hadn't done anything really wrong had I? His mouth twitched under his moustache. Was he smiling at me? I wasn't sure so I pretended I was thirsty and reached for the glass.

Miss Trevethan turned on him, obviously quite angry. 'And I have a bone to pick with you, Captain Karim! Why did you let me call you Constable all the time? You should have corrected me at the start. It was very rude of you.'

'A bone to pick with me? Is that another one of your strange English idioms?' I didn't like to ask what an idiom meant.

'I'm sure you know what I mean. Why didn't you say anything? Were you trying to embarrass me?'

The horrid policeman bowed slightly. 'Certainly not, Miss Trevethan. I have nothing but respect for you. It just didn't seem important or of any relevance at the time. Now, perhaps you and I could have a discussion somewhere else?' He spoke to her but looked at me. 'I would like to discuss a few things with you, if you can spare me a few minutes? We'll see if there is a room free.'

He turned and walked away without even waiting for her answer. She actually said, 'What a rude man,' so it was probably a good thing he didn't hear her. 'I won't be long, Effie. I promise I'll come back, and we can finish our conversation. Don't you go anywhere, will you?' She winked at me and followed the horrid policeman out of the ward.

32

He obviously wanted to talk to her about me. What was he going to say? Did he still think I was a thief? I had put that golden statuette he'd found in my bag but only in a panic before I got into the box. There's no way I was going to steal it, honest. What would I have done with it, anyway? I could hardly walk into an antiques shop and try and sell it. Pawn it, perhaps? I giggled to myself at the thought of strolling into old Shylock's shop round the corner and asking how much he'd give for a carved lump of gold. Then a terrible thought struck me that made me go quite cold and faint. They wouldn't, would they?

Chapter 5

Beattie

He really was the most insufferable man I had ever met: arrogant, rude and utterly cold-hearted. But I wanted to know what was going to happen to Effie, so I followed him, aware of the eyes of the women and children that lay in the beds following me. Some smiled at me, most didn't. What did they think of me? Did they respect me because I was British or despise me for the same reason and wish me gone? Would they prefer to be ruled by their own kind? This hospital probably wouldn't have existed if we had not occupied their country decades ago; nor would the schools their children went to every day. Did politics even interest these women, most of who were of the lower classes?

When I arrived at the reception desk Captain Karim was speaking to a nurse, who nodded and led us into an empty office. They spoke Arabic but I recognised the word '*qahwa*' and realised he had asked her, or probably ordered her, to make us both some coffee.

I decided to take some control and show him I wasn't a complete fool. 'There was no need to tell her to make coffee. She has better things to do with her time.'

He looked at me for a few seconds, his brow furrowed. 'I wasn't telling her to make a cup of coffee. Why do you think I was?'

I damned my need to impress this man and my tendency to blush when embarrassed. 'My apologies. I must have misheard.'

He tilted his head condescendingly in acknowledgement of my mumbled apology. 'I'm under no obligation to do so but out of courtesy to you I wanted to give you an update on the case and tell you what we are planning to do about Miss Bloom.' He waited as if he expected me to fall to my knees in gratitude. I didn't, of course. 'I have notified the situation to the Parquet who, as I'm sure you are aware, decide whether there is a criminal case to answer. If there is, it is they who carry out the full investigation and prosecution.' He paused but I nodded my understanding. My father had explained to me many times that he is adviser to the Ministry of the Interior, who is responsible for the police, whereas the Government prosecution department, called the Parquet, is the responsibility of the Ministry of Justice.

'And is there? A case to answer?'

He smiled a genuine smile; he looked almost pleasant.

'No. We agreed that she is neither a drug-smuggling criminal nor a thief of artefacts, but merely a victim of very unfortunate circumstances. But...' He reverted to his stern expression and for some ridiculous reason I felt nervous. I realised I would hate to be cross-examined by this man. 'But she must be sent home as soon as possible.'

'Of course. I'm sure that is what everyone wants. Have you managed to get hold of her parents? Well, her foster parents?'

'Foster parents? What does that mean?'

'It means they are not her natural parents but are paid to look after her. She told me earlier that she'd been left outside an orphanage when she was a baby and stayed there until a few years ago when it closed down. Since then she, and a few other children, have been living with these foster parents.'

He looked puzzled. He was probably struggling with the concept of someone with a heart large enough to be willing to look after a child who was not their own. 'So, her own parents abandoned her, and she is now being looked after by another couple? Their name isn't Bloom, it's Foster?' His puzzled expression remained. 'So, they are foster parents called Foster or is this one of your funny English nicknames?'

I hadn't thought of that. 'I'm not sure, to be honest. Effie calls ....'

'Why do you call her Effie when the library card says May?'

I didn't want the captain to laugh at her, so I didn't tell him about Effie being short for Nefertiti. She did indeed have the straight, black hair, the black eyes and the sallow skin, but her very non-Egyptian button nose rather put paid to the likeness. 'It's a long story and not particularly relevant. Back to the Fosters, if indeed that's their name. I'm sure she gave me the right address yesterday, so someone can go round there and speak to them.'

'We are in touch with your police in London. The address has been passed on and a request for them to purchase a ticket for the girl to fly back to London.'

I knew from experience the cost of a ticket. 'I doubt they'll be able to afford that.'

He raised one eyebrow, something I've never been able to do with any finesse. 'Well, someone will need to buy it and quickly.'

I felt myself blush again, but this time in anger. 'Don't worry, Captain Karim, we'll get her a ticket. I'll pay a visit to the consulate myself and discuss it with them. There must be a fund somewhere to cover this sort of eventuality.'

'Perhaps you could hold one of your jumble sales to raise money?' Captain Karim snorted with laughter and looked a little sheepish at his dig at one of our favourite past-times. For just a moment he was almost human. 'In the meantime, she will have to stay somewhere else. The doctor says she is fully recovered now so there is no need for her to remain here.' He didn't say it out loud, but I could hear him add, 'taking up the bed that could be used by an Egyptian, who is really ill.'

'Where do you intend to put her? Not in a jail, surely?'

'Of course not, Miss Trevethan. What do you think I am?' He seemed to be waiting for an answer. Should I say a hard-hearted monster? Perhaps not; best to say nothing. He must have realised I wasn't going to say anything. 'I have arranged for her to stay at the *Maison pour les enfants de Dieu*. Do you know of it?'

I nodded. I had helped raise money for it on many occasions and knew it to be a small orphanage, run by French nuns. They would keep Effie safe until we could arrange for her to fly home. I forced myself to be pleasant. 'Thank you, *Capitaine*. When is she to go?'

'There is no reason why she should not be taken there now. I wondered ...; His face softened, and he looked at me almost kindly. 'I wondered whether you could explain it all to her and perhaps go with her? She seems to be frightened of me, I don't know why.' He had the decency to give a small smile. 'She would perhaps not be so scared if you were there.'

I was amazed that he even had the empathy to realise how she might feel being taken to such a place. 'Of course. I'd be happy to tell her your plan and to accompany her to the orphanage. How will we get there?'

'It's just down the road and easily within walking distance. Constable Hassan will escort you there. He's the officer that you sent packing earlier on, but he bears no grudges and will not lead you astray.' Was Captain Karim trying to be funny? It seemed unlikely but he was smiling, which was contagious, and I found myself smiling back. We shook hands and I went back to the ward on my own.

The poor girl looked terrified although Captain Karim wasn't with me.

'Now don't worry, Effie.' She still looked terrified. 'Captain Karim has just told me that they're not going to charge you with anything.' She visibly relaxed. 'But he said you do need to be sent home as soon as possible.'

She tensed again, and the blood drained from her face, her lips trembled, and tears appeared and hung precariously from her lower lids. 'They're not ... they're not ...'

'They're not what? What are you worried about?'

'They're not going to send me back in a box, are they?' I could hardly hear her whisper.

I nearly choked trying to turn a laugh into a cough. 'Oh, my poor sweet, of course not! You don't think I'd allow them to do that, do you? No, you'll go back by aeroplane but in a seat this time. But we need to sort out all the paperwork and purchase a ticket.'

She wiped her tears and snotty nose with the back of her hand. 'Ma and Pa Foster don't have no money, Miss. They can't afford to buy no airyplane ticket.' She started to cry. I gave her my handkerchief. 'Don't you worry about that; something will be sorted out. In the meantime, you need to stay somewhere.'

'They're not going to put me in jail, are they? 'Cos I ain't no criminal. Can't I just stay here?'

'No, Effie, you're not going to jail but you can't stay here, either. The doctor told Captain Karim that you're well enough to leave now and they need the bed for a woman or child who is sick.' I hesitated; she wasn't being sent to jail, but to her it might seem almost as bad. 'You're going to stay at a home for children who have no parents to care for them.'

'It's an orphanage, then.' A statement, not a question.

'Yes, it's an orphanage but it's very small and only has a few children there, only about ten, I think. It's run by French nuns and the children are well looked after. It will only be for a few days.'

'I don't know no French.'

'No, I know, but I'm sure some of them speak English. But if not, well, I'm sure a girl as clever as you can manage just for a few days, can't you?'

Flattery got me nowhere and Effie looked sulky and unconvinced. 'When do I have to go to this 'ere orphanage?'

'Well, there's no time like the present, is there? So, let's get you dressed.' My voice came out far too loud and I winced internally at my forced jollity. Her clothes were folded on the table: a pair of black lace-up shoes; a pair of long white socks with suspect dark stains on them; a thick dark blue pleated skirt; a none too white vest; a dark blue polo necked sweater and a dark blue coat, slightly shabby.

'These will have to do for now. The orphanage will have some more suitable clothes.'

'What's wrong with my clothes? They're very suitable. That's my best coat.' She looked quite put out.

'They're very suitable for a cold winter's day in London, but not for here in Cairo. January in Egypt is like an English summer. You need a cotton dress. Just wear your skirt and vest; you won't need your jumper or coat.'

Effie looked shocked. 'I'm not walking around in just my vest!' She started to rifle through the pile of clothes, looking for something. 'Where are my knickers?'

Ah. Being soiled, they must have thrown them away when they undressed her. 'Your skirt is long enough; no one will notice. Actually, women only started wearing knickers about one hundred and fifty years ago. You'll be like one of your Georgian ancestors.' Another piece of useless information I had picked up from school.

She looked at me as if I had gone completely mad. 'I don't know anyone called George and I ain't walking around with no knickers; you can't make me.' She pulled the sheet up to her chin and lowered her eyebrows; she was obviously not going anywhere unless she was what she considered to be properly dressed. This time I turned a laugh into a sigh and went in search of a pair of knickers.

Chapter 6

Effie

I regretted insisting wearing my jumper and coat as soon as I had put them on, but I wasn't going to admit it to her. I felt hot and ridiculous all bundled up as I walked down the ward next to Miss Trevethan, who looked cool and elegant in her summer frock. She smiled and nodded at the patients, who stared at us in a none too friendly manner. Maybe they were cross with me for taking up one of the beds. I looked out for the big nurse who had been so kind yesterday because I wanted to thank her, but she must have been on a different shift.

When we stepped out of the front door into the open air I thought I was going to faint. It was like that day when I had gone into the back of old Ma Jones's laundrette, and she had opened one of the huge machines letting all the steam out all over me. I'd been able to run away from that heat but I couldn't run away from this; it was everywhere. The air itself was hot, far hotter than in England on a summer's day. It got up my nostrils, in my mouth and ears, under my skirt and through my clothes. It felt as if my blood was going to boil. The sweat on my forehead started to trickle down into my eyes and every inch of my skin was clammy. I couldn't bear it and I tore off my coat, letting it fall to the floor and pulled my jumper over my head, adding it to the pile. My hair was mussed up and I felt embarrassed being in just my vest and skirt but at least I could breathe again, and I no longer felt as if I was being hugged to death by an invisible blanket of fire.

'Go on, you might as well say it, Miss.' Miss Trevethan tried to look all innocent. 'Just say "I told you so" and get it over with.'

She laughed, a guffaw not a silly titter. 'I told you so. I told you so.' She didn't stick her tongue out, but I bet she wanted to.

Whilst I was picking up my clothes and brushing the dirt off them as best I could, two people came up to us: one was the policeman Miss Trevethan had sent packing this morning and the other was an old man in a white dress and a red hat. The policeman looked unsure of himself and shuffled his feet; the old man was more confident and Miss Trevethan spoke to him in some foreign language. He handed her a parasol, which she took and put up even though she had her sun hat on. I know from Billy that people with ginger hair need to keep out of the sun else they'll turn into a tomato instead of a carrot.

Miss Trevethan listened politely to the old man then turned to me. 'This is Lateef. He works for my father and today he's my driver. I've told him we'd prefer to walk; I expect you'd rather do that, wouldn't you? See a bit of Cairo?'

I certainly did. What I could see already was so different to what I'd expected. I'd only ever read books on old Egypt, so I thought there'd be a pharaoh walking around, or being carried on a bed by slaves and girls that looked like me protecting him from the sun with large fans made from feathers. I thought I'd be able to see the Pyramids and the streets would be lined with statues of their gods. I thought I'd see the Nile with small boats sailing on its gleaming surface and men ploughing the fields with oxen. I thought I'd see women walking along effortlessly carrying pots on their heads. I thought I'd see lots of palm trees. Instead, what I saw looked like an Egyptian version of where I lived in London, only more colourful.

The street we were being led down by the policeman was narrow and clogged with people walking, riding on bicycles, pushing hand carts, leading donkeys and sitting in the outside cafés shaded by sun-bleached, stripy awnings. It took me a while to realise that the customers were mostly Arab men; the women were at the tables outside the shops, buying vegetables, breads, copper pots and pans, brightly coloured jewellery and sweets which, I couldn't help but notice, were covered in a

41

layer of flies that young boys half-heartedly tried to swat away. There were children, both boys and girls, running around, looking like street urchins in the East End only their skin was darker. They seemed to come from everywhere and they veered towards us like iron filings to a magnet, just like in the experiment Miss Roberts showed us at school last term. I don't know how they dared with a policeman just a few steps away but they all held their hands out to Miss Trevethan, saying something like '*Bucksheesh, bucksheesh*' Even I knew this meant, 'Give us some dough, Missus.'

Miss Trevethan started to look a bit panicky, and I can't say I blame her because the children were circling us and preventing us from moving forward, but the old man she called Lateef shouted out something and swung a stick he was carrying left and right, left and right, not caring whose shins he struck; I barely avoided being hit myself. The children ran back out of the way; some laughed, all shouted words I could only guess weren't very polite. The policeman hadn't altered his stride and was now some way in front. Lateef called to him; whatever he said made the man go red in the face and he stopped and waited for us to catch up and glared at the hovering children for good measure.

Miss Trevethan still looked a little flustered and I thought it might help if I held her hand. She smiled down at me. 'It's all right, Effie, most of the children in this part of town beg. But one of the first things we Brits are told when we come out here is never, ever give them money.'

I heard scuffling behind us and when I turned, I saw a dozen or so children following us. They weren't laughing or shouting or holding out their hands and their expressions weren't friendly. Some older men joined them, a couple in blue shirts and one was carrying a flag with what looked like an eye drawn on it. He saw me looking at him and he sneered and spat onto the road. I squeezed Miss Trevethan's hand and when she

42

saw me looking behind me, she turned as well. I heard her gasp and say something to Lateef, who turned also and strode forwards to catch up with the policeman. Suddenly Miss Trevethan shrieked, and she put the hand I wasn't holding to her head. It came away with blood on her fingertips. 'Lateef!' we both screamed his name. The two men came running back to us, both shouting at what had grown to be a crowd behind us.

Miss Trevethan took a handkerchief out of her dress pocket and dabbed it onto the cut. It wasn't bleeding much but I expect it stung. 'Are you all right, Miss? What was it, a stone? Does it hurt?'

'I didn't see what it was. Something small, hard and sharp. It just stings a little bit. I'm so sorry, Effie, this isn't the Cairo I wanted to show you.'

'But why did someone throw a stone at you?'

'Some Egyptians don't want us Brits to be here. It's too difficult to explain now. Let's get you to the orphanage, you'll be safe there.'

There were loads of questions I wanted to ask but Miss Trevethan was walking ever so fast and dragging me along with her. The policeman walked in front and Lateef walked behind; not much protection against a thrown stone. Even though I was only in my vest I was getting hotter and hotter, and I desperately needed a cold drink of water but there was no stopping Miss Trevethan. I barely had time to glance at the passing shops, houses and people but I could hear. The air was full of sounds: shop keepers hawking their goods; men and women shouting to each other across the street; small children screaming as they ran between the grown-ups' legs; donkeys braying as they plodded along carrying baskets overflowing with stuff; the sound of the feet of the crowd that still followed us; the thwacking sound of a man beating a donkey that obviously couldn't go any further. I wanted to stop and rip the stick from the man's hand, but Miss Trevethan was forging

43

ahead, not looking to left or right, determined to get me to the orphanage.

We went down a few more streets and eventually stopped outside a plain stone building, its only decoration being the steps leading up to the closed, wooden door and the black iron bars at each window. It looked like a prison, but it was the orphanage; same thing to my mind.

The policeman banged on the door. Miss Trevethan was breathing heavily after her rush to get here and somehow our hands had swapped and she was now holding mine. I didn't mind. There was a creaking sound and the door opened just enough for whoever was inside to peer out. The policeman spoke and the door opened wider; he turned to us and beckoned. I really didn't want to go inside; all I could see through the gap was blackness and I'm frightened of the dark. Miss Trevethan also seemed uneasy, and she stood stock still. The policeman frowned and shouted to her, presumably telling her to bring me up the steps and into the building. Miss Trevethan didn't seem to hear him, and I began to hope that she'd just turn around and take me away again. But the policeman became very policeman-like, marched down the steps and grabbed me by the arm, pulling me away from Miss Trevethan. I squealed and tried to pull myself away.

'*Arrêter!*' She said more; I have no idea what she said but he loosened, though not released, his hold and stopped pulling me along.

'*Désolé. Ce sont les ordres du Capitaine Karim.*'

I recognised the horrid policeman's name and gathered that he was just following orders. Miss Trevethan closed her eyes and sighed, nodded her head slightly and led the way up the steps and into the darkness.

The first thing I noticed when I walked – well, was pulled - through the door, was the smell of disinfectant. The second was the silence. When I was at Saint Gussy's, there was always

44

noise: children chatting, laughing, crying; nuns chastising, complaining, instructing. Here, there was nothing other than the sound of us breathing. Whoever had opened the door had disappeared and the policeman looked around in confusion; I expect he wanted to hand me over to someone and get back to catching criminals, although I suspect he wasn't much good at that.

The silence was shattered by the sound of heavy footsteps coming towards us. We all turned towards the noise and I for one expected to see a giant with size ten boots. Instead, there appeared round the corner a very short, very sweet-looking old lady, wearing the garb of a nun. Her face lit up when she saw us, and her face broke into the broadest smile I have ever seen. She nodded her head at the two men, curtsied to Miss Trevethan and held both her hands out to me and said, 'I am Sister,' she pronounced it seester, 'Margarita. Come, little one.' Her accent was French I assume as Miss Trevethan had told me the orphanage was run by French nuns. The policeman, who was still holding my upper arm, let go and pushed me towards her. She was still smiling, and her arms were open to hug me, but I looked into her blue eyes and there was no warmth there.

Chapter 7

Beattie

I didn't want to leave her. She looked so small and vulnerable standing there with her socks at half-mast under her knobbly knees; her grubby vest half tucked into the top of her skirt, half not; her eyes fixed on mine, pleading with me. She clutched her worldly goods to her skinny chest and stood unyielding as Sister Margarita tried to embrace her.

She would be safe here with the nuns. Wouldn't she? It would only be for a few days. Wouldn't it?

Effie continued to watch me as I walked backwards towards the door, not wanting to lose eye contact with her. I mouthed, 'I'll see you tomorrow' and blew her a kiss. She didn't respond.

Why did I feel so guilty? Why did I feel as if I was abandoning her? What else could I have done?

The policeman had disappeared, leaving Lateef and me on the doorstep of the orphanage. I expect he was going to report to Captain Karim that Effie had been delivered safely. I wondered whether he would mention the attack on me; I suspect not. We had to walk back through the same streets we'd just come down, in order to get to the car. I felt nervous and scanned the milling throng, looking for a disgruntled looking young man in a blue shirt, clutching a stone in his fist but I saw no one fitting that description. I'd always felt safe walking the streets of Cairo but the demonstration yesterday and the stoning today made me realise that I had been too complacent of my right to be there and the acceptance of my being so by the Egyptians. Rather than being welcomed by all, I was beginning to appreciate that I was barely tolerated by some and abominated by the rest.

We reached the car unscathed and Lateef took me home, where I was surprised to see my father's hat and walking stick still in the hallway; he should have been at work. Why was he still here? I went to his study and knocked on the door. 'It's me, Pa.' I waited for him to invite me in, which he did but not before I'd heard a rustling of paper and the opening and closing of a drawer.

I didn't come into the study very often; it was my father's private domain, which I, and everyone else in the house, respected. Daddy and I have a very special relationship. Mama died when I was fourteen but he didn't just send me away to boarding school and forget about me; instead, he took over the role of mother whilst still carrying on the role of father and wage earner. When I came home for the holidays he didn't leave me in the hands of a servant or his secretary but rather made sure he spent time with me doing what my mother would have done: he came shopping with me and waited patiently whilst I tried to make up my mind which dress to buy; he not only bought me a pony but had riding lessons with me and soon became a competent rider, which I did not; he made time every day to sit and listen to my news and to offer guidance or commiseration if asked; he came to my bedroom every night to say and kiss me good night. He tried so hard to fill the gap left by my mother's death and it's only recently, as I've become an adult myself, that I've appreciated what he did, and still does, for me.

His face looked flushed and his hair, still a lovely chestnut brown with just a few grey hairs at the temple, looked as if he'd spent all morning pulling his fingers through it.

'Is everything all right, Pa? Why are you still home?'

'Oh, just some correspondence; nothing for you to worry about, nothing at all. Did you go and see that little girl? What was her name again?' I knew he was changing the subject, but I decided to let him for now.

'Her real name is May, but she likes to be called Effie, short for Nefertiti. She could be an Egyptian with her black hair and eyes and her darker skin. She was abandoned as a baby

47

outside an orphanage in Bloomsbury I think it was. Poor little mite. That's where she is now.'

He looked confused. 'Where? At an orphanage in Bloomsbury?'

'No, silly, in an orphanage in Cairo. That policeman I told you about, who, by the way, is a captain not a constable, arranged for her to stay in a local orphanage called the *Maison pour les enfants de Dieu*, run by French nuns. We've raised money for it in the past. He asked me to go there with her and that's where I've just been.'

'That seems a perfectly reasonable thing to do in the circumstances. I know he's contacted the police in London, who are trying to find her parents. Although if she was in an orphanage ...'

'The address she gave me was of her foster parents, who are apparently called Ma and Pa Foster. I don't know if that's their real name.'

'Well, she should be used to living in an institution. It'll only be for a few days, anyway. She'll come to no harm there. Is that blood on your forehead?' He sounded concerned and put his hand out as if to wipe it away.

I didn't want to worry him, but I knew I should tell him. He needed to be aware of the hostility on the streets. 'Someone threw a stone at me when I was walking Effie to the orphanage.'

'You walked. Alone? Where was Lateef? Why didn't you go in the car?'

I explained the reason for walking and who I was walking with, and he looked thunderous.

'What was that policeman's name? I'll have his guts for garters.'

'I have no idea and there was nothing he could have done. The stone came out of nowhere and could have been thrown by anyone although it was probably a young man in a blue shirt.'

I thought I'd have to explain but he didn't look surprised and for a fleeting moment he glanced at the drawers of his table, his shoulders sagged, and he looked far older than his years.

'They're turning against us again. I know there's been unrest over the last few weeks; the demonstration you witnessed yesterday was not the first nor, I suspect, will it be the last. But that they should attack you personally; that is intolerable. Beattie, I'm sorry, but I'm going to have to forbid you to walk anywhere anymore, and you must always have someone with you. I can't let you have Lateef all the time, but I'll make someone else permanently at your disposal as soon as I can. I'm sure it will pass but the streets aren't safe at the moment.'

'I don't understand what they want. I thought they were given their independence years ago, but Marcus said that it was in name only. Is that right?'

Daddy bobbed his head, a combined nod and shake. 'In 1919 there were widespread violent demonstrations and quite a few of the demonstrators were killed. In 1922 we, the British that is, agreed that Egypt would no longer be our protectorate and gave them their independence. But we all know it was nominal only. We're still here advising their ministers; owning the largest businesses; influencing key decisions and, of course, we still control Sudan, although King Farouk does insist on calling himself the King of Egypt and Sudan.' He laughed. I didn't see what was so funny. 'The plan is to withdraw eventually, but at a time of our own choosing, which is not now.'

'Marcus said one of the factions was a right-wing group called the Blue Shirts. There were definitely men in blue shirts at the demonstration and following us today and I'm sure, though I can't prove it, that it was a Blue Shirt who threw the stone at me.'

'They're certainly one group but there are many more, a lot of them students. We've heard rumours of demonstrations all over the country and that strikes are planned, which will do no one any good, especially the Egyptians themselves.'

'Why don't we just leave then, if that's what they want and we're going anyway?'

My father looked at me sternly. 'We will not be bullied into leaving, Beattie. These people need to understand what we've done for their country, and we need to make sure that Egypt doesn't slide into chaos and misrule as soon as we've left.'

I opened my mouth to say that it seemed that we were the bullies, but then I closed it with no words spoken; it was not an argument I was going to win, not with my father.

'Promise me that you'll not go out on your own, and that you'll always go in the car. Promise me, Beattie. And tell me if there are any more incidents. I know you like to be independent, but this is important. I don't want to have to lock you in your bedroom.' He smiled at me to take the sting out of his threat. 'On a different note, there's a cocktail party at Shepheard's this evening, to say a fond farewell to the old King and welcome the new. We'll leave at seven and hopefully be home by eight. We only need to show our faces.'

'If only you would marry, Pa, I wouldn't have to accompany you to these awful social events. Surely there's some woman out there that would take pity on you? You're not such a bad catch despite being old.'

He snorted with laughter. 'Not so much of the old, thank you. You do realise if I did marry again, you would have a stepmother and, as you know, they are invariably wicked and want to eat their step daughter's heart.'

'You never read me that fairy tale!'

'Anyway, I'm far too old to marry and I'm unlikely to meet anyone at the Turf Club or the Embassy, where I really should be going. What are you going to do?'

'I'm going to the tennis club. I said I'd meet Marcus there for lunch. I'll sit and write some letters in the afternoon.'

'Make sure you go in the car; I'll send back Lateef after he's taken me to the club. You could sort through your wardrobe and choose one of the many expensive dresses you've made me buy you over the last few years. Your young man will be there, talking of marriage, as we were.'

I blushed from my neck right up to the roots of my hair. 'Stop it, Pa! He's not my young man and he hasn't even asked me out on a proper date, let alone to marry him, as you well know. He's just a good friend.' Unfortunately.

We walked out of the study together and I was surprised when he stopped to lock the door. Everyone knew it was his private study and apart from one of the maids, who cleaned it regularly, no one ever went in there. There was nothing of value other than his own space, which couldn't be stolen. He didn't offer an explanation and it was only after he had gone that I realised I hadn't asked him what the correspondence was that made him late for the club.

I had left before the post this morning, so I went to the vestibule table to see if there was any for me. There hardly ever was but today a thick, cream-coloured envelope with my name and address scrawled flamboyantly in purple ink heralded the fact that Aunt Edith had written one of her missives. When I picked my Aunt's envelope up I noticed another one underneath, much smaller with just my name typed, no address, so it must have been hand delivered. I put both letters in my pocket and walked up the stairs to my bedroom and sat in my rocking chair by the open window overlooking the back garden. First-time visitors from England always expect to be surrounded by sand and are invariably astonished at how green and lush the gardens are. I could hear the tinkle of the fountain, the gardener hoeing the soil and the rattle of the seeds in the long pods that hung from the tree known locally as the Beard of the Pasha; I could see the fig and olive trees, doum palms and vines growing over the trellises; I could smell the jasmine, the damp earth and the ham being boiled for dinner. It was a world away from the bustling streets of the city and people intent on harm.

The letter opener I had in my hand fell to the floor and woke me from my reverie. I remembered the letter from the unknown person and slid the replica dagger under the barely sealed flap. Inside was a folded lined sheet of paper that had obviously been ripped from a notebook. I opened the letter up and my eye was immediately drawn to the bottom, where someone had sketched, amateurishly but still recognisably, the eye of Horus.

I read the typed lines, all in capital letters, each word screaming at me.

NEXT TIME IT WILL NOT BE A PEBBLE.

GO HOME, MISS TREVETHAN. YOU ARE NOT WANTED HERE.

Chapter 8

Effie

We both looked in horror at the spreading pool of piss on the floor.

Sister Margarita stepped out of its path and the hands that had only minutes ago wanted to embrace me now gripped my upper arms. Her smile, false though I knew it had been, faded and she looked at me in disgust. She spat words at me that I didn't know but could understand.

'I'm so sorry. I'm so sorry. I'm so sorry.' I whispered these words like a mantra and wished she would let me go so I could wipe my eyes and nose. I was leaking from everywhere except my ears.

The outside door opened, and another nun came in humming gently to herself. She sang out '*Bonjour!*' when she saw us then stopped in her tracks as she took in the scene.

'*Ah, Sœur Suzanne, Dieu merci.*' Sir Suzanne? What a strange name for a nun. Sister Margarita spoke to her quickly then thankfully let me go and strode heavily away. The other nun, Sir Suzanne, came towards me and I cringed from her.

'*Puavre petite.*' She spoke so gently and kindly that I burst into tears. '*Venez. Venez.*'

She took my hand and pulled me along and I went willingly, clutching my bag to my chest, squelching in my sodden socks and shoes. She chatted brightly not seeming to expect an answer and I was happy to oblige. We went along an empty corridor, our footsteps echoing off the walls, only an occasional picture of Jesus or a wooden cross breaking the monotony. I supposed the other children were at their lessons. We stopped at a door and Sir Suzanne indicated that I should wait whilst she went inside. She came out less than a minute later carrying some clothes. We eventually went through another door that opened onto a courtyard that was as hot as the hell the nuns used to tell me I was destined for. Sir Suzanne led me across, my feet sinking inches into the hot sand, reminding me of the day last summer when Ma and Pa Foster had taken us all to Brighton. We had caught the train at Victoria at eight o'clock in the morning and one and a half hours later we were sitting on the beach at Brighton, along with a million others. It was nowhere near as hot as it was here and I remember Ma and Pa Foster sat huddled in their cardies and coats but us kids didn't feel the cold; we stripped down to our pants and vests and spent all day running down to the sea, braving the cold water up to our knees then running back again, our feet sinking into the sand, just as mine were now. How I wished I was back there now.

The courtyard was enclosed by the main building on one side and a jumble of wooden structures on the other three sides. Sir Suzanne took me into one of the wooden buildings that was evidently a washhouse. It was dark inside, despite the door being open and there being a couple of small windows at the front and on the rear wall. I could just see that along one wall was a single stone trough containing five or so chipped enamel bowls and along the opposite wall was a long wooden bench with holes spread evenly along it. The place stank worse than our privy at the bottom of the garden after Pa Foster had been reading the sports pages. Sir Suzanne turned on a tap and held one of the bowls underneath. There was a dreadful noise as the water juddered its way along the pipes and spewed out into the basin, forming a murky puddle at the bottom. She indicated with actions that I should take my clothes off. Now, I'm not shy when it comes to my body, not after years in an orphanage then more years sharing bed and bath with the other kids at Ma and Pa Fosters. But I'm nearly twelve now and Ma Foster says I'll soon need to keep my body to myself.

I was trying to think how to say this to Sir Suzanne when she started to untuck my vest from my skirt. My instinctive reaction was to slap her hand away and shout, 'Gerroff!' The change from smiling and chatty to furious and vicious was instantaneous, emphasised by a slap to my cheek so hard that I was thrown against the edge of the trough. I cried out at the pain in my ribs, and I wet myself again.

Sir Suzanne hissed and launched herself at me. She yanked my shoulder bag over my head, hurting my ears in the process, then grabbed the bottom of my vest again and pulled it roughly over my head. I couldn't stop her; I was still too shocked from the slap to fight back. She tugged my skirt and knickers down and chucked them away from her. I stood in my socks and shoes; it wasn't cold, but I was shivering as if I was standing naked in Leicester Square on a January morning.

She eyed me; I eyed her back.

Her stare shifted to over my shoulder, and I sensed someone standing in the doorway. She said something and the person came in. I turned and saw a young girl; I knew it was a girl because her black hair was pulled into a tight ponytail, and I knew she was young because she had a thumb stuck into her mouth. Her round black eyes flitted from the nun to me and back again. Ma Foster always said I was a skeleton covered in skin, but this girl was even skinnier, truly a bag of bones. Her legs were like a sparrow's and weren't quite straight and her face looked like one of the mummies in the museum, her skin taut over her cheek bones and lines that no child should have.

The girl came up to me and took hold of my arms with a surprisingly tight grip. She didn't look at me but studied my shoes as if she had never seen any before. Her feet were bare. Sir Suzanne took a square linen from the pile of clothes she had brought with her and put it into the water in the basin to wet it. Then she picked up a piece of red soap that lay on the edge of the trough and rubbed it onto the cloth. Before I could warn her, she began to scrub me, starting with my face and then continuing down my arms and chest and onto my privates. I

55

tried to stop her by shouting and wriggling and finally succeeded by kneeing her in her chest as she bent down to do my legs. The only reason she didn't fell me with her next slap was because the girl continued to hold me tight. Sir Suzanne's face was all twisted and she was screaming at me; she was so close I could feel her spit hot on my cheeks, burning my skin like acid.

'Get it off, get it off!' I screamed but she didn't understand. Instead, she pushed the girl away, grabbed one of my arms and literally dragged me out of the washhouse, across the yard to one of the other wooden buildings. There was a large padlock on the door. I felt the sun burning my back, already sore from Sir Suzanne's harsh scrubbing and the reaction of the carbolic soap on my skin, which Ma Foster said was more sensitive than a newborn baby's. She reached under the apron that she wore over her dark blue habit and brought out a metal loop that held dozens of keys of all sizes. Her first attempt at opening the padlock failed, but with much muttering, which I don't think was a prayer to her God, she succeeded with her second and she opened the door just wide enough to shove me in before closing and locking it again.

It was pitch black. I mean absolutely pitch black and hotter than hell, if there is such a place. I was terrified of the dark thanks to the nuns at Saint Gussy's and I waited to see if my eyes would adjust so that I could see anything but there were no windows and no chinks in the wooden walls to let any light in at all. I felt the blackness wrap itself around me and start to suffocate me. I could feel the panic uncoil itself from the pit of my stomach and start to slither up into my lungs, squeeze my heart and throttle my throat. I wished I had my bag with me so I could get at the torch I always carried in there.

There was a scrabbling sound from somewhere followed by a loud whimper, which I quickly realised was me. Were there rats in there? Was this my punishment, to be eaten alive by

56

rats? I remembered that I was still wearing my shoes and socks. Were rats attracted to the smell of piss? They lived in sewers didn't they, so they must do. I hastily crouched down, pulled them off and flung them as far away from me as I could. I stayed crouching, listening but I couldn't hear anything other than my own hysterical breathing and the hammering of my heart against my ribs. I forced myself to breathe slower and quieter; I couldn't do anything about my heart.

There was another ratty clawing sound behind me and in sheer desperation I scuttled forwards on my hands and knees, but I didn't get far. Something solid obstructed my path and, now sobbing frantically, I seemed to be blocked at every turn. I lay on the floor and blubbered in fear and pain; the grains of sand rubbing into the sores the carbolic soap had caused. There was another shuffling sound that came slowly closer, and I screamed and curled up as tight as could be and waited in horror for the end.

I prayed. I prayed to God, the Holy Spirit, Jesus, Mary, Joseph, St. Peter, St. Augustus, St. Christopher and then because I couldn't remember any more saints I prayed to Nefertiti and Tutankhamun for good measure. The dragging sound came ever closer. I felt something soft against my ankle and I screamed and screamed and tried to pull myself away, but I was penned in by the barricade. 'Hail Mary, mother of God, save me.'

I kicked out and there was a yelp, a very unrat-like sound. I cautiously put out my hand, ready to pull it away again if I felt anything that could be a rat but instead, I felt something warm, soft and smooth. It wasn't a dog, cat or any animal that I recognised. I let my fingers wander and felt flesh and bones and material. It was another person! Why didn't they speak?

'Hello?' There was a loud, wet sniff. 'Who are you? Why don't you speak?' The person made a mewling sound, and I suddenly felt a small, warm body curl up against me. Arms wrapped themselves around me and I felt a head rest on my chest. The person, a child surely, probably a girl as the orphanage was only for girls, cried softly and I felt her hot tears on my skin. I put my arms around her as best I could and found that I was no longer frightened, not now there was somebody even more scared.

'Have the nuns put you in here? Was it Sister Margarita or Sir Suzanne?' The body tensed at one of the names, I couldn't tell which. 'Well, you're safe now. I'll look after you. What's your name?' There was no answer and I realised she wouldn't speak English. 'Never mind, shall I sing a song? It won't matter if you don't understand the words.' So I sang 'Twinkle, twinkle little star' followed by 'Diddle, diddle dumpling, my son John' and then 'Here we go round the mulberry bush'. By the time I finished she was asleep.

The darkness was absolute, so I didn't know what time it was; all I knew was that I was hot, thirsty, hungry and sore.

I also knew that I was no longer scared of the dark.

And that I was going to escape from that place if it was the last thing I did.

Chapter 9

Beattie

The note didn't become less threatening with re-reading, in fact it became more so. I realised that in all probability the stone-thrower knew who I was when he took aim. In which case, was the incident planned rather than it being on the spur of the moment? But why target me and why send me such a letter? What did they hope to gain? Did they really think I had any influence at all and could persuade the British to leave? Then I remembered how my father had put some papers into a drawer and locked it before inviting me into his study. Had he had a similar letter? Were all the British diplomats under threat? Was he at risk of something far worse than a stone to the forehead?

I leapt from the rocking chair. I had to do something. Was he in danger at this very minute? Was he lying somewhere bleeding and broken? I had to know. I ran downstairs, determined to carry on running out of the house and straight to the club but at the bottom of the stairs I cannoned into Lateef, nearly knocking him over.

'Oh, Lateef, is Daddy all right? Is he badly hurt?' In my anxiety I spoke in English.

Lateef looked puzzled. I trawled through my mental French dictionary. '*Papa va bien? Est-il blessé?*' Lateef continued to look puzzled, obviously wondering why I should think that Papa might be hurt. '*Sir Trevethan et dans son club. Je suis là pour vous emmener au tennis.*'

My relief came out of my mouth as a sob. No one had beaten him to death, thank God.

I wanted to know if he seemed worried. '*A-t-il paru onquiet?*'

Lateef considered for a moment. '*Un peu, peut-être. Tous les messieurs avaient un air inquiet.*'

Maybe they had all had letters. Maybe others had had stones thrown at them. Maybe Marcus had. I was desperate to get to the tennis club and asked Lateef to take me there immediately.

We lived in the *Ismailiya* quarter. It was no longer the most fashionable residential area but the plethora of European consulates, banks, department stores, hotels and palaces still made it a desirable district. The tennis club was on *El Gezira*, a large island in the middle of the Nile. To get there we had to drive down the *Shâri Fuâd El-Auwal*, which I had gone down many times before. Today I felt none of my usual excitement at being part of the cosmopolitan throng bustling up and down this long straight boulevard, as wide as those in Paris from which it had been copied. Today, I nervously scanned the pavements for groups of men: men in blue shirts; men carrying banners; men with the eye of Horus emblazoned on their robes; men far too interested in me. Lateef must have sensed my unease because he drove faster than normal, angrily banging on the horn when a car suddenly pulled out in front of him from a side street causing him to stamp on the brakes. Was this a ploy to make us stop so that others could attack us? I looked around me feverishly shouting, 'Go, go, go!' then felt foolish as I saw the driver of the other car was an old man who could hardly see over the steering wheel.

We carried on over the *Bûlâq* Bridge and onto the northern part of the island and down the *Shâri El Amîr Fuad* to where the tennis courts were located. Normally Lateef would just drop me by the entrance to the grounds but today he drove right up to the door of the club house and stood by my side as I tried to decide where to go first. The sight of the players in their whites, the whack of the balls on rackets or hitting the net, the grunts of triumph or despair calmed me, and I told Lateef he could go and have some lunch. He couldn't eat with us, of course.

'Aah, there you are. Come on, I'm starving.' Marcus bounded out of the club house, his sun-bleached hair still damp and tousled from a shower, his linen suit crumpled from not being hung up properly. He radiated good health and *joie de vivre.*

'I take it you won your game?' Marcus gave me that grin that always makes my toes curl and my knees weaken. I didn't want to spoil his mood, but I had to know. 'Marcus?'

'*Oui, ma chérie?*'

If only he meant it. 'Are you all right?'

'Yes, why? Don't I look all right?'

'Nothing out of the ordinary has happened today?'

Marcus's jovial demeanour changed instantly into one of concern. 'Has it for you?'

'I received a letter.'

'Ah.'

'What do you mean, "Ah"?'

'You got one too, did you? Now I'm sure there's nothing for you to worry about. The paters will sort it all out. It's just a few students getting a bit out of hand.'

'One of them threw a stone at me. Look.' I lifted my fringe so he could see the cut. I hoped he would reach out and touch it, but he didn't. He did look shocked though.

'One of the blighters did that? Was he caught?'

I explained the reason for my promenade that morning and the incompetence of the policeman sent by Captain Karim.

'I know you like wandering round by yourself, Beattie, but until this is sorted out you really need to be driven everywhere and never go anywhere alone.'

'You sound just like my father.'

'Good. Now let's go and eat. I said we'd meet the others there.'

I would have preferred to be alone with Marcus. I really didn't feel like being sociable but being with Marcus in a crowd

61

was better than not being with him at all and maybe some of the others might have more news on the threatening letters.

They'd kept seats for us – unfortunately not together. The two men, like Marcus, had obviously already had a game and had showered; the two girls were dressed in readiness of a game later in the afternoon when it was cooler; I was the only one who had no intention of playing. I would no more want to attempt to hit a ball over a net than to eat a scorpion; sport of any sort not being my forte. I sat between Gerald Docherty and Jane Smith, whose plain name belied the fact that she was in fact an heiress to a fortune the rest of us could only dream of. Marcus sat between PP - for his friends it stood for Percival Pritchard, for the rest of us it stood for Pompous Percy - and Lady Grace Cartwright, who flirted outrageously with Marcus whenever she saw him. My biggest fear was that one day Marcus would succumb to her charms and I prayed it wouldn't be today, or any day to be honest.

We were all the children of advisers, who were ultimately responsible to the High Commissioner, Sir Miles Lampson. The advisers, who were all British, advised ministers, who were all Egyptian. It was common knowledge that the ministers were just figure-heads and it was the advisers who held the real power. So it was men like my father, Marcus's father, the father of these four sitting here, that actually ran Egypt. It was this incongruous state of affairs that some Egyptians now wanted to resolve, seemingly by threats and actual violence.

When Marcus and I joined the table; they were discussing the letter that PP's father had received that morning. Marcus confirmed his father had received one, threatening death and destruction to his family and friends if they didn't leave Egypt. I said I thought mine had received one too, but it hadn't been shared with me. The others promised to investigate whether their fathers had been recipients also. They all went quiet when Marcus and I told them we had also received a letter and when I told them of the contents of mine, Grace looked around her nervously as if expecting an attacker to leap from behind the potted palm. There was much harrumphing from PP and Gerald of 'bally this,' and 'damned that,' and 'know what's good for them,' and 'put them in their place.' The girls were more sympathetic and practical with, 'Oh, poor you, how frightful!' and 'Do you have something to cover that scab?'

'Well, they don't frighten me. They're just riff-raff, and the country wouldn't last a week if left in their hands. We put them down in 1919 and we'll do it again.' PP being his usual pompous self.

'That revolution led to a general strike throughout Egypt with the whole country almost grinding to a halt and even worse, more than eight hundred people, mostly Egyptians, were killed. We supposedly gave them independence in 1922 and I personally think they are entitled to be outraged that some fourteen years later we still effectively rule their country.' Oh, bravo Marcus!

'Poppycock! What utter rubbish you talk, Marcus. You don't agree with him, do you Gerald?'

'Absolutely not! We've got a good life here and Father's promised me a promotion. He says I'm a natural diplomat; I know how to handle these natives and it's not by being kind and understanding.'

Why had I not realised before how utterly ridiculous these two men were and how they cared only for themselves, not for the inhabitants of the country they were meant to serve. I decided it was time to speak out. 'I actually agree with Marcus. I don't agree with their threatening and hurting us, but I do agree that we have been here for too long and should give them their country back.' There was a deadly silence for a few seconds then everyone started talking at once.

'You can't be expected to understand the situation, Beattie.' Because I'm a female and females don't have a brain.

'Just leave it to us.' Because I'm a female and females can't actually do anything of any use.

'You're bound to agree with Marcus.' Because I'm a female and females can't possibly have their own opinions.

'Shall we agree to differ and order lunch?' Marcus was the only man at the table who didn't work for the Diplomatic Corps but he was by far the best diplomat.

I didn't have much of an appetite and picked at my meal of lemon sole and braised vegetables. The conversation thereafter was inane; I found their voices, all but Marcus's, irritating and I began to have a headache. I gave my apologies and acknowledged their false concern, apart from Marcus who really did look worried for me. He came with me to find Lateef, who had had his lunch and was sitting outside under a palm tree smoking a cigarette.

'Thank you for siding with me earlier on.'

'I didn't side with you, Marcus, I merely said what I thought. Lateef, can you take me home now?'

'Do you really have a headache? Or do you just want to get away from those imbeciles?'

'Both. Are you going to the cocktail party tonight?' Marcus pulled a face and nodded his assent and opened the car door for me. 'I'll see you there then.' He shut the door and stood watching as we drove away. I turned round as we exited the grounds, and he was still standing there.

When I got home, I went up to my room and sat rocking in my chair. My headache soon eased, and I had just decided to look out what I would wear that evening when I remembered the other letter I had received. Aunt Edith was the elder of two sisters, the younger by two years being my mother, Evelyn. Whilst my mother had been a social butterfly born for soirées and champagne, her elder sister was an eccentric who gave not a hoot for society or for what it thought of her. She lived in Luxor, which is on the east bank of the Nile about three hundred miles south of Cairo. She had never married, a fact she daily gave thanks to the Lord, and lived in a large, dilapidated house that used to belong to a minor Egyptian grandee. She spent her days painting and being rude to the tourists who frequented the temples of Luxor and Karnak. I always enjoyed her letters and often laughed out loud at her escapades, which I'm sure she exaggerated for my entertainment. I loved my Aunt and although she was nothing like what I remembered my mother as being, she was now the nearest thing I had to a mother.

My mother had been visiting Aunt Edith for an extended stay when I was about fourteen when she had died unexpectedly. Aunt Edith had been wonderful with me when I went down with Daddy afterwards and to this day, I can't understand why he refused to even mention her name. He knew we wrote to each other, but he never asked what news she had and, although I was very aware he didn't like it, I visited her about twice a year. I'd tried to talk to Aunt Edith about Pa's antipathy, but she just pursed her lips and shook her head, saying she'd tell me one day.

Chapter 10

Effie

While the little girl slept, curled up inside my own curved body like we were two pieces of jigsaw, I planned. We would escape that very night. We, being me of course and the little girl, I could hardly leave her behind, could I? From my experience of Gussy's there'd be a door, or a window open somewhere that we could slip through. If not, we'd find Sir Suzanne's bedroom and steal her keys when she was asleep. Then we'd look for Miss Trevethan. I was sure Cairo wasn't all that big and it shouldn't be too hard to find where she lived. When I told her what the nuns had done to me, to us, she'd not send us back; I was sure of that.

The girl was snuffling in her sleep, but it didn't stop me from dozing until the door was opened and a nun walked in. I was surprised it was still daytime and for a few seconds I was blinded by the light that spilled into the room, revealing it to be nothing more than a glory hole. It was full of broken bits of furniture, mouldy cardboard boxes that barely held in their contents, what looked like rusty farming equipment and even a ragged old rocking horse that had lost its rockers and had made a comfortable nest for generations of mice. The floor was sandy, and I could see the narrow path the little girl had managed to crawl along from her hiding place to mine.

The nun looked young and pretended to be nice, but I knew better and wasn't going to be deceived again. She pulled me gently to my feet and waited whilst I hopped around in agony from cramp; she sighed and tutted at the welts on my body as she helped me dress into a cotton shift she had brought with her; no knickers though. She also had my bag which I slung over my shoulder and held on to tightly; it was a reminder of who I was. I went in search of my socks and shoes whilst she turned her attention to the still-sleeping girl.

'*Ma pauvre Mimi.*' She lifted her easily and clutched her to her breast whilst I just stood staring with my mouth open, ready for the nausea that threatened to spew out.

Her legs stopped after just a few inches from her body, the stumps smooth and rounded like the end of a copper's truncheon. I shuddered at the thought that I might have touched them. The rest of her looked normal enough, until she roused from her slumber and turned her head, looked at me and smiled – I think. Between her nose and mouth there was a big, black nothing. I gasped and stepped back, knocking the back of my legs against something metal and sharp. I couldn't help myself. Her smile, if that's what it was, left her face and she started to cry. Big, fat tears dripped from her big, black eyes, snot dribbled from her nose and disappeared into the hole, but she made no sound. The young nun frowned at me, held Mimi even tighter, stroked her back and spoke to her quietly. She then walked out of the prison and beckoned me to follow her across the courtyard towards the washhouse.

I wasn't going in there again. I stopped dead in my tracks and folded my arms to show my determination. The young nun turned back and lightly touched a sore on my arm saying, '*Pas de savon*' and shook her head. I hoped she meant she wouldn't use the soap on me again, so I followed her into the washhouse. There were others in there; a fat nun was overseeing about fifteen girls. They were all, apart from the nun of course, stark naked, all skinny, all darker than me and all staring at me. All except the girl who had held me earlier whilst Sir Suzanne had abused me, and she had the decency to look away. The fat nun shouted something at them, and they all carried on washing themselves with dirty looking rags. Some sat on the privy, swinging their skinny legs, just like I always did. I really wanted to go for a piss, but I felt too shy and convinced myself I could hold it in until I'd escaped from that place. The girls were chattering and laughing and, I must say, looked happy enough although I know from my time in an orphanage that laughter and smiles are a good cover to true feelings. The young nun handed me a damp, unsoaped cloth and left me to dab myself all over whilst she sat Mimi in the trough and washed her from head to toe – well, to the end of her stumps.

When we left the washhouse, I was surprised at how dark it was. Night had literally fallen out of the sky. The air was cool, so much so I wished I had my jumper over my thin, cotton shift. The other girls got into a line that wriggled its way after the fat nun and disappeared into the main building. The young nun, carrying Mimi with one arm and holding my hand with the other, followed them but then veered off down a different corridor. She took us into a large kitchen that was empty of people. Cooking was obviously over for the day; the pots and pans hung gleaming on the walls and the work surfaces were clean and clear. There was just one pan left on a cooker, steam still escaping from around the rim of the lid.

There was a long wooden table, damp from being scrubbed and the young nun sat Mimi on a stool, the stubs of her legs sticking out like two thick sausages and indicated that I should sit next to her. I couldn't look at the girl and moved my stool away a little so that I was in no danger of touching her or being touched by her. I knew I was being horrible and that it wasn't Mimi's fault, but she gave me the creeps. No wonder she was in an orphanage; who would want to keep a freak like that? I knew I wouldn't be taking her with me when I left.

The young nun ladled the contents of the pan into two bowls and put one in front of each of us along with a spoon. My stomach reminded me that I hadn't eaten since the two pieces of toast that morning in the hospital, which seemed a lifetime ago. My hunger, however, disappeared with the noises Mimi made as she slurped down the food, whatever it was. The young nun gave an exaggerated pout at my full bowl and just when I was going to take a taste, she snatched it away and emptied the contents back into the pan. She then lifted Mimi into her arms again and gestured for me to follow.

I did wonder about making my escape then, but I could see that there were other nuns and older children still prowling the corridors, so I decided to wait until everyone was fast asleep. The young nun went up some stairs, along another corridor and into a room that was dark but with enough light filtering from outside through the shutters for me to see a row of about eight beds, most with the bump of a girl asleep, or more likely pretending to be. There were a few stifled giggles that the young nun ignored. She walked down to a bed that had no one in it, pulled back the top sheet and blanket and lay Mimi gently down. She continued to hold back the bed coverings and tilted her head, obviously wanting me to get in. I put my shoes, socks and bag under the bed and as I couldn't see Mimi's deformities, I forced myself to slide onto the bed and let the nun tuck me in.

She bent to kiss Mimi, who made a contented purring sound, not unlike Ma Foster's cat, Tom, when he stretched out in front of the fire. She came to my side of the bed, but I turned my head away so that she knew not to take liberties with me. She sighed then walked away and once the door was shut there was only the sound of breathing, snuffling and giggles, which stopped as soon as the door opened again and a harsh voice – it sounded very like Sister Margarita's – shouted something that shut everyone up.

I didn't feel tired although it was nighttime, so I lay on my back, right on the edge of the bed as far away as possible from Mimi, and thought. I thought about my life back in London with Ma and Pa Foster and the other children; I thought about my visits to the British Museum and of some of the pieces I particularly liked; I thought about my unexpected trip to Egypt; I thought about Miss Trevethan and the horrid policeman; I thought about my escape plan; I thought about my mother.

According to Billy my mother was an East-End tart and my father a dirty Arab sailor who had his shore leave and then left. But he can't possibly know who my parents were, not even the nuns did. All they could tell me was that I was left in a Moses basket on the steps of the orphanage, wrapped in a pink crocheted blanket, clutching a crotched rabbit – which was on my pillow back home – and an envelope with a ten pound note inside. Tarts can't crochet and they certainly wouldn't have ten pounds to give away. There was no letter explaining why she couldn't look after me or saying what the date of my birth was or what she had called me for the couple of months she had been able to keep me. I am convinced she was made to give me up because of her reputation; perhaps she was a princess, an Egyptian princess who'd fallen in love with someone not considered suitable, a stable boy or a teacher. Perhaps they'd tried to run away when I'd been born but they'd been captured, and she'd been sent back to Egypt, and he'd been shipped off to Australia and I'd been sent to an orphanage. Perhaps she was in Cairo and at this very minute thinking of me.

I was desperate for a piss. I peered under the bed and was glad to see a pot. I got out of bed carefully, pissed in the pot as quietly as I could and clamped my mouth tight shut so that I didn't groan with the sheer pleasure of it. Afterwards I stood by the side of the bed and listened. I could hear shouting and music wafting in from outside and I could hear the sound of eight girls breathing deeply but I couldn't hear anything else. I picked up my bag, shoes and socks from where I'd left them under the bed and tiptoed towards the door, stopping every few steps to make sure that I hadn't woken anyone up. For one horrible moment I wondered if the nuns locked the door at night, but they didn't; it opened easily and quietly. The corridor was lit by very dim, bare light bulbs every few yards, but it was enough for me to see that there was no one there. I pulled the door behind me but didn't shut it completely in case it made a loud click. I walked down the corridor, keeping tight against the wall, keeping to the shadows.

I heard her before I saw her. The heavy footsteps and harsh voice told me it was Sister Margarita. The shadows were dark but not dark enough to hide me. I turned the handle of the next door I came to and breathed a sigh of relief as it opened, and I was able to slip in. It was a bedroom and whoever was in there was not having a restful sleep. She tossed and turned, muttered and moaned, even yelled out at one point, but she didn't wake up. I was worried that Sister Margarita would hear the noise and come in to investigate but I needn't have worried. I had the door open a little and managed to watch as she continued to shout at a poor nun who slouched by her side. It was the young nun who had actually been very nice to me; she was having her niceness sucked out of her by the older nun's unkind words. I wondered what she'd done to deserve it. Perhaps just being nice was reason enough.

I waited until the two nuns had passed by and turned a corner before I slipped out. I'd managed to catch a glimpse of the sleeping nun and was disappointed that it wasn't Sir Suzanne. It would have been so easy just to steal the keys and walk out the front door. I was still confident that I'd find a way out. If Sister Margarita and the nice nun were still up then others may be too and I'd left my bed too soon but I didn't want to go back. I remembered that the kitchen had been empty and wouldn't be used until the next morning, so I made my way there, keeping to the shadows and making as little noise as possible, just like the famous Flannelfoot, the cat burglar. I managed to slip into the kitchen without meeting any more nuns. It was dark but not pitch black and my eyes soon got accustomed so I didn't need to use my torch. I could see the pan on top of the cooker and my stomach grumbled in anticipation of a bowlful of its contents. I didn't want to make a noise, so I carefully removed the lid and just ate the stuff with the ladle. I think it was a stew, but I didn't really care what it was or that it was lukewarm; it was quite tasty, and I ate and ate until I was stuffed, then ate some more.

Chapter 11

Beattie

Shepheard's Hotel was only a short distance away. Normally we would have strolled through the gardens of *El Ezbekiyeh* to get there but this evening Daddy insisted we go by car, although it hardly seemed worth getting into it just to get out again almost immediately. Daddy was obviously anxious, which made me anxious. He held onto my elbow from house door to car door and from car door to hotel entrance and both our heads moved constantly from side to side as we scanned the passers-by.

Shepheard's is undeniably the most famous hotel in Egypt, possibly the whole world. It takes up most of one side of the street *Shâri Kamil* and the interior is excessive in its opulence. It does nothing by halves, from its stained-glass windows, huge granite pillars – for aesthetic rather than structural necessity – Persian carpets, crystal chandeliers, lush greenery both inside and out, baths in most of the bedrooms and electric lighting throughout. I usually enjoyed an event here but this evening I saw it with the eye of a *fellahin*. Surely the ordinary person would feel nothing but contempt for the British who stayed here with their smart clothes – many in uniform – over-sized cars and voices, their fat wallets and bellies, their arrogant sense of superiority, whilst they themselves were banished in their own city to the hovels of Old Cairo? I looked into the eyes of the young man who took our coats and led us into one of the salons that had been hired for the evening, searching for contempt and loathing but found nothing other than politeness and servility.

The salon was dazzling. It had two enormous crystal chandeliers hanging from the ceiling and crystal lamps every few feet on every wall. Each table had pristine white tablecloths that hung down to the patterned tiled floor and were laden with silver platters of canapés, tartlets, tiny triangles of crustless sandwiches and other morsels deemed suitable for a cocktail party. There were waiters, all Arabs, in dark suits carrying silver trays with crystal glasses filled with champagne. The sparkle of the room was outdone only by that of the jewels that hung from the women's ears and around their wrists and throats.

There was a hum of conversation that I guessed, from the worried faces, was all about the letters that many had received. There was a tension in the room that was almost tangible. Daddy finally released my elbow, and I was free to mingle if I so chose, which I didn't. I stood by the wall and looked for Marcus. I saw him standing with his father and mother listening intently, along with others in a large group, to the High Commissioner. The men were nodding their heads and standing more upright and pushing their shoulders back; they were obviously being given a pep talk by their supreme commander. I didn't want to join the group, so I tried to get Marcus's attention by staring at him, which usually worked but not this evening.

I looked around to see if there was anyone else there I could bear to talk to when PP, Pompous Percy, handed me a glass of champagne and stood by my side, rocking backwards and forwards on his heels and surveying the room like a general reviewing his troops.

'You're looking particularly ravishing this evening, if you don't mind me being so bold as to say?'

I knew I did. I had worn my emerald green velvet dress because it went well with my red hair and white skin. And because Marcus liked it.

'Thank you kindly, Sir Percival.' I did a mock curtsey. 'This is pretty ghastly, isn't it?' I knew PP loved these occasions.

'Whatever do you mean, Beattie? We're here to toast the past and the future. And to show that we're not frightened by a few letters sent by illiterate Arabs.'

'Why do you say they're illiterate? My letter was written in perfect English.'

'You are such a tease, Beattie. When are you going to give up on that ignorant archaeologist and come and marry me? We'd make a great team, don't you think?'

'I think you should keep your voice down before the ignorant archaeologist knocks your head off.'

'Ah, Marcus. Good to see you, old fellow. You scrub up quite well, considering; you look almost human. I was just telling Beattie here that she should marry me. What do you think?'

I choked on my champagne and Marcus looked startled. 'Well ...' He looked at me with an eyebrow raised. 'If Beattie wants to marry you, then of course I offer you both my heartiest congratulations but ...' He grinned. 'She's always told me that she'd never marry anyone in the Diplomatic Service, even if he were the last man on earth. Unless you've changed your mind, Beattie?'

PP looked slightly affronted, but I didn't deny having said it, because it was true. He shrugged then salved his pride by saying, 'I was only joking, anyway. I don't have time for all that sort of thing, especially not now. I think I'll go and see if Sir Lampson needs me to do anything.'

Marcus waited until he was out of hearing range. 'Not unless Sir Miles wants any filing to be done, which is unlikely, don't you think?'

I snorted with laughter but then felt guilty because although PP was pompous, he was still one of our friends and I wouldn't want any harm to come to him.

'Would you?'
'Would I what?'

'Would you marry him if he asked?'

I looked at him in horror. How could he ask such a question? How could he not see that the only man I wanted to marry was him? Why are men so bloody blind?

'No.'

Our conversation, such as it was, was interrupted by a scream. Marcus grabbed my arm but then sheepishly let it go as the scream was followed by loud complaining in a very posh voice, emitted from the bright red lips of Mrs Featherington, who was chastising a waiter for spilling a tray of vol-au-vents down her very ample bosom.

Was I the only one who noticed another waiter nod his head at the culprit and give him a supportive smile?

'We should mingle.'

'Must we?'

'We must.'

So we mingled. I even commiserated with Mrs Featherington and tried not to stare at the greasy stain down the front of her purple, silk dress that looked very much like the outline of North America. After about half an hour someone rapped on the table, asked for silence and for us all to raise our glasses. There was a short spurt of activity as glasses were held out to be refilled then Sir Miles Lampson, High Commissioner, said in a sonorous voice, 'The King is dead, long live the King!' We all repeated the words and sipped or guzzled our champagne. The mood was shattered, both figuratively and literally, by a waiter dropping a tray full of glasses onto the tiled floor. I peered to see if it was the same hapless man who had spoiled Mrs Featherington's dress, but it wasn't. It was the one who had smiled at him.

'The waiters are clumsy tonight.'

'I don't think they're accidents. I think it's being done on purpose.'

Marcus nodded in agreement. 'I think you're right. Let's hope it doesn't escalate to anything worse.'

I felt a shiver of fear. 'Do you think it might? Should we tell someone?'

'I'll wander over and have a word with Father. Why don't you go and find yours? I'll catch up with you.'

I watched as he ambled his way through the crowded room. As PP had pointed out, he looked good in his evening suit, though I preferred him in his working gear with a layer of sand in the creases of his clothes, his skin and in his tousled hair. I was making my own way to find my father when there was a splintering sound, a thud and screams. Everyone turned towards the large window that looked onto the main street. I could see lights refracted off cracks that radiated from a hole in the centre. The screaming had stopped and in the moment of silence, whilst everyone was still in shock, the sound of muted chanting could be heard. Someone translated, 'British go home.'

A voice, military, shouted out, 'It's just a stone thrown through the window, nothing to worry about. My men will go out to disperse the crowd. I suggest we carry on, stiff upper lip and all that.' My upper lip felt anything but stiff and I just wanted to go home. People started moving: anyone in uniform headed for the door; the waiters bore their culinary gifts to guests who had lost their appetite; wives sought their husbands; those at the bottom of the career ladder went in search of those at the top and I went looking for my father.

He was standing in a group with men I recognised as being his equivalent in other ministries, along with their wives and sometimes their adult offspring. I stood next to Marcus and wished he would hold my hand. Daddy was speaking.

'I suggest we all stay for another thirty minutes or so then make our way home. Please make sure you don't walk; if you need a lift let me know. I'll inform the Minister of the Interior of what's happened, and I believe there will be more army patrols tomorrow; the soldiers' presence should calm things down. We need to keep our heads and carry on as normal, but the women need to stay indoors for the next few days if possible but if their outing is urgent then they must be escorted and driven. Any questions?' I glanced at Grace, whose main purpose in life was shopping, but she didn't say anything; she probably considered buying clothes she didn't need to be urgent and so exempt from any embargo.

There were no questions and Daddy very deftly turned the conversation to '*La Traviata*,' which was playing at the Royal Opera House. He was rather a connoisseur of opera and had everyone entertained with his poor opinion of Alfredo as Violetta's lover and I prayed he wasn't going to burst into song to illustrate his point. As soon as thirty minutes had passed, I caught his attention and indicated, through eye rolls and nods of my head that I wanted to go home.

The street was far less busy than normal at that time of night except for a surfeit of military and police personnel milling around the entrance to the hotel. I recognised Captain Karim giving orders to a group of policemen. He seemed to sense my gaze and turned and nodded his head in greeting. I was glad he couldn't see my blush. We had our own soldier who escorted us the few steps to our car, and I saw that everyone was being similarly shepherded. I sat by Daddy's side in the back of the car, and he took my hand, engulfing mine in his large, capable one.

'I wish you weren't here, Beattie.'

'I hope you mean that in a positive way.'

He squeezed my hand. 'Of course, my dear. I don't know what I'd do without you, but I don't want you here if things are going to get ...'

'Dangerous?'

'Let's just say, unsettled.'

'Well, I'm not leaving you here and I don't suppose you'd come away with me, so that's rather an impasse, isn't it?' He leant back in the seat, closed his eyes and gave a long sigh; his grip of my hand relaxed and I realised that he was exhausted. 'Let's just get home; you need your sleep. We can talk more tomorrow.'

'Ah, to sleep, perchance to dream.'

We spoke no more until we got home. I kissed him goodnight at his study door, where he said he had just a few things to do.

All the excitement at the cocktail party had drained me and I felt weary as I climbed the stairs to the upper floor and to my bedroom. Even fifty years ago I would probably have had a maid help me undress but in these modern times I was left alone to undo the tiny pearl buttons at the front of my bodice, which were pretty but fiddly, and to haul the heavy material over my head, causing my hair to stand on end with static. How pleasant it must have been just to step out of one's clothes and know that someone else would pick and hang them up. I smiled to myself at my fanciful thoughts and sat down at my dressing table to do something with my hair. Luckily I wear it short so it only needed a quick brush. It was when replacing the brush, a silver backed one that used to belong to my great grandmother, that I noticed the box.

It was just a plain white, cardboard box about six inches long by four wide and four deep. There was a red ribbon tied rather crudely around it and fastened into a semblance of a bow. Just my name was printed on the lid. Was it from Marcus? He hadn't said anything at the party, and he would surely have written Beattie, not Miss B. Trevethan? I undid the bow and lifted the lid.

At first I thought it was a black, shiny brooch, made perhaps of obsidian.

It was only when it raised its tail that I realised that it was a scorpion. A very much alive scorpion.

I bolted off the seat but then stood absolutely rigid, hardly daring to breath. I couldn't remember, were black ones deadly? Would a scream startle it? Would it notice if I moved ever so slowly to the door? How much provocation would it need to attack me? It lowered its tail. Was that a good thing? I didn't know much about scorpions but I did know that they preferred the dark; there was no way on this earth I was getting close enough to put the lid back on.

I stood like that for minutes and a soft knock on my door nearly had me jumping out of my skin. 'Beattie, are you still awake?' I didn't want to make a sound that might startle the scorpion but then again, I didn't want Daddy to think I was asleep and leave.

'Mmmm.'

'Can I come in for a minute?'

'Mmmm.' This one came out wobbly.

'Are you all right, Beattie?'

'Mmmm.' This one came out slightly hysterical.

He had the presence of mind to open the door slowly and to just pop his head round. He took in my posture and the direction of my stare. He could see the box but not what was in it. 'Is it dangerous?' he whispered.

'Mmmm.'

'Wait there.' He slid away. I almost laughed; I wasn't going anywhere.

He seemed to be away for hours, but it was probably only for a few minutes. He came quietly into the room along with one of the Arabs who looked after the garden. I don't know where he had found him at that time of night. The Arab was wearing thick leather gloves, and he was holding a dense, canvas bag in one hand and what looked like a long pair of tweezers in the other. My father stayed by the door watching anxiously. The Arab, having given me a huge, toothless grin, strolled over to the dressing table, calmly picked up the scorpion with the tweezers, put the squirming body into the bag, tied it up, grinned at me again and left.

I laughed. I didn't stop laughing until Daddy hugged me to him, stroking my hair and telling me everything was going to be all right, just as he had done when I'd fallen off my pony and hurt my knees as well as my pride. He smelled of old cigar smoke and recent whisky.

'What if there's another one, hidden somewhere?'

'Sleep in your mother's bedroom tonight and I'll have the whole house checked tomorrow.'

'How did it get here? Someone must have put it there. Was it one of the staff?'

'We'll find out tomorrow.'

I extracted myself from his embrace and walked over and stared into the box, to make sure it was empty.

It wasn't.

Lying at the bottom of the box was a piece of paper upon which was drawn in thick, black ink, the Eye of Horus.

Chapter 12

Effie

I huddled under a table for what seemed hours, waiting for the silence that only comes when everyone within is asleep. I think I might have dozed for a short while. As I sat clutching my knees I got colder and colder, even my feet, although I was wearing my piss-stained socks and shoes. By the time I crawled out my teeth were chattering and I was shivering uncontrollably. I realised I'd have to find something more to wear than the cotton shift they'd given me. I wish I knew where they'd put my clothes; it would be ridiculous to die of cold in such a hot country. I also needed to find some knickers.

I decided that my escape would have to wait until I'd found something to keep out the cold. I remembered the room where Sir Suzanne had got my shift and wondered what other clothes might be there so, with the torch making goblin-like shadows on the walls, I made my way down the corridor until I found the door. It was locked. I'd read in a comic that you can pick a lock with a hair pin; shame I didn't have one. In my frustration I shook the handle and whispered, 'Open Sesame!' but to no avail.

Against the wall opposite was a long, low table covered by a tasselled runner made of a dark material just like Ma Foster's curtains in her parlour. I lifted off the crude wooden cross and the crucified Jesus looked on indifferently as I wrapped the runner around me a couple of times. I already felt warmer.

I knew all the outside doors would be locked but the windows wouldn't be. The ones on the ground floor were shut at night to stop someone getting in from outside, although why anyone would want to beats me, but there was nothing to stop me opening one from inside, climbing through and jumping the few feet to the ground. I chose a window at the side of the orphanage and found myself in a narrow, dark passageway that stank of rotten vegetables and shit. I pulled my shawl tightly round me, put my bag over my shoulder, crept to the entrance of the alley and peered round the corner of the building.

I recognised the street that fronted the orphanage, now empty of people, the shop doors closed, the awnings rolled up and the chairs and tables taken inside. I wanted to get as far away from the place as possible, but I didn't know which way to go to get, where? Where was the best place to go? I only knew the way back to the hospital and I didn't want to go there. Ma Foster had always told us to find a policeman if we ever got lost, but I certainly wasn't going to do that; they'd just bring me straight back here. I really wanted to find Miss Trevethan, but I didn't know where she lived. I realised that in my determination to escape from the nuns I hadn't given enough thought as to where I would go afterwards.

Then I had a brainwave, or thought I had, anyway. I remembered that Miss Trevethan said she'd come and see me tomorrow, or was it already today? All I needed to do was to hide somewhere until the morning then catch her before she went inside. But I didn't want to hang around here, so I turned right, away from the orphanage and, keeping as far to the side of the road as possible, started walking.

I didn't need my torch to see as there was enough light from the occasional lamp. I had to be able to get back later on so I kept to the main street and avoided going down any of the alleys, although I would have felt much safer in the darkness they offered. The road abruptly came to an end, and I had the choice of going left or right. I instinctively turned left, feeling that this was taking me further away from the orphanage. I had to remember the way back: right at the corner where there was a barber shop, its distinctive red and white pole just like the ones in London.

Out of the silence there came a strange wail that rose and fell in a sing-song fashion. It seemed to come out of the sky, but I couldn't see anything when I looked up, only the night sky dotted with stars like silver sequins on black velvet. I realised I was no longer alone on the street. There were people, mostly men, coming quietly out of doors, all with heads bowed, sandalled feet shuffling in the sand. They were all going in the same direction as me, seemingly drawn by the hypnotic sound. It made me think of the Pied Piper of Hamelin, who played his pipes to lure the rats away from the town, and then the children because the townsfolk wouldn't pay his fee. Where were they all going? No one took any notice of me, so I continued walking with them, curious to see their purpose.

It was only when we arrived at their destination, a white stone building with a domed roof, that I remembered I hadn't taken note of the twists and turns we had made. I felt a moment of panic but then calmed down; I could just follow them back again for they would surely return home soon. The wailing was loud now and came, I realised, from a tall tower attached to the building. Most of the people were going through a doorway and I walked in with them because I wanted to know what they were all up to. When I had only taken a step inside the ornate doorway a man took me roughly by the arm, pushed me out of the door and pointed down the street. He didn't say anything, but he looked furious. I went in the direction he indicated and realised that it was just the men who had gone through the first door and the women were going through a different door, stopping only to remove their sandals before going inside. I hurried up, removed my shoes and socks, although I didn't know why, and walked in; I was the last person to enter. I noticed that all the women had their heads and mouths covered, just their dark eyes showing. I knew that women and girls had to wear hats or scarves on their heads in a Roman Catholic Church. Was I in a church then? What God did Egyptians worship these days, I wondered? Was it the same God as ours?

I tried to rewrap my shawl, but I kept covering my eyes as well. Whilst blindfolded I heard a giggle and hands gently removed mine, unwrapped the cloth and wrapped it again so that everything was covered apart from my eyes. I nodded my thanks and smiled at the young woman who had helped me. She took my hand and led me to a small, tiled pool sunk into the floor where others were washing their hands and feet. Once they had shaken off the droplets they went into another room, their feet still bare. The helpful woman waited whilst I squatted and washed in the pool. The water was warm and none too clean, but it refreshed me. When I stood up, she took my hand again and led me into the room where the other women had gone. There were about seven of them, all kneeling on the floor, all facing the same direction. The helpful woman knelt down, so I thought I had better do so as well.

There was an intricately carved screen at the front of the room and through the gaps I could see the backs of the men. I thought it very old-fashioned that men and women were separated; for goodness' sake, it was 1936! A man from the other side of the screen started sing-speaking and suddenly all the women leant forward and put their foreheads to the floor. The helpful woman wiggled her fingers at me, and I gathered I should do the same.

We each had a mat; mine was dark red with swirly patterns in gold and green, smelt musty and felt gritty. The man continued chanting and the women didn't make a sound. Were they praying silently? Should I? God hadn't answered any of my prayers so far, so I didn't think he'd bother listening to me now. Anyway, it was time to raise ourselves into a kneeling position again. Over the next few minutes, the women alternated between kneeling upright, bowing their heads, raising their hands and bending right over. I copied them as best I could but was relieved when it all seemed to be over, and

85

they all stood up. They chattered and hugged each other, and the helpful woman turned and started talking to me.

I shrugged my shoulders and rubbed my finger along my closed mouth. She seemed to understand my lie that I was dumb and put on a sad face before starting to chatter again. I put my hands over my ears to indicate I was also deaf. I nearly burst out laughing at her expression but then felt guilty at my deception. She hugged me and led me to the other women, who also hugged me. I really wished I could speak to them; they seemed very nice and would surely help me if they knew the pickle I was in.

We went out of the room and put on our shoes and sandals together. Then they all started back the way they had come. I followed, walking with the helpful woman, who kept looking at me, smiling and nodding her head. By now I realised that I could see things clearly; it was lighter and there was a glow to my right as the sun started its journey through the sky. I remembered that the sun rose in the east, well it did in England, I assumed it did in Egypt too. I wasn't sure if this information would help me.

The people who I was walking with stopped off at their homes and went inside or started opening up the shop doors, unrolling the awnings and putting out the chairs and tables. The helpful woman turned to go down an alley. She waved goodbye at me, and I waved back. I felt guilty as I imagined her telling her family all about the strange deaf and dumb girl that had turned up at her church, not knowing any of the rules. I wondered if she would look out for me over the next few days and when she would stop bothering.

The noises of the city grew as the sun rose and I wondered what time it was. I kicked myself for not thinking about such a simple thing as time. I had no idea what time it was now, and I had no idea what time Miss Trevethan would come. She may not come until the afternoon. She may not come at all. My plan to wait outside the orphanage for her now seemed stupid and for the first time since escaping I felt scared and alone. I went through a long list of 'what ifs' in my head and none of them ended well. I needed to find someone who could help me but who? Where was I going to find someone who spoke English and who wouldn't take me to the police? Then I asked myself a question I never thought I would. Should I just go back to the orphanage? What's the worst that could happen?

It didn't take me long to realise that the worst that could happen would be that they told Miss Trevethan that I'd died or run away or something so that she forgot about me, and they'd put me back in the windowless room until I really did die. I'm not a cry-baby but tears soaked into my makeshift shawl, making darker spots on the dark material and my snot left a slug-like trail where I wiped my nose.

Then I smelled new baked bread. I realised that I was hungry despite having gorged myself on the stew last night. I couldn't think of anything else but food. I followed my nose to where the smell was coming from and watched as the baker put rolls and loaves onto a table outside his shop. My mouth watered and my stomach rumbled. The man kept popping back inside to get more but he left a young boy outside to make sure no one stole anything. I knew I had some pennies in my purse, which Ma Foster had bought for my ninth birthday. It was made of real leather, and I treasured it. I was loath to spend my bus money home, but I decided my need for food was greater. I walked up to the guardian boy and held out the pennies in my hand. He took one and turned it over in his hand, frowning at the head of King George. Could I still use it now that he was dead? He called to the man, probably his father, and showed him one of the pennies. The man also frowned, rolled his eyes and shook his head. He shouted something at me and threw the coin onto the floor, which was quickly followed by the ones I had given the boy.

How dare he! I crouched down and rubbed my fingers over the sand, searching for my coppers. When I had found them all and put them safely back into my purse I stood up, accidentally knocking the table, causing some of the rolls to fall to the floor. Without thinking I grabbed two and ran for it, followed first by the man's shouts and then his footsteps as he chased after me. I wasn't the fastest runner in my class for nothing. I seemed to have wings on my feet as I flew down the street, avoiding people, donkeys and cars. I turned corners and crossed roads and just kept on running. I could now hear nothing but my heavy breathing and the sound of my own shoes on the ground. Eventually I ran out of steam and had to stop. I ducked into a shop and looked out and listened. There were plenty of people ambling past but no running man calling out 'Thief!' in Arabic.

I smiled sweetly at the wizened old shop keeper then slowly stepped out onto the pavement. I stood for a few minutes then felt safe enough to cross over the wide road and into the wrought iron gates that opened into a public park. I found a seat overlooking a wide river rather like the Thames and devoured one bread roll and then the other without pause. Birds that looked just like the pigeons in Trafalgar Square flew down from the palm trees and pecked in the sand looking for crumbs.

I leant back in the seat. I'd lost my shawl during the chase, but it was warm now and I didn't need it. 'Now what am I going to do?' I spoke out loud. Neither the birds nor I had an answer.

Chapter 13

Beattie

I was so shocked that my words came out as a croak. 'What do you mean, she's missing?'

Sister Margarita sat behind her desk looking distressed; standing behind her was another nun, much younger, who had not been introduced. Sister Margarita looked directly at me with her clear, blue eyes; the other one looked down at the floor.

'*Je suis désolé*, Miss Trevethan. *Sœur Françoise*,' she indicated to the downcast nun, 'put Mademoiselle Bloom to bed last night with the other young ones and she was *bien, assurément oui*. The rooms, they are checked before the nuns sleep and she was there, *vraiment*. But this morning, well...'

I had convinced my father that my visit to see Effie was urgent, but I had had hardly any sleep, and I was finding it hard to take in what she was saying. 'So, she wasn't in her bed this morning. Couldn't she have just got up early and gone somewhere else? To the bathroom? Or to another room? Have you looked in the rest of the building?'

'*Bien sûr*. We have looked ...' she swung her arm in a circle. They had looked everywhere.

But why would she leave the orphanage? She didn't know anyone; she didn't know Cairo. She was safe here.

Wasn't she?

I looked more closely at Sister Margarita. She was smiling but there was a hardness about her mouth and eyes, and I realised that I didn't trust her. 'Did anything happen yesterday that might have upset her?'

'*Mais non, rien.*'

I noticed the young nun glance at Sister Margarita before inspecting the floor again. What was down there that was so fascinating? God?

'*Sœur Françoise?*' She didn't look at me, merely shook her head. She was either extremely shy or extremely guilty. I looked boldly at Sister Margarita. 'Perhaps Sister Françoise could show me around the orphanage? I would like to see for myself.' And I would like to talk to her without her Mother Superior being there.

'That won't be necessary, Miss Trevethan. One of my men is searching the place as we speak.'

I turned in my chair to see Captain Karim standing by the door. I hadn't heard him knock; he probably hadn't. I found to my surprise that I was pleased to see him although I didn't want him to know so I just glared at him. He doubtless knew about my encounter with a scorpion by now as there were policemen at the house when I left.

'What was the young lady wearing, *Mère Supérieur*? Let us all speak in English, if you please.'

'Of course, Capitaine. I will translate for Sister Françoise.' She spoke to the younger nun and then translated her mumbled answer. 'Sister Françoise says that she had a white, cotton dress, like all the other girls wear. She has taken her socks and shoes and her bag, which is, *toile*, how you say?'

'Canvas', Captain Karim and I spoke at the same time.

The policeman looked at me and smiled then he turned to Sister Françoise and asked the question I had already asked. 'What happened yesterday that has made Miss Bloom run away?'

Sister Margarita translated the question and listened to the answer. There was no need to translate the '*Rien, honnêtement.*' I thought she looked scared, and I didn't believe her nor, I suspected, did Captain Karim.

He turned to me. 'You know the young lady better than anyone, Miss Trevethan. Do you have any, er ...' he tilted his head whilst he searched his mental English dictionary, 'inclination as to where she might go?'

I didn't know her well, though. We'd only had a few conversations but in that time I'd grown to like her and my worry at her disappearance had added to the mass of rock in my stomach that had grown over the last few days since the demonstration. 'I suppose she might try and find her way back to the hospital. It's the only other place she knows, and she might remember the way. But ...'

He held up his hand to stop me talking and stepped out of the room. We heard him talking to someone then he came back into the room whilst the other person, so I assumed, went to check the hospital. 'Anywhere else she might have gone? Your home? The British Embassy?'

'She doesn't know where I live but I suppose she might ask someone where the Embassy is. But she'd have to find someone who speaks English. Or,' I remembered her keen interest in Egyptology, 'perhaps the museum?' The more I thought about it the more likely I thought that she would go there; she'd feel safe there, protected by the gods. 'I could go there. I would like to help find her.'

He seemed to consider for a minute. 'Are you sure?' I nodded. I didn't want to go back home until it had been thoroughly checked out and the person who had put the scorpion in my room identified and hung, drawn and quartered. 'I'll send a constable with you.'

'Not the one from yesterday, if you please.'

He didn't react but rather said goodbye to the two Sisters and held the door open for me. As I brushed past him, I smelt cigarettes, apple and sweat, a surprisingly pleasant concoction. Only once outside and walking down the corridor together did he ask, 'Why not the constable from yesterday? He is young and perhaps inexperienced, but he will make a good policeman in time. Did he do something wrong?'

'He didn't do anything wrong himself, but he was incapable of stopping anyone else doing wrong.' I told him about the

91

stone-thrower, surprised that the constable hadn't told him about the incident. Perhaps he was too ashamed at his failure to apprehend the culprit.

Captain Karim looked concerned, which I felt pleased about. 'You have become something of a target, haven't you, Miss Trevethan? To be fair to the young policeman, no one could possibly have stopped someone from a crowd throwing a stone.'

'Perhaps, but he just didn't even try to see who had done it.'

By this time, we were standing on the top of the steps that led up to the front door. I found the orphanage oppressive and a little claustrophobic and I was glad to be outside, breathing in the smell of drains, animal droppings and petrol; it seemed fresher somehow than the air inside.

'On a different, but not unrelated matter, Miss Trevethan, I understand that you have also received a rather ...' another search of his mental English dictionary, 'disturbing letter. I don't suppose you have it with you?' I shook my head. 'Did you keep it?' I nodded. 'In that case, could you please have it sent to me? I wish to study all of them; they may give a hint of who sent them. I already have the paper that was left in the box with the scorpion last night. Sir Trevethan said you had no idea who left you that little gift?'

'No, I don't. I hope it wasn't any of our staff but that would mean someone from outside put it there, which is even more worrying. But I would have thought it was perfectly clear who has been targeting me. The Blue Shirts.'

Captain Karim shook his head. 'The Blue Shirts certainly want the British out of Egypt, but they are not the only ones and they do not use the Eye of Horus as their signature. No, that is another group, and I would very much like to know who is in it.'

'I'll have the letter sent round to Head Quarters later today.'

A young police constable came out of the orphanage and spoke to Captain Karim in Arabic. From the shakes of his head and the uplifting of his shoulders I knew that he had found no trace of Effie in the orphanage. I waited until he had finished his report before admitting, 'I don't trust those nuns. I'm sure they did something to Effie, to Miss Bloom, to make her run away.'

This time it was the Captain who shrugged his shoulders. 'Perhaps, but it is not likely to be a police matter. Our priority must be to find her.'

'I don't want her sent back there.'

He studied me for a while, I felt quite embarrassed under his scrutiny. 'We'll see. Let's find her first. Constable Mohammed will accompany you to the museum and I will send some men to the Embassy. Constable Mohammed will report back to me at Head Quarters, hopefully with the girl in hand. Good morning, Miss Trevethan, and happy hunting.' He gave a wry smile then turned on his heels and strode away, his khaki uniform standing out from the whites and blacks of the *fellahins*' attire. His English was excellent, and I wondered where he had learnt it. He was beginning to interest me, and I would ask my father if he knew his history.

Omar, the driver Daddy had assigned to me, was parked at the bottom of the steps. He was about my age, tall and skinny; he drove well and spoke reasonable English, but I didn't feel as safe with him as I did with Lateef. I wondered if there was a gun in the glove box and whether this gangly youth knew how to use it. Omar had the back door open for me and he pointed to the non-driver's front door to Constable Mohammed, who looked boyishly excited at being driven in a Ford motorcar.

It didn't take long to get to the Museum of Egyptian Antiquities located in Tahrir Square. It's a large, red-stoned neo-classical structure with a lower and upper floor. The building is in the shape of a fat T, with the top of the T being the front with a magnificent domed and pillared entrance in its centre, and the fat stem behind. I went to the museum most days because Marcus was there and I suppose I had stopped noticing how enormous it was, but as I walked into the entrance with Omar and the young policeman, I realised we had very little chance of finding Effie, especially if she didn't want to be found.

I suggested to Constable Mohammed, by pointing up the stairs, that he took the upper floor, and we would take the lower. I asked Omar to remind him that Effie might look like an Egyptian but that she was English and would be very frightened and he must not scare her. Although he grinned and nodded my heart sank as he walked away; even if he found her how would he ever convince her to go with him? It would be far better if it was me who found her.

The ground floor houses what Baedeker, the tourists' and my essential guidebook, calls the 'ponderous monuments.' Here is the last resting place of the statues of Rameses II, Amenhotep and Amenophis III, to name but a very few. In one section there are even two large wooden funeral boats built to transport dead Pharaohs to the afterlife and there is an abundance of stone sarcophagi. There are around fifty rooms, all filled with large artefacts from the beginnings of Egyptian history, all of which would be fascinating to Effie. Luckily there were not many people in the museum, and we were able to look in many of the rooms quickly to determine there was no one there at all. Other rooms, however, had groups of tourists and we had to look carefully to see if Effie was one of their number.

It occurred to me that just as we were moving from room to room, so may she be. She may always be in the next room, and we'd never catch up with her. Omar asked a few of the guides if they had seen a young dark-haired girl with black shoes and a canvas shoulder bag, but they all shook their heads; some laughed at him.

My feet and my heart ached as we plodded from room to room. I knew with absolute certainty that we wouldn't find Effie here and we were on a fool's errand. But I couldn't give up; what if she was in the next room? It took two hours to check the ground floor. When we arrived back at the entrance the young constable was already there. Alone. I didn't really think he'd have found her, but I was nonetheless disappointed. I watched him go off, presumably to report our failure to Captain Karim, feeling despondent and worried. Where could an eleven-year-old girl go who doesn't know the language, who doesn't know the city? What if she was hurt? What were we going to do with her even if we did find her? I didn't know what to do or where to go so I went where I always went to find comfort – to Marcus.

I made my way to the workshop, which was underground, dogged by Omar, who followed his orders to keep close to me to the letter. Before I reached it, I saw Marcus walking abstractly down the corridor towards me, studying a piece of paper in his hand.

'Oh, Marcus! The most awful thing has happened.'

He looked up, startled, and opened his mouth but I didn't let him say anything. 'Effie has run away from the orphanage. Well, the nuns say she's run away. We've looked everywhere here, and Captain Karim has had the orphanage searched and is sending someone to the Embassy and the hospital but what if she's not there? I'm so worried about her; she'll be so frightened. And, I was thinking, what if she hasn't actually run away. What if the nuns lied because they've actually killed her? I don't know why they would have, but I don't trust that Sister Margarita and as for Sister Françoise, there was definitely something very odd about her. I just don't know what to do. Oh God, what on earth are we going to tell her foster parents? "I'm terribly sorry but we seem to have lost your daughter." Foster daughter. Just because she's fostered, they'd still care, wouldn't they? Even if they didn't, I care! I really liked her and, and ...' I ran out of words and just stood, sobbing.

He took my arm gently and led me into his workshop to comfort me in private but there was someone else in there, sitting on a stool hunched over something on the table. She looked up and turned towards us. 'I think I know who it is, Mr Dunwoody. Oh, hullo Miss Trevethan.'

Chapter 14

Effie

Miss Trevethan's hug hurt more than the slap that had preceded it. When she had nearly squeezed the breath right out of me she took me by the shoulders and shook me, all the while both crying and laughing.

Mr Dunwoody finally came to my rescue and gently took her hands off me and handed her his handkerchief. Why he didn't just hold her in his arms to comfort her I don't know; even I could tell that was what he wanted to do and what she wanted him to do. Having wiped and blown as necessary, Miss Trevethan sat on a stool and looked at me. Her eyes were shining with unshed tears; they reminded me of some bright green moss I had once seen on the side of a tree in one of the London parks. Although Billy had hair the same colour as Miss Trevethan, his eyes were more the colour of stagnant water.

She smiled and took my hands in hers. 'I'm so glad I've found you. I hoped you might come here but then when I was walking around I realised how very big it is and thought we'd never find you. Why did you run away, Effie? I was so worried.'

'You was worried about me?'

'Of course I was.' I felt a warmth spread over my cheeks, down my neck to my chest, legs and arms and right to the tips of my toes and fingers. 'Why did you run away? Did the nuns do something to you? Were you scared? Did they hurt you?'

'Beattie, stop asking questions. Let her speak, my dear.'

'Them nuns were cruel.' I didn't want to say anything about pissing myself with Mr Dunwoody there so I stared intently at Miss Trevethan hoping she'd read my mind. She didn't but he did.

'I tell you what, I'll just go and find something to eat and drink and leave you two here if that's ok?' He took our silence

97

as a 'yes' and quietly left the room. I heard him speak to someone then his footsteps as he walked down the corridor. Only when I was absolutely sure he was gone did I continue with my story.

'When you were gone, I was so scared I wet myself and Sister Margarita turned right nasty. She handed me over to another nun who she called Sir Suzanne but she weren't no knight, I can tell you.'

Miss Trevethan looked puzzled then broke into a wide grin. 'French for sister is *sœur*, which sounds exactly like the English word 'sir' like Sir Lancelot of the court of King Arthur. Sir Suzanne.' She chuckled and so did I, glad she hadn't said anything about me pissing myself.

'Sister Suzanne, then, seemed quite nice to begin with, all chatty and smiles but she turned into a monster when I tried to stop her washing me.'

'Why on earth didn't you want to have a wash?'

'She used carbolic soap, and my skin can't take it. Look.' I held out my arm where there were still some weals visible. She stroked one and the hairs on the back of my head stood up on end.

'Do they hurt?'

'Not so much now. I struggled to get away from her and I might have hit her on her chest. Not hard but she went berserk. She dragged me still stark naked and threw me into a shed which had no light at all. I hate the dark.'

'Oh, Effie.' That's all she said, whispered really, but it was like a key that opened a door that held back all my tears. I couldn't stop myself crying like a baby. She got off her stool, put her arms around me and rocked me as if I really was one. I had soaked her blouse with my tears and snot before she remembered to give me Mr Dunwoody's handkerchief, which was very wet by the time I'd finished my bawling. I didn't have a pocket in my shift, so I balled up the handkerchief and held it in my fist in case either of us needed it again. I decided not to tell her about Mimi; I wanted all her sympathy for myself alone.

Miss Trevethan got back onto her stool and told me to carry on with my story. 'Eventually another nun came and let us, me out. She gave me some food and put me to bed. She seemed quite nice, but she probably wasn't.'

'That might have been Sister Françoise. She was with the Mother Superior, that's Sister Margarita, this morning when I was told that you'd gone missing. She said nothing about what you've just told me; she said you were perfectly all right and there had been no problems at all. No wonder Sister Françoise looked so uncomfortable; she knew the truth but couldn't say anything. So, how did you escape and how on earth did you end up here?'

'Once I was in bed I waited until I thought everyone was asleep and made my way to the kitchen. I knew it was empty and I waited a while then climbed out of a window.'

'Weren't you scared? Wasn't it dark? Where did you go then? Oh, I'm sorry. I shouldn't ask so many questions. I'll shut up.' She bit her bottom lip to stop any more words flowing out.

'I was a bit scared but not as much as if I'd stayed with the nuns. I wanted to get as far away from them as possible, so I just followed the road.' I didn't tell her about my visit to the church or my stealing the bread; she didn't need to know that. 'I walked for a while, it got light, and I found myself by a river.'

'The Nile. Goodness, that is quite a long way from the orphanage. How did you know where to go to get here?'

'Well, to be honest, I didn't. I followed a group of English tourists intending to ask one of them for help. By the time I'd plucked up courage to approach one they'd reached the museum, and I remembered that Mr Dunwoody worked here. I followed them in but one of them guards saw me and pulled me away. I tried to tell them I was English and wanted to see Mr Dunwoody but they just wouldn't listen.'

As if he was waiting for his name to be mentioned the man himself came in bearing plates of filled rolls, pastries and fresh fruit. I had eyes only for the pastries, the bread earlier only having filled up a very small hole.

Whilst I ate Mr Dunwoody took up the story. 'I was sitting here working away, trying to determine the identity of the cartouche on the bottom of that scarab I showed you. Do you remember it? A very fine specimen that ...'

'Yes, Marcus. I remember. Just tell me what happened next.'

'Well, as I said, I was sitting here when I heard the most awful hullabaloo. There was a lot of shouting, mostly in Arabic but I heard, louder than everyone put together, this voice shouting "I'm English. I want to see Mr Dunwoody. I'm English.' Mr Dunwoody had put on a squeaky voice and Miss Trevethan laughed. 'I went upstairs to see what all the fuss was about and there was this young lady, struggling against the two burly guards who were holding her. Quite a crowd had gathered, and I heard an American lady say "She says she's English. She sure don't look English to me, she looks more like one of those Arabby street brats who are always begging for money and trying to steal your purse."' His American accent was awful, but Miss Trevethan laughed again. I didn't think it was all that funny but then I wasn't in love with him. 'I went over to see if I could help and I only recognised her when she saw me and cried out, "Oh, Mr Dunwoody, don't you remember me? I'm Effie. I'm the girl you found in the packing case."'

He looked at me and grinned. I grinned back. I pointed to the sketch I had made of the cartouche. 'I think I've found whose name that is in that old book you gave me to look at. I think it might be Akhenaten. Do you agree?' I desperately wanted to be right and get his approval.

'Yes, you might well be. Let me take a look.'

'Not now, Marcus. We need to agree what we're going to do with Effie. I absolutely refuse to take her back to the orphanage and we ought to tell Captain Karim that she's been found. We also need to get her some proper clothes. She does rather look like a street Arab in that outfit, apart from the socks and shoes.'

My stomach lurched and I nearly choked on my pastry. 'Please don't take me to the police, Miss Trevethan. They'll just take me to the orphanage and I'm not going back, I'm not!' My cheeks were red hot, and I was finding it difficult to breathe.

'Don't worry, Effie, I won't let anyone take you back; the place ought to be shut down. Perhaps we should go to the Embassy, I think someone there was working on your case. We can see if they've managed to contact your parents.'

'Foster parents,' I corrected.

'Yes, your foster parents and how they intend to get you back home.'

I liked both Miss Trevethan and Mr Dunwoody and now I was safely with them I realised I didn't want my adventure to be over. 'Could I have a look round the museum first? There's so much more here than at the one in London.'

The two grown-ups glanced at each other, and Mr Dunwoody raised his eyebrows. 'She's got to see the Tutankhamun artefacts, Beattie, if nothing else. Why don't you show her around whilst I go to Police Headquarters and tell Captain Karim we've found her, then I'll go onto the Embassy and get an update. After that we can discuss where Effie can stay.'

We both thanked him, and he left; Miss Trevethan's eyes followed him out of the room and beyond.

'Why don't you just tell him, Miss?'

'Tell him what?'

'That you love him?'

Miss Trevethan's face went the colour of one of the tomatoes no one had eaten. 'What a thing to say! You're only ten. What do you know about such things? I'm not in love with him. No, not at all. We're just good friends.'

'If you say so, Miss. But he's in love with you.'

I watched to see if her face could get any redder; it could. I handed her the damp handkerchief I had been clutching but instead she searched in her pocket for one of her own; a useless dainty piece of cotton with a lace trim and the letter B embroidered in the corner. Once she had calmed herself and her cheeks had returned to the normal white, she ate the last bit of pastry I'd been planning to eat myself, told me to pick up my things and led the way out of the door into the corridor. She didn't seem cross with me but was certainly flustered. There was an Arab squatting by the door, obviously waiting for Miss Trevethan. He stood up, eyed me suspiciously and followed close behind as we went up to the ground floor.

I hadn't had the chance to look around before; I'd been too busy trying to fight off the guards, but now I stared in wonder at the huge, red statues that gazed down on us. Many of them were damaged, which was hardly surprising as they were thousands of years old, but they still radiated power and even though it was warm I shivered as they looked into and through me with their blank eyes.

Miss Trevethan pulled me along. 'I'm sorry, Effie, but we don't have time to look at everything. I think you'll want to see the things that were found by Carter in the tomb of Tutankhamun. Come on, they're upstairs.'

On the way we passed a number of glass cases in which lay mummified bodies. One looked particularly short, and I stopped to read the type-written piece of card stuck askew to the side: 'Unknown child found in the tomb of Thutmosis III.' She must have been important or the son or daughter of someone important for her to have been mummified. How sad that she had died young; how sad that she should end up being gawped at by tourists.

'Did you know,' I wanted to show off my knowledge to Miss Trevethan, 'that the Ancients believed that the heart was the seat of the soul so left it in the body? It would be weighed in the scales of justice against the feather of Ma'at. The liver, lungs, intestines and stomach though were put in canopic jars, like these here.' I pointed at a glass fronted case that held over thirty jars. 'I hope this little girl can find hers; she'll need them in the afterlife.'

Miss Trevethan laughed, took my hand and dragged me into a large room that took my breath away. It was full of pieces of furniture and glass displays of every size and shape, each one crammed full of items, all found in the young king's tomb only a few years ago. 'Just imagine,' I whispered, 'moving a stone block, squeezing through a small gap, holding up your lamp and ... and seeing all this.' Miss Trevethan wanted to show me Tutankhamun's death mask. The gold, inlaid with jewels and lapis lazuli glittered in the lights and his dark eyes looked out scornfully at us lesser mortals. The heads of the cobra and vulture that he had on his forehead seemed to follow me as I walked around the room, making me feel uncomfortable. I wondered if any of these items carried the curse. The mask was indeed beautiful but I was more interested in the other items that told the story of the people that lived at that time: gold-plated and ebony bedsteads; gilded couches that looked most uncomfortable to sit on; parts of chariots that perhaps carried Tutankhamun himself; ivory inlaid walking sticks; alabaster vases; lotus-shaped cups; colourful fans, opened ready for a woman to pick up and cool herself. There was so much more it was overwhelming. It was the jewellery that mesmerised me the most: exquisite brooches, earrings, necklaces, amulets and rings, all looking as if they had just been worn and were waiting to be worn again. Gold and lapis lazuli dominated, but there were flashes of turquoise, purple amethyst and red carnelian.

I was standing staring at a display of scarabs when Miss Trevethan touched my shoulder and made me jump. 'I've had the most marvellous idea.'

Chapter 15

Beattie

My plan was perfect; I would take Effie to Luxor to stay with Aunt Edith. It would not only solve the problem of what to do with her, but it would also mean I would get out of Cairo for a while, something Daddy was very keen for me to do. When I explained my proposal Effie could hardly contain herself and jumped up and down, until she realised she was making the scarabs rattle. But then she looked worried.

'Would I be allowed to go with you? The police won't say I have to stay in Cairo?'

'I don't see why they would. They're not going to say they don't trust me, the daughter of the adviser to the Minister of the Interior. We'll have such fun, Effie. My aunt is a bit eccentric, but I know you'll love her, and she'll love you. We'll be able to visit the Valley of the Kings and see the temples of Luxor and Karnak.'

Effie's expression changed to unadulterated joy again then back to distinct worry. 'What if Mr Dunwoody finds out that everything's in place for me to go home?'

'Pshaw! The Embassy doesn't work that quickly. Don't worry, you're folder will be at the bottom of a very high pile. We'll have gone and come back, and they won't even have reached it.'

'Promise?'

I shouldn't have, of course. 'I promise.'

'You could ask Mr Dunwoody to come with us.'

Why did this child, who knew nothing of these things, keep going on about Marcus and me? How could she possibly know how I or he felt? I admit, though, she did seem to know how I felt. What if she was right about Marcus? If he did... like me ... then why didn't he make it known to me? Was he, like me, unsure how or when our life-long friendship had become something more? He was two years older than me, and our families had lived near each other in Kent when our fathers were both working in London. To begin with I was just the annoying little girl who followed him around and ruined his games, but he got to like me better when I was a willing Indian captive, a mediaeval princess trapped in the dragon's cave, a witch burning at the stake, or a young girl kidnapped by Bedouins. He, of course, was always the rescuer, apart from the time he forgot about me, and my mother found me after hours of searching, tied to an oak tree and sobbing my little heart out. I forgave him, of course.

We were educated at different schools, and he went to university whereas I went to be finished off, but we always got together during the holidays. He impressed me with his knowledge of ancient Egypt, I him with my ability to walk across a room without dropping a thick Charles Dickens book balanced on my head. I was thrilled when my father was posted to Cairo to find that the Dunwoody's were going, and that Marcus was training to be an archaeologist. We soon started meeting up again and I spent much of my days now following him around the museum, typing labels and his almost illegible notes. When did I start to love him? Probably when I was four, when we were pretending to be a married couple and he pecked me on the cheek as he had seen his father do to his mother. Twenty years of unrequited love is a long time but I'm nothing if not patient and Effie, bless her stained, cotton socks, thought he might love me too.

'We'll need an escort so yes, perhaps I'll ask him. I'm sure he'll jump at the chance to visit the Valley of the Kings again. Speak of the devil.'

Marcus scanned the room for us and seeing us, strode over. 'That's all done, then. I've left a message for Captain Karim and went to the Embassy to see the bloke responsible for Effie's case, a Mr Jones. He's a grey man in a grey suit and I'm not at all sure he's the slightest bit capable. I'll have a word with my father and see if he can chivvy it along a bit.'

'There's no need, Marcus. I'm going to take Effie with me when I go and visit Aunt Edith. It'll kill two birds with one stone, so to speak. We can telegraph her foster parents and tell them we'll return her in a few weeks or so.'

'What about school?' Marcus could be something of a kill joy.

'What better education than travelling through a new country and visiting ancient temples and tombs? She'll be able to teach history when she returns, won't you Effie?'

She grinned and nodded with great enthusiasm. 'Will we be all right travelling on the train by ourselves, Miss?'

What a little monkey she was. 'I expect Daddy will insist Omar accompanies us.' We all glanced his way; he was squatting on the floor, his back against the wall, looking bored.

'Do you think he'd be able to stop a gang of them Blue Shirts, Miss?'

'I think they're only in Cairo, Effie.' I was so desperate to ask Marcus to come with us, but I just couldn't get the words out of my mouth, which had gone drier than the Sahara.

'Maybe you could take us, Mr Dunwoody? You could show us around all the sites.'

Was it my imagination or did Marcus blush? 'That's certainly an idea. It depends on what Lord Trevethan says.'

I wanted to scream, 'Yes, yes, yes, come with us!' but I merely shrugged and noticed Effie shake her head in despair. 'I think the first thing we need to do is to get you a new wardrobe of clothes. We'll go to see Jamila. She makes all my clothes. She'll be able to run you up a new wardrobe in just a few days.'

Marcus tousled Effie's hair, which she didn't seem to mind. I wouldn't have minded it either. 'If you're going shopping, I'll leave you to it. If it's all right with Beattie, how about tomorrow I take you to see the pyramids?' Effie's eyes opened wider than I would have thought possible, and she looked beseechingly at me. How could I refuse? Not that I wanted to. I nodded. 'We'll go early in the morning before the tourists arrive and then I thought we could pay a visit to El Lisht. It's a necropolis. There's no one working there now but it's not far away and I think you'd find it interesting. We could have a picnic. Would you like that?' He looked first at Effie and then at me. How blue his eyes were and how grateful I was to him for making such an effort to entertain Effie. Or was he trying to entertain me?

'That would be splendid. I'll pack the picnic. How early is early?'

'Let's say seven o'clock. We can spend a few hours at the Pyramids then get to El Lisht in time for lunch. Right, you girls have a lovely afternoon, whilst I ruin my eyesight poring over worn hieroglyphics, and I'll see you tomorrow.'

He winked at Effie and smiled at me and started to walk away. He was just going through the doorway when Effie ran after him and pulled on his arm. He bent down to hear what she was saying, glanced at me and I'm sure he blushed again. What was she saying to him? He gave her a nod then left and Effie came sauntering over, looking innocent.

'What was that all about?'

'I just wanted to thank him. I can't believe it, Miss Trevethan. The pyramids! And the Valley of the Kings!' She looked at me in horror. 'This isn't a dream, is it? I'm not going to wake up and find myself back in the orphanage? Oh, please don't say it's a dream.'

I laughed and tousled her hair. She pulled away and straightened her locks. 'No, it's no dream, Effie. Come on, let's go and get you kitted out.'

'Miss,' she looked around her as if to make sure no one was listening and then she whispered, 'I need some knickers as well. The nuns never gave me any. I'm walking about without none, and I don't like it; it ain't right.'

'No, you're right. It ain't, isn't, I mean. Jamila will run you up half a dozen pairs in no time.'

In fact, Jamila had someone run them up whilst we were still in the shop, discussing what clothes a young girl of ten years and eight months would need for a foray to Luxor. We agreed on a couple of night dresses, four simple cotton dresses, a best dress for Sunday, four short-sleeved blouses and two pairs of shorts, socks, a light jacket and a warm cardigan for the evening. When Effie was handed the pile of knickers, she put one on there and then. 'That's better,' she sighed in relief. We stopped at another shop to buy her some sandals before Omar drove us to the orphanage. I wanted to tell Sister Margarita to her face exactly what I thought of her.

Effie refused to go inside. She was actually shaking with fear, and I didn't have the heart to force her to face her nemesis. I left her hunched in the back of the car, with Omar as her guard. I told him no one, whoever they were, must be allowed to open the door and drag her out. He nodded in understanding and wore a determined look. He reached into the glove compartment and pulled out a revolver which he laid on his lap. I hoped it wouldn't be necessary to shoot any nuns.

I knocked on the door, which was opened by a nun I hadn't seen before. I asked for the Mother Superior and said I had a very urgent matter to discuss with her. She left me standing whilst she went to see where Sister Margarita was and whether she was free to see me. She came back just a few minutes later and beckoned for me to follow her to the room I had been in only this morning.

'Ah, Miss Trevethan. *Asseyez vous, s'il vous plait.* How very nice to see you again.'

'I wish I could say the same, Sister Margarita.'

'I pray you don't have bad news about Miss Bloom?'

'It's you I have bad news for.' I waited whilst her face went through expressions of curiosity, fear and finally obstinacy. She finished up with her lips set in a thin, straight line and her eyes the colour of blue granite. She didn't ask if Effie had been found; she just waited for an explanation.

'I'm sure you'll be pleased to hear that Effie, Miss Bloom, has been found and she is quite unharmed. Well, I'll re-phrase that. She's not been harmed since she was in your care yesterday.'

Still the nun said nothing. Merely glared at me and raised her eyebrows.

'She still has the weals on her skin where she was forced to be washed with carbolic soap.'

'That, Miss Trevethan, was an unfortunate accident due to her not being able to speak French and explain her - *sensibilité.*'

'And was her being thrown into a dark room for hours on end with no clothes also due to a misunderstanding?'

'She was put there to think about her actions, which were not those expected of a well-brought up English girl.'

'And what actions were they, pray?'

'She soiled herself – twice – and caused physical harm to Sister Suzanne. This was not acceptable *et devait être puni.*'

I felt myself redden in anger. 'That's what it says in the bible is it? Didn't Jesus say, "suffer little children to come unto me"? I don't think he meant make them suffer if they are scared out of their wits.'

Her lips went so thin they almost disappeared. 'She was a disobedient child. Thank you for coming to tell me that you have found her. I don't think it would be – *approprieé* – for her to come back.'

I stood up so suddenly the chair fell backwards. 'It would not only be not appropriate it would also be cruel. When you should have shown her love, kindness and forgiveness, you

110

showed her nothing but intolerance and brutality. I really don't know how you can call this place the *House for the Children of God* and then treat them so badly. I can't stay here any longer. Good day.' I stalked across the door and flung open the door. I turned in the doorway and gave my parting shot. 'I happen to know the Right Reverend Jean Garnier rather well. Be assured I will make my dissatisfaction known to him.' I slammed the door, childish maybe but rather satisfying.

Chapter 16

Effie

I couldn't take my eyes off the gun. Omar sat motionless in the front seat, his right hand resting lightly on the wooden handle. I wondered how long it would take him to raise it, point and fire? Didn't you have to unlock them? 'Have you ever shot anyone?'

He looked at me in the mirror; I could only see his eyes. 'Many times, young miss. You have nothing to fear.'

Was he joking? Why and when would someone like him shoot anyone? 'Did you kill them?'

'Of course.' His eyes crinkled; was he squinting or smiling? I didn't really believe him but although I didn't like the nuns neither did I want him to have the death of one on his conscience. The only person to come out of the orphanage, though, was Miss Trevethan, looking like thunder. Her face was a red that didn't go well with her ginger hair, and she didn't need a gun; her looks alone could kill.

'That woman is absolutely insufferable.' I didn't know what insufferable meant but I guessed it wasn't a word of praise. Miss Trevethan sat back in the seat and told Omar to take us home.

'Who did you see? Were they cross?'

'I only saw Sister Margarita and was she cross? No, she wasn't, anything but. She explained exactly why they did what they did, as if it was the most natural thing in the world to lock a young girl away for hours on end in a dark hole.' It was a dark room not a hole, but I didn't like to interrupt her. 'She said it was all a misunderstanding about the carbolic soap and she effectively blamed you for not speaking French. She was really horrible, Effie, really horrible. It scares me to death to think what those poor girls must suffer at that place.' She took a deep breath and relaxed into the seat. 'Well, I've told them what I think of their Christian behaviour. I don't suppose it will make

112

the slightest difference but I'm going to speak to the bishop and tell him what goes on in that place. Ah, here we are.'

We pulled up outside a large building that looked very like the posh terraced ones in London. It was white and the steps to the front door led straight from the pavement. There were balconies at all the windows. We went up the steps and Miss Trevethan used her key to open the front door, which was very shiny black with a huge brass knocker in the shape of a lion's head. We walked into a large hall that had a black and white tiled floor, just like a draughts board.

'My father won't be home yet.' Thank goodness, I wasn't sure I wanted to meet him. 'I'll stay in my mother's room, and you can have mine. Come on, I'll show you where it is.'

'I thought your Ma was dead.'

'Yes, she died ten years ago. We still call it her room. Silly, I suppose. Here's mine. I'll get one of the girls to change the bedding. Do you want a bath? We have hot water, you know, all very modern.'

The room was enormous. It had light coloured wooden furniture, cream wallpaper decorated with different types of flowers and matching curtains that hung limply. The windows were wide open but there was no breeze. I looked out but everything was blurred. 'What's this in the window? Is it to keep you in?'

Miss Trevethan laughed. 'No, it's to keep mosquitoes out.'

'What are they?'

'Tiny little insects that suck your blood.'

I looked at her in horror. Was she joking? She didn't look as if she was. 'Are they vampires?' Billy had shown me one of his Dracula comics.

'No, but they can really irritate the skin and their bites itch something terrible. They seem to find me particularly tasty, so I have a mosquito net around the bed as well. Don't look so worried. It comes with living in a hot country. Now, do you want a bath?'

The thought of lying in a bath in the middle of the afternoon seemed almost sinful so I nodded. Miss Trevethan went to tell someone to get a bath ready and left me to settle in. There wasn't much I could do other than put my bag on a chair and sit at the dressing table. I stared at the girl in the mirror. Behind her was a double bed with crisp, white sheets, a cover that matched the wallpaper and curtains and pillows piled high. It had a canopy above it from which hung drapes of material tied back; I suppose this must be the mosquito net she talked about. I thought of the bed back home that I shared with Dora and Betty and sometimes the boys; we kept each other warm but there was never any room to turn over or stretch out, there was always an elbow, a knee or a foot in the way. I thought of the bed I'd slept in last night, sharing with the freakish Mimi; the very thought of her still made me shudder. Was it only last night? So much had happened since. The girl in the mirror looked back at me and she suddenly grinned.

'We're going to the pyramids tomorrow. Can you believe it? And to some archaeological site. Mr Dunwoody is taking us. And then Miss Trevethan and me are going to Luxor. Luxor! Is this really happening? Do you think we'll wake up tomorrow back in London? Do you miss home?' The girl in the mirror shook her head adamantly. 'No, me neither. Don't suppose they miss me much either.' The girl in the mirror shrugged. 'Do you think we'd recognise our mother if she walked past us?' The girl in the mirror frowned then shook her head reluctantly. 'No, me neither. Maybe Miss Trevethan could help us. She probably knows everyone in Cairo.' The eyes of the girl in the mirror sparkled and she nodded enthusiastically.

'Who are you talking to?'

I blushed. 'Just myself.'

'Oh, I do that all the time. Comes with being an only child, I suppose. Come on, the bath is ready.'

I winked at the girl in the mirror, and she winked back; she left the room when I did. I expected to go down to the kitchen, but Miss Trevethan led me along the corridor and into another room. Its walls were tiled in white; there was a large white sink, a white toilet and an enormous white bath with silver taps. Everything gleamed. The steam rose from the bath water and the smell of something flowery filled the air.

'We all share the same tin bath back home. We bathe in age order so I'm fourth. The water is always lukewarm, grey and scummy by then.' I thought I'd have made Miss Trevethan laugh but she didn't; she looked sad. I started to take my clothes off.

'Do you want me to leave you? I can send one of the girls in to help you wash your hair.'

I didn't want to be left alone. 'Could you stay? I might drown, the water is so deep.' This time she did laugh. The water was covered with a dense mountain range of bubbles, and they clung to me as I stepped in and lowered myself into the warmth. The bath was longer than me so I could stretch out fully. I put my head back and felt my hair fan out.

'Shall I wash your hair for you?'

I felt embarrassed that someone like her should wash the hair of someone like me, but I couldn't resist her offer, so I nodded, leant my head further back and closed my eyes. I heard her kneel by the side of the bath and felt her fingertips as they rubbed the shampoo into my hair. My scalp tingled deliciously, and I couldn't help groaning in pleasure. She hummed as she rubbed and poured clean water from a jug to rinse out the bubbles.

'Sit up, that's you done. Have a soak and I'll take your clothes to be washed and find you something to wear until they're dry, which won't take long.'

115

I wished the others could see me, living it up in such luxury. But I didn't really want them there; this was my adventure, and I didn't want to share it. I moulded the bubbles into peaks and troughs then buried my face in a handful, making myself sneeze. I don't think I've ever felt so clean. I lay back and just wallowed. The water began to cool and the palms of my hands to wrinkle. I got out of the bath and was wrapping a large towel around me when Miss Trevethan came back in.

'Oh, that's perfect. Just keep that on until your dress is dry. We're only going to be sitting in the back garden so no-one will see you.' She held out her hand and I gladly took it and let her lead me downstairs. We went into a room that was full of books, more books than the local library down the road from us. It had a couple of comfy looking armchairs, and I could imagine Miss Trevethan curled up on one, reading. 'Do you want to choose yourself a book to read? The ones over here are my old children's books.' She took one out. 'Do you like horses?' I can't say I'd ever thought about them, so I just shrugged. 'Well, just take a look and take whichever ones you want.' I put my finger on the spine of each book and read the titles under my breath: *The Story of Doctor Doolitle*, *Just William*, *Emily of New Moon*, *The Magical Land of Noom*, *Child Whispers*, *When we were Young*. I didn't recognise any of them.

'Do you have any books on Egypt?'

'There are a few travel ones over here. This one,' she picked one off the shelf, 'is by Amelia Edwards, and is called *A Thousand Miles up the Nile*, which says it all, really. She made the journey fifty years ago; she was a fascinating woman and very adventurous. There are a few etchings of the things she saw but this one might be more interesting to you. It's a catalogue of the museum in Cairo. It tells you a bit about each of the artefacts that were on display a few years ago and it's full of pictures.'

116

I was a bit annoyed that she thought I could only read a picture book, but the catalogue did look really interesting, so I took it eagerly. I followed her as she crossed the library, picked up a book that was lying open on the arm of one of the chairs and went out through the open French windows into the garden. There was a table and four loungers placed under a large tree, whose spread-out leafy branches provided shade from the sun that burned my skin in the short distance from the house.

I was glad to see a jug of lemonade, with ice cubes still visible though melting even as I watched. I was even gladder to see a bowl of fruit and a plate heaped with crustless sandwiches so small they were not even a mouthful. Miss Trevethan poured the lemonade, allowing a couple of ice cubes to drop into each glass and told me to help myself to the food; I was more than happy to oblige. I'm not sure what the sandwiches were filled with, but they were delicious, and I had to stop myself from eating the whole lot. I bit into a peach and instantly regretted it as warm syrup dribbled down my chin and onto the towel. Miss Trevethan didn't shout at me, she just pushed a plate, knife and serviette over to me then settled back to read her book.

'I'm afraid I'm rather addicted to crime. I'm a huge fan of Agatha Christie. Have you heard of her?' Miss Trevethan held the book up so that I could see the cover. The title, *Death in the Clouds,* was written across the sky by the fumes from an aeroplane.

'I have, actually. Ma Foster loves her too. She gets them out of the library.' The towel I was wearing was thick and making me too hot, so I just loosened it a bit to allow the heat out, settled back and started to browse the catalogue. I hadn't had a good night's sleep and the warmth, and the buzz of insects lulled me.

I was lying on a couch; a young girl peeled grapes and popped them into my mouth whilst above me an enormous peacock fan, held by someone unseen, wafted from side to side.

I was on a boat, gliding slowly down the Nile. On either side there were tall palm trees bent over with the weight of the coconuts they bore; dark haired and skinned people, my people, stood on the banks waving and cheering, the children running excitedly alongside the boat. There were others on the boat: Ma Foster was sitting knitting; Billy and Cyril were leaning over the side, trying to stroke the snout of a crocodile; Dora and Betty were sitting on the deck playing with scarabs; Miss Trevethan was reading a book; Sister Margarita was in a wooden pen, being poked at by Dick.

The world suddenly went dark as a black shadow fell over me and a deep voice thundered from the heavens, 'It's all right for some.' I leapt off the lounger, forgetting that my towel was no longer tied around me and stood completely naked in front of a tall, thick-set man, who didn't bat an eyelid. He reached down, picked up the towel and handed it to me. 'You must be Effie. I'm very pleased to meet you. I'm Beattie's father.'

Chapter 17

Beattie

Early the next morning, I went into my room, now Effie's room, to find her still fast asleep. She was curled on her side with her thumb firmly in her mouth, which would explain her slightly protruding front teeth. I pulled the curtains open first followed by the mosquito net around the bed, put my hand on her shoulder and gently shook her, speaking softly, 'Time to get up, Effie.' She stirred but showed no signs of awakening, so I shook a little harder and spoke a little louder, 'Time to get up, Effie.' Still she slept on. I shook her with one hand, tickled her bare tummy with the other and shouted, 'Time to get up, Effie.'

She opened one eye, then the other. 'No need to shout. I heard you the first time. Gawd, what time is it?'

'Time to get up. Come on, you've got half an hour to get ready and have some breakfast; we don't want to keep Marcus, Mr Dunwoody, waiting. Your clean clothes are here. Can you remember where the bathroom is? Good. Come downstairs when you're ready, the breakfast room is just to the right. I'll see you in a few minutes.'

I'd only just sat down and taken my first sip of tea when Effie came in. She hadn't brushed her hair and I doubt she'd had time to wash but apart from that she looked fresh and wide awake.

'Did you sleep well, Effie?' Daddy looked up from his newspaper and grinned at her, not a polite smile but a wide, boyish grin of pure pleasure.

'Oh, yes thank you, Mr Trevethan, it's the most comfortablest bed I've ever slept in. Did you? Sleep well, I mean?' Effie blushed a little. Last night she and Daddy had chatted together all evening; she telling him about her life so far and he telling her about what a dreadful daughter I had been, which she found hilarious. She had obviously been exhausted after her escapades and almost fell asleep at the dinner table, but she didn't seem to want to leave him. In the end, he had to pick her up and carry her to bed where, so he told me later, he had kissed her good night and she had clung to him and had a little cry. I'm not sure he hadn't also shed a tear or two but I didn't probe.

Daddy nodded. 'Yes, I slept like a log. So, you're off to see the pyramids followed by El Lisht? There's not much to see there now but I think you'll find it interesting. Beattie told me her plan to take you to visit her Aunt Edith at Luxor. I think it's an excellent idea and don't worry, I'll make sure your foster parents are told. Now, I need to go; I've got an early start, going on a fact-finding mission to some of the surrounding villages with the Minister of the Interior. It should be fun but not as much fun as your day.' He got up and folded his napkin carefully. As he passed behind Effie he tousled her hair, making it stick out even more. 'Have a good day and don't let her boss you about too much.' It wasn't clear which of us he was speaking to.

Effie may have been as skinny as a twig, but she had the appetite of a locust and devoured a cooked breakfast and several slices of buttered toast in the time it took me to eat an orange and drink a cup of tea. I never ate much in the morning; I usually saved myself for a hearty evening meal and I knew that the picnic we took with us today would be substantial. Effie was still chewing when Marcus popped his head round the door.

'Morning both. You two ready for the off?'

Effie swallowed noisily and stood up so quickly she knocked the chair over. She looked flustered and her cheeks went flame red when Marcus strode over and picked it up before she had a chance to. I suppose she just wasn't used to people doing things for her. I told Marcus to get the hamper and checked my holdall again to make sure I had everything Effie

120

and I would need for a day out. I knew Effie was excited but so was I, though perhaps for a different reason.

It took about half an hour for Omar to drive us to the Pyramids of Giza. As we drove along Marcus gave a running commentary to Effie, who bounced in the seat and not just from the poor road surface. We parked where the road ended, got out of the car and just waited whilst Effie was silently overawed at the sight of the three huge pyramids in the distance. They looked as if they had been forced up from the desert so that their points could reach the heavens.

'Can we go nearer?'

'Of course. But first let's go and look at the Sphinx. He's just behind us.'

Effie's mouth dropped open even more as she took in the giant reclining lion with the head of a king.

'We believe it was created about two and a half thousand years BC, so that makes it about four and a half thousand years old. It wasn't fully excavated until about fifty years ago. The Great Pyramid is considered to be one of the Seven Wonders of the World, but I think this ought to be on that list. It's magnificent, isn't it? Let's go round it.'

Effie walked up to it and stroked the warm limestone blocks that formed the base. I'd seen the Sphinx many times and had perhaps become a bit complacent but seeing it through Effie's eyes was like seeing it for the first time and I was as amazed and overcome as she obviously was.

'Are they going to put his nose back?' Effie asked.

'They can't find it and they don't want to make a new one, so they've decided to leave it as it is.'

'It was knocked off by Napoleon during a battle, wasn't it? That's what I've read.'

'Not him personally but yes, one theory is that it was knocked off by a cannon ball in one of the French battles in the late seventeen hundreds, but there are others. Some think it's due to erosion, others to vandals in Ancient Egyptian times who removed it in order to stop it breathing and so effectively kill it.'

Effie didn't question the logic of killing a stone statue; she merely nodded and continued to walk around it. When she had done the circuit and had returned to the front, she took out her sketch pad. 'Do I have time to just make a quick drawing?' Without waiting for an answer, she sat on the sand with her legs crossed and started to sketch.

Marcus grinned at me. 'It's great showing her these things, isn't it? She's so enthusiastic and interested. I'll go over and hire some camels to take us to the Pyramids. She'll probably want to climb to the top. Will you?'

I'd done it once before and it was exhausting. Each block is about three or four feet high, and you have to have an Arab behind to push and an Arab in front to pull. I had stopped counting at two hundred blocks, and I was only about halfway up. I didn't relish the thought of climbing it again, but I didn't want to appear a pathetic female in front of Marcus, so I nodded and hopefully looked as if I was keen and able.

Effie had finished her sketch by the time Marcus returned, followed by three grumpy looking camels, each led by its driver and followed in turn by a horde of grubby urchins who raced up to me, holding their hands out and shouting '*Baksheesh, baksheesh!*' I shook my head and ignored them. The drivers coaxed the camels to sit down so that we could mount them. They are the most inelegant creatures; first they go onto their front knees then they sit on their back legs and finally they curl their front legs under them. I saw Marcus mount his quite easily and Effie just clambered on managing to show the whole world her knickers. My camel turned its head to glare at me, snorted and showed me its long, yellow teeth in a grin or more likely a grimace. I was extremely glad that I was wearing slacks, but I was still uncertain as to how to mount the beast. My driver, who looked not a day under one hundred years old, was unfazed by my reluctance to clamber onto the camel's back like an eleven-year-old, placed a block of wood so that I could step onto it and swing my leg over with a modicum of modesty. When I was astride with my hat set straight, I glanced at the other two to find them grinning at me, both looking relaxed and far more comfortable than I was.

Their drivers made strange clicking noises and tapped the knees of the camels, which slowly hauled themselves back to their feet. They got up in reverse order: onto their front knees first then they straightened their back legs before straightening their front, which meant that for a while the rider was precariously tilted forward and having to hang on for dear life. Marcus, of course, was a dab hand and knew to lean back at the appropriate moment but I watched Effie with gleeful anticipation, convinced she would flounder and probably fall off. But she was a natural and seemed to know instinctively which way to lean and she grinned at me triumphantly when her camel was upright. My own driver started to click, and I braced myself. Despite knowing the theory my timing was all wrong and I suddenly found myself thrown forward before being thrown back again as it straightened itself. When it was standing it made a sound that I'm sure was a snort of disdainful laughter. My hat had fallen off and I waited for the driver to hand it to me.

Out of the corner of my eye I saw a movement but before I could register what or who it was my camel gave a start and bolted. I instinctively threw myself forward and clung to the saddle's pommel. The camel – and I - swayed from side to side and it seemed to be doing its best to throw me off, but I continued to hang on tightly. I opened my eyes to see the ground hurtling past beneath its great flat feet and I had visions of my battered and bloody body if I should fall off at this speed. I raised my head slightly to see where we were heading, to find the pyramids looming over us. I cursed the fact I couldn't remember the Arabic for 'Stop!' and that I had never learned to ride a camel. I wondered if Marcus was trying to catch up with me but I daren't look back; perhaps it was his indistinct shouts I could hear.

Suddenly the camel veered to one side to avoid another camel that was in our path, its driver waving his arms and shouting. I felt my body slip inexorably sideways and knew that with nothing to stop me my fear of a battered and bloody body was about to come true. I tried to grip the pommel harder, but the weight of my sliding body was too great and eventually I had to let go. I threw myself away from the camel to avoid getting tangled in its legs. I felt stabs of pain as I bounced over the stony ground. I eventually came to a stop and ended up on my back, my legs bent, looking up at a beautifully blue sky that seemed to be whirling round and round. I could feel the sun on my face. I cautiously began to straighten my legs.

'Don't move, Beattie!' The blueness of the sky was replaced by the blueness of Marcus's eyes as he bent down and peered at me closely. 'Don't move, my dear. You may have broken something. Do you hurt anywhere?'

I hurt everywhere. I wriggled my toes and fingers and flexed my wrists and ankles. There was no excruciating pain. 'I don't think I've broken anything. Help me up please.' I raised my arms, but he didn't take them.

'You may have hurt your back. Just lie still. I think we need a doctor to check you over before we move you.' His concern was gratifying but I didn't feel as if I had broken anything, so I stretched out my legs and raised myself onto my elbows. 'For goodness' sake, Beattie. Why don't you ever do as you're told?'

'I'm all right, Marcus, honestly. Just a bit bruised that's all. Help me up please.'

Marcus hesitated then when he saw I was trying to get up anyway he took hold of me under the arms and lifted me gently to my feet. I staggered a bit, and he steadied me. He brushed some sand off my face and kept his hand cupped under my chin. 'I was so worried. I don't know what I'd do if anything happened to you.' Did he really say that or was it just wishful thinking?

Chapter 18

Effie

There was nothing I could do. I watched in horror as Miss Trevethan's camel galloped – no, galloped isn't the right word – as Miss Trevethan's camel galumphed across the desert. I wanted to go after her but before I could even begin to think how to get my camel moving the driver pulled on my foot and yanked me off, leapt onto the camel's back without making it sit and raced after the runaway camel. I was left lying on the sand with a group of grubby children surrounding me and laughing.

'Shut up you dirty Arabs!' I got to my feet and turned slowly around, looking at each of them in the eye. They looked back, one spat, another sneered, most grinned. 'One of you made that camel bolt. It's all your fault.' My voice came out as a squeak such was my anger. 'If anything happens to Miss Trevethan I'll ...' What would I do? What could I do? 'I'll tell Captain Karim. He's in charge of the police and he'll put you all in prison. For ever and ever.' They didn't understand, of course and they continued to surround me, spit, sneer and grin.

I looked over their heads and couldn't see a runaway camel, but I could see three camels standing in a group and some people huddled, looking down at something. Oh God! Had Miss Trevethan fallen to her death? Was she all broken and they were trying to put the pieces back? I had to get to her. I knew the children wouldn't move if I asked nicely so I just barged through, shouting at the top of my voice, 'Out of my way, coming through!' I heard a few yelps as my elbows came into contact with chest or head, but no one tried to stop me and when I looked back there was no one there. It was as if they had turned to sand and become part of the desert. I picked up Miss Trevethan's hat that was still on the floor and started walking.

126

It was hard work; I wished I had the feet of a camel as my own sank almost up to my ankles with each step.

It was still quite early in the morning, but the sun was getting hotter, and I was glad my head was covered by the straw hat Miss Trevethan had insisted I wore. By the time I reached where everyone was standing my face was burning, my mouth was dry and every inch of my skin was covered in sand. I was relieved to see Miss Trevethan all in one piece. She was standing, leaning on Mr Dunwoody. She was wearing slacks and a long-sleeved blouse, worn to protect her from the sun but as luck would have it, now also from the stones. There were small tears in the knees of her slacks, cuts on the backs of her hands and a nasty looking graze on her cheek bone.

'Are you all right, Miss? You did really well hanging on for so long.' She gave a wan smile but seemed content just to stand there with Mr Dunwoody's arm around her. It looked to me as if he never wanted to let her go again. 'You know that was done on purpose, don't you?'

Mr Dunwoody nodded but Miss Trevethan looked surprised. 'Was it? How do you know? What happened?'

'One of them little brats ran over and stuck something into the camel's bottom. I don't know which one it was, they all look the same, don't they?'

Miss Trevethan looked around her nervously but there was no one there other than the three of us and a couple of old men who were looking after the camels; they didn't look as if they were a danger to anyone. Mr Dunwoody gave her a squeeze. 'It was probably because you didn't give them any baksheesh. They couldn't possibly know who you are and there were no adults around other than the camel drivers.'

Miss Trevethan didn't look convinced. 'I never told you about the scorpion, did I?'

Although she looked pale, I noticed that already her nose and cheek bones were turning pink. I held out her hat to her. 'You need to wear this, Miss, else you'll burn.'

Miss Trevethan managed a laugh. 'I'm meant to be looking after you, not the other way round. Thank you, Effie.'

Mr Dunwoody seemed to come out of a dream; he gave his head a shake. 'What am I thinking? Come on; let's get you away from here. We'll go to the Mena House Hotel, and you can clean up those cuts and we can have some refreshments. Should we go home afterwards? I'm sorry, Effie, but I don't think we can see more of the Pyramids today. Do you think you can bear to ride a camel back, Beattie? It's a long way and it's difficult to walk in the sand.'

'What's that you were saying about a scorpion, Miss? And no, Mr Dunwoody, of course I understand we can't see the Pyramids.'

'I'm never going on a camel ever again. I'll walk, thank you. And no, I don't want to go home afterwards. We can go onto El Lisht, can't we? There won't be anyone else there, will there? I'll tell you about the scorpion when we're in the hotel.'

Having answered everyone's questions she began to walk slowly back the way her rampant camel had run. She was wearing sturdy shoes and managed the terrain far better than I did in my sandals, but she did stumble every now and then and Mr Dunwoody was always there to steady her. I was left to manage on my own. I turned to look back at the Pyramids. I was disappointed I wasn't going to be able to explore them. I could see tourists being hauled up the high blocks, but no one had reached the top yet. I imagined the view would be wonderful and I longed to be up there looking over Cairo in one direction and the endless desert in the other. I would have loved to go inside. I knew from my reading that the Pyramids were riddled with tunnels and burial chambers, some real and some fake to confuse robbers. I'd be able to see the walls that had vivid paintings still preserved and lie in an empty sarcophagus pretending I was a mummy.

But it was not to be, so I reluctantly turned my back on them and plodded on. The sand was hot and burning my feet through the soles of my sandals. I tried to walk faster but I sank even deeper, so I slowed down again and just gritted my teeth. When I reached the car there was not only Miss Trevethan and Mr Dunwoody but also Omar, who had the ear of a young boy firmly in his grip. The boy was hopping from one foot to another, and tears had cleaned a track down his dirty face.

'What's going on? Who's this?' I knew though. 'Is this the boy who frightened Miss Trevethan's camel?' They all nodded.

'There's a police station by the hotel. We could take him there.' Mr Dunwoody said something in Arabic and the boy laughed then spat at his feet turning the sand a dark brown. As quick as a flash Omar pulled the boy so he was facing him and slapped him twice across the face, leaving two bright red handprints.

'Stop! *Arrêtez!* Leave him. Omar. He's just a boy. Someone probably gave him a few piastres to do it. There's no point taking him to the police, Marcus. We can't prove it was him. Just let him go, Omar.'

Omar seemed reluctant to release him but when Miss Trevethan repeated her command he shoved the boy away from him, shouting words that could only have been curses. The boy stopped when he was far enough away from grasping hands and raised his arm so that we could all see the Eye of Horus that was roughly drawn on his forearm. I heard Miss Trevethan gasp and saw her cling to Mr Dunwoody. The boy made a very rude gesture and ran off laughing.

Omar went to run after him, but Mr Dunwoody ordered him to stay put. 'Just take us to the Mena House. I'll get a message to Captain Karim later on today. He needs to know what's happened and that this Eye of the Horus gang are recruiting children. Not that he's going to be able to do much about it.'

We got into the car which was as hot as Ma Foster's oven when cooking a Sunday roast. Miss Trevethan sat back with her eyes closed so I asked Mr Dunwoody, 'What's the Eye of Horus gang?'

'You were there when Miss Trevethan had a stone thrown at her, weren't you? We think this was because she is British. A small number of Egyptians want us out of their country and there have been a few incidents making life a little uncomfortable for us. There seem to be a couple a different gangs, one is called the Blue Shirts for obvious reasons and the other bears the Eye of Horus as its sign. I think the sooner Miss Trevethan goes to Luxor the better.'

I glanced at her but although she looked as if she was asleep, I didn't think she was, so I said nothing and instead took her hand in mine. The hotel was only a few minutes' drive away and we were soon there. The hotel was enormous and very grand. There was a wooden veranda along the front of the building and people were sitting in the shade drinking tea and lemonade. They looked and sounded rich; most of them were English or American. Arabs in long, white dresses and red upside-down plant pots on their heads – I couldn't remember what they were called – hovered in the background. One opened the car door for us. He frowned at the state of us: Mr Dunwoody in his rumpled shorts and shirt; Miss Trevethan in her torn and grubby slacks and blouse with the graze on her face weeping blood and me, who looked like one of the street Arabs. But Mr Dunwoody spoke to him firmly and the man bowed and waited for us to follow him inside.

The hall was bigger than Ma and Pa Foster's whole house, possibly even the whole terrace. It had a white marble floor and white walls with high arches leading into other rooms and alcoves that contained pieces that looked as if they should be in a museum. There were huge plant pots containing full grown palm trees that nowhere near touched the ceiling.

'Shut your mouth, dear.' Miss Trevethan smiled at me. 'It's rather splendid, isn't it?'

'You can say that again.'

'It's rather splendid, isn't it?' We all laughed at her childish joke, and I felt a warmth inside as I realised how much I liked her.

The Arab led us into a large, empty room that was obviously a restaurant and pulled the chair out for Miss Trevethan at a table by a glass wall. I was put in a chair with my back to the window but as soon as he had taken our order and left, I moved my chair so that I could enjoy the uninterrupted view of the three pyramids we had just left. I took my sketch book out of the bag and started to draw. It should have been simple, after all they were just simple pyramid shapes, but I found it difficult to show the sheer size and impressiveness of them.

'Effie, would you come with me and help me tidy up a bit?'

I didn't really want to leave off drawing, but she needed my help, and it was the least I could do. I actually burst out laughing when we went into the ladies' room; it was so ridiculously extravagant. More marble and palm trees, with a wall of mirrors and a row of enormous sinks with what looked like gold taps. Each pan was in a cubicle bigger than our living room at home.

'This is very grand for a place where all you want to do is piss.' Miss Trevethan raised her eyebrows and looked around as if she hadn't noticed the decor before; she nodded and smiled at me in the mirror. She ran some hot water into a bowl and took a serviette off a pile that stood by every sink, and she started to dab at her cheek. 'Here, let me.' I took the cloth from her and told her to sit on one of the red velvet chairs that looked like a small throne. I gently washed her face and her hands; she

131

winced occasionally but made no sound. 'You need to put some antiseptic cream on these. Do you have any?'

'Yes, at home. This'll do for now. They're only scratches; none of them are deep.'

I felt my eyes fill up and I had the sudden urge to hug her, so I did. 'It could have been a lot worse, Miss. You was real lucky. Well not lucky for someone to spook your camel, but lucky you managed to get off without breaking anything. I think Mr Dunwoody was shocked. You should ask him again to come with us to Luxor.'

'You're a minx, Effie, do you know that? Would you like to use the facilities whilst we're here?' I didn't know what she meant and must have looked puzzled. 'Do you want to, er, have a piss?' She blushed and put her hand to her mouth as if she'd sworn like an East-Ender after a Saturday all-nighter.

I did and it's the grandest piss I've ever had.

When we got back, the table had been laid with tea things and a plate of dainties. Why did they make the rooms so large but their cakes and biscuits so small? Mr Dunwoody poured the tea from a silver teapot into three white china cups, each sitting on a white china saucer, each with a silver spoon. I don't like tea but didn't say anything so just sipped at it, trying not to pull a face. The biscuits and tarts were lovely though and I had to restrain myself from scoffing the lot.

'Are you all right, Beattie? You've got a bit of colour back into your cheeks. That graze looks a bit nasty. Are any of the other cuts bad? You'll get some bruises all over by tomorrow. Are you in pain anywhere?'

'Marcus, stop asking questions, or at least give me time to answer them. I'm perfectly all right, honestly. It was a shock, I can't say it wasn't and I was quite frightened at the time, but, as Effie just said to me, I was lucky and there's no lasting damage. What worries me is that this seems to be another attempt by this

Eye of Horus gang. You don't think there will be any of them in Luxor, do you?'

Mr Dunwoody frowned but didn't shake his head. 'I don't know, which is why I'm going to come with you.' I couldn't stop myself from grinning, but stopped quickly so that the other two wouldn't see. I'm sure I saw Miss Trevethan's lips curl up as well. 'I'm due some holiday and I'd actually like to explore the temples and the Valley of the Kings a bit more. I didn't really get time to look around when I was working there. Will your Aunt be all right with me coming?'

'I sent a letter to Aunt Edith yesterday so she should get it today or tomorrow, depending which trains it goes on. I'm not going to wait for a reply; she's bound to say it's all right. I told her there were a few of us coming to stay; I didn't say who exactly. She has plenty of room and she adores you, Marcus. I'd like to go the day after tomorrow; we can get the train tickets from Cook's later today.' I felt pleased that Mr Dunwoody was coming and felt sure I had helped him make the decision by telling him at the museum that Miss Trevethan really liked him and wanted him to go but was too shy to admit it. I felt my role as matchmaker was going well.

Mr Dunwoody nodded in agreement. 'You said something earlier about a scorpion. What was that all about?'

Chapter 19

Beattie

I told them about the scorpion in the box and the piece of paper with the Eye of Horus that had been left at the bottom. I didn't want to scare Effie so I tried to make light of it, but I could see her eyes and mouth getting rounder and rounder. My throat was dry, so I stopped talking, sipped at my tea and took a bite out of one of the few remaining biscuits.

'Was it put in your bedroom?' Without thinking I nodded at Effie's question. 'But that's the room I was sleeping in last night! What if there had been another one? They can kill you, can't they?'

'One of our gardeners removed the one in the box and the whole house was searched from top to bottom yesterday and your bedroom again just before you went in. The gardener said if it had bitten me, it would have been painful, but it wouldn't have killed me. I think they just wanted to scare me.' Which they were most successful in doing.

Marcus took my hand, and his eyes were full of concern. 'Do you know who put it there? Was it one of the staff?'

'The police questioned everyone. Most of the staff have been with my father for years and we think they are extremely loyal but there was one new gardener who started only a few weeks ago. They couldn't find anything to incriminate him but as he was the only real suspect my father told him to go. Daddy said he didn't seem that bothered.' Effie didn't look very reassured and had gone a rather grey colour. 'Don't worry, Effie. We'll be in Luxor soon, away from all this. But it's worth always checking your shoes before putting them on in case a scorpion has made its bed there.'

'Are there any other horrid animals in this country? What with them mosquitoes that bite,' Effie scratched at a small red lump on her arm, 'scorpions that can kill you and camels that spit and try and break you?'

'They have cats, dogs, donkeys and horses just like they do in England.' Though most of them are starved and mistreated.

I reached for another morsel to eat but the plate was empty. Effie looked embarrassed, brushed a crumb off her lap and said, 'Sorry.'

'Shall we set off for El Lisht, Beattie? It's about thirty miles from here so it will take about an hour and a half to drive there. We can find somewhere sheltered to have our picnic then perhaps we could all do some sketching? There are still some carvings there I would like to record, and I want to show Effie some of the chambers that are still accessible. Shall we go?'

My head spun a little as I stood and my joints ached, but I soon recovered and managed to walk out without stumbling. The car was hot inside; I handed Effie a fan and we both sat and tried to cool ourselves as we drove south along the road that followed the west bank of the Nile. I had only made this journey by car a few times and I found it hard not to follow Effie's example and press my nose against the window, closed to keep out the dust thrown up by the tyres, to take it all in.

The banks of the Nile are incredibly lush and fertile, and crops of grain, figs, melons, pomegranates, vines and flax have been successfully grown in the narrow strip since the time of the Ancient Egyptians and probably before. The farmers still ploughed the land using oxen; the land was still watered using channels filled by the Nile's water. They still transported their produce over land using camels or donkeys or on the Nile in a felucca. We passed groups of women washing clothes at the side of the river whilst their naked children screamed and splashed in the shallows; we drove through small villages where the men sat and smoked under the shade of a tree and skeletal cats and dogs slunk in the shadows searching for scraps. We marvelled at ruins of buildings, some ancient some new, silhouetted against the cloudless blue sky.

After about ninety minutes Marcus told Omar where to drive off the road and onto a dirt track that led to the edge of El Lisht. I was concerned that Effie wouldn't find the site interesting enough, especially after what she had seen that morning, but I needn't have worried. Effie's eyes were bright with excitement as she cast them over the ruins of the royal burial ground. I could see that Marcus was dying to explain everything to Effie and that she was dying to be told but we had to have lunch first. There were remains of buildings covering the whole site and we chose one that had once been a temple to set up camp. As well as the basket stuffed with everything that could possibly be required on a picnic, the car boot held a folding table, four folding chairs, a large parasol and an ice box holding bottles of lemonade. The two men soon had all the equipment out whilst Effie and I laid the table. I thought there was far too much food but then I remembered Effie's appetite and hoped that in fact there would be enough.

I asked Omar to sit with us, but he looked quite shocked and went to squat a distance away, his back against a stone wall. I piled some food onto a plate and asked Marcus to take it over to him. I saw Omar shaking his head and Marcus nodding and thrusting it at him. Eventually Marcus's insistence won, and Omar took the plate but continued to look uncomfortable and embarrassed although he did finish all the food.

Marcus began to lecture us about the necropolis where we were now enjoying our picnic. 'Those two pyramids over there are quite small compared to the three we saw at Giza this morning, aren't they? That one over there is where Amenenhat I was buried and the other was for his son Senusret I. The pyramids collapsed a long time ago and both have more than halved in height. The burial chamber of both men are flooded so are now impossible to get at, which is a shame. Some of these collapsed ruins surrounding the pyramids are the burial chambers of the Pharaohs' families or of their high officials and their families, whilst others are temples or offering halls. I'll take you to a burial chamber which we can still enter and show you some carvings on the walls.'

Effie was listening avidly and writing quickly in her notebook, her pink tongue peeping out of her slightly open mouth. 'Was much found when they discovered this place?'

Marcus shook his head. 'No. The site was excavated for a few years at the end of the last century by a French Egyptologist and then this century up to a few years ago by the Metropolitan Museum of Art in New York but the tomb robbers had effectively cleared everything out. No one is working here now. One of the things the Americans did find was the undisturbed tomb of a woman called Senebtisi, her name is all they really know about her. But she must have been someone of note to be buried here. She was entombed in a set of three coffins and her mummified body was covered in jewelled collars, amulets, anklets and necklaces. Finding something like that is an archaeologist's dream!'

Marcus stood up and looked out over the ruins. 'Imagine what this must have looked like before it all collapsed.' There was a moment's silence as we all imagined. 'Come on Effie, I'll show you around. Are you coming Beattie?'

My body ached and I felt sleepy and as much as I wanted to be with Marcus all I really wanted to do was nothing more than doze. 'No thanks, I'll let you two go and explore. I'll sit here and read.' I watched as they clambered over and around the blocks of stone that littered the ground then beckoned to Omar to come and clear everything away. I moved my chair so that I was fully in the shade, took out my book so that it looked as if I at least intended to read and closed my eyes. I could hear Marcus and Effie chattering and laughing together; then their voices became muted so I supposed they must have gone underground. I was desperate to sleep but my head was full of what had happened that morning and what I still needed to do before we went to Luxor in a few days' time. I listed in my head everything I would need to pack for myself and Effie; I hoped her new clothes had been delivered to the house today. I was so pleased Marcus was coming. I began to imagine spending time together, just the two of us. Would I dare say anything to him? Should I? What if Effie was wrong and he didn't feel the same way about me? I didn't want to ruin our friendship but how I yearned for it to be more than that.

'Omar, please don't let us forget to stop at Cook's on the way home this evening. We need to buy some train tickets; we're going to visit my aunt in Luxor.'

'Yes, your father mentioned it to me this morning.'

'Are you coming with us? Don't you have a family that needs you? Mr Dunwoody is coming too so he can take care of us.'

'I have not been given any orders by my master. My job is to guard you and now the little Miss so if I am told to go to Luxor with you, I will.' He closed the lid of the picnic basket which was a lot lighter now that most of the food had been eaten and was carrying it to the car when he stopped and stared at something.

'What is it, Omar? Can you see Marcus and Effie?'

'No. They went in a different direction. But there are some men coming out of the ground.'

I stood up and walked to his side and looked in the direction he was pointing. There were indeed three, no four, men emerging from the ground. They didn't look like *fellahin* as they were all wearing what looked like uniforms. They were coming in our direction, no doubt alerted to our presence by the sound of our voices and as they came closer, I could see they were in fact all policemen. What on earth were they doing in El Lisht?

As they neared, I recognised the man in front.

'Good afternoon, Captain Karim. Fancy seeing you here.'

His startled look was quickly replaced by a polite smile. 'Good afternoon, Miss Trevethan. May I ask what you're doing here?'

I felt myself bristle with irritation. 'Why shouldn't we be here? There's no reason for us not to be, is there?'

'Us? Who else is with you?'

'I'm not sure it's any of your concern, but Mr Dunwoody and Effie, Miss Bloom, are here also.' Captain Karim and the other three policemen looked around. I flung an arm in the general direction they had gone. 'They're probably down a hole somewhere, as indeed you were just now. Are you all interested in archaeology?'

Captain Karim didn't answer my question but spoke to the other men in Arabic and they all went off in the direction I had indicated Marcus and Effie had gone.

'Where are they going? We have every right to be here.'

Captain Karim smiled with his lips but not his eyes. 'I'll explain when the others are here. Please, sit down.' An order rather than a request.

I found the silence unsettling. 'I hope you got Mr Dunwoody's message that we had found Effie?'

'Yes, I did. You just said she is here now? You have decided to take responsibility for her?'

'I have indeed. If I had my way that orphanage would be shut down.'

'And what would happen to all the children that they care for? They would end up on the streets begging, stealing, being abused, very likely dying before the year was out. Is that better than their life at the orphanage? They don't all have people like you to look after them.'

He was right of course but I wasn't going to admit it. 'Mr Dunwoody was also going to send you a message later today. I

139

was attacked again today by a member of this Eye of Horus gang. Well, I wasn't attacked but the camel I was on was deliberately startled so that it bolted. It was sheer luck that I didn't break a bone when I fell off.'

He didn't seem particularly surprised. Had he already been told? If so, by whom? 'That is most unfortunate; I hope you weren't hurt too much? Are you sure it wasn't just an accident? Camels can be quite unreliable.'

'I'm absolutely sure. Omar here caught the boy, who was very pleased to show us the drawing of the Eye of Horus on his arm.'

'It's a shame you couldn't detain him, he might have given us some information about this mysterious gang. They do seem to have you in their sights. Perhaps you should do as they ask and go back to England? You'll be safer there.'

I felt my back straighten and hackles rise. 'You suggest we give in to them? Perhaps you should find them and stop them terrorising innocent people!' He raised an eyebrow but didn't respond. 'Anyway, I am getting away for a while. I'm going to Luxor the day after tomorrow to stay with my aunt. I'm taking Effie and Mr Dunwoody is going too.'

'That is an excellent idea. And your Aunt is?'

'Why on earth do you want to know her name?' He just raised an eyebrow and looked at me, waiting for an answer. 'Miss Edith Goodley.'

We both turned as we heard the sound of multiple footsteps. Marcus looked furious and Effie looked frightened. One of the policemen held Marcus's upper arm and was practically dragging him along. The one pulling Effie looked like a giant compared to her. He was unusually tall, a good few inches taller than Marcus's six feet two. He reminded me of a gorilla with his shorter-than-they-should-be legs and his longer-than-they-should-be arms and his mop of black, unruly hair poking out from under his tarbush. As they got nearer, I saw he had a strange, vacant expression; when he saw me looking at him, he smiled, a gold tooth glinting in the sunshine.

'Mr Dunwoody, please just come quietly. I will explain everything in a few minutes.'

The policeman let go of Marcus's arm and he strode over to me. 'Are you all right? Do you know what's going on?' I shook my head. Effie came and stood by my other side and clung to my arm. I felt her shivering.

'Please sit down, Mr Dunwoody, Miss Bloom. There, now let me explain. We have reason to believe that this place is being used by criminals. We are trying to find where they might be hiding their goods.'

'What sort of criminals?' Marcus was still fuming. 'They're not here now, surely? Where's their car? What makes you think they're here?'

'All very valid questions.' Captain Karim was very polite, but supercilious. 'We have very good reason to believe that they use some of the burial chambers to keep drugs in. They bring them here before distributing to the local villages. As I'm sure you are aware drug use is still a huge problem in Egypt and we must all do our very best to stamp it out. We were given a tip off a few days ago that this place is being used for, er...' he tilted his head, 'nefarious activities. That's the right word, yes?' Marcus nodded. 'So, now we are here to do a search. If there is indeed evidence of any criminal activity, then we will keep watch until we catch them.' He looked at Marcus and then at me. 'We cannot risk having innocent people caught up in this, so I'm afraid you will need to leave.'

Marcus ran his fingers through his hair but seemed to accept the Captain's story. 'Do we have to go now? Can't we stay for just a few hours more?'

Captain Karim shook his head and looked *desolé*. 'I'm sorry but no. You don't want anything else to happen to Miss Trevethan do you? You need to go home now and don't come back. I understand you are escorting Miss Trevethan and Miss Bloom to Luxor? You will be safe there.' He stepped back and held out an arm, pointing towards the car. 'Now, if you don't mind, please leave.'

We all walked to the car, looking and feeling like naughty school children being sent home for being cheeky to the headmaster. As we drove away, I turned to see the four of them standing motionless in a row, watching us leave.

20

Effie

It was dark but there was a dim light coming from a small opening in the roof. Too small for me to get through. How had I got in? I could see that I was in a burial chamber, its walls covered in the most exquisite carvings that I knew I had to copy into my notebook. Where was it? I scanned the ground around me but saw only sand. My stomach churned in panic. I couldn't lose that notebook; it had all my notes, diagrams and translations of hieroglyphics. What was that over there? Not my notebook but something that scurried across the sand towards me. A scorpion! I tried to move out of its path, but my legs were made of stone. I could feel it though, its eight feet tickling me as it ran up my shin and over my knee. I tried to brush it away, but my arms were being held in a pincer-like grip. I could feel hot breath on my neck and knew by his smell that it was the policeman with the gold tooth. When the scorpion reached my thigh, it stopped and looked at me. Then it bit me, ran back down my leg, across the sand and into a dark corner. I felt no pain, but I watched in horror as my legs began to crumble into dust and I felt myself tumbling to the ground. I screamed and screamed.

'Effie, Effie, it's all right, dear. It's all right. It's just a dream. Husha, husha. You're all right, You're safe. Take deep breaths. There, that's better.'

I was no longer in a small, dark confined space and it was Miss Trevethan who was holding me. I looked round in panic but there was nothing to spoil the whiteness of the crumpled sheets.

'There was a scorpion. It bit me. But my legs were stone. And I couldn't find my notebook and I needed it to copy down the carvings. And that policeman, the one with the gold tooth, he was holding me and wouldn't let me go. Then ... then ...' I couldn't remember what happened then.

'Oh, my poor dear. You've had a horrid dream with lots of things from today all mixed up. I know you're worried about your notebook, but Marcus will go and see Captain Karim today and ask them to give it back. I'm sure they'll have picked it up when they were doing their search. If they didn't then he'll insist someone is sent to get it. Now, let's get these sheets changed and you into one of your new nighties.'

The whiteness of the crumpled sheets was spoiled after all, by a damp, yellow stain.

The next morning, I was pleased to find Mr Trevethan still at the breakfast table. I hadn't seen him the previous evening; Miss Trevethan said he was probably at his club. I wondered if it was like the Girls' Club I was made to go to on a Friday evening? I'll have missed last week's. Good.

His face was covered by his newspaper but when he heard me pulling out my chair, he put it down and smiled at me. He had such a nice smile; it made me feel safe and warm inside. 'Ah, good morning, Effie. Beattie told me what an exciting day you all had yesterday but did you enjoy seeing what you did manage to see?'

'Oh yes, sir, I thought the Sphinx was the best. I made a drawing of it in my notebook but ...' I caught my breath as I remembered that the last time I had seen my notebook it was on the floor of the chamber after I had dropped it when the policeman with the gold tooth had dragged me out. 'They made me leave my notebook. They needn't have done that, need they? That was just mean.'

'Beattie told me about that. Don't worry, Effie, we'll get it back for you. In the meantime though, I found this that you can have.' He stood up, went to the sideboard, picked up a sketchbook and handed it to me. 'It used to belong to Beattie.' I

144

opened it and stroked the pages, which felt like velvet. All the pages were blank. Mr Trevethan gave a short laugh. 'Look, she hasn't used it at all. She was always much more into reading than sketching. You'll make much better use of it than she ever did.' He sat down at the table again and buttered a piece of toast, covered it in a thick layer of jam and handed it to me. 'So how much of El Lisht did you actually see?'

My mouth was full of toast, and I tried to speak but sprayed the tablecloth with crumbs and tiny drops of jam. I wiped the mess with my fingers and just made it worse.

'Don't worry about that. My fault for not handing it to you on a plate. Finish that slice, then tell me what you saw.'

I gulped down the rest of the slice. 'Mr Dunwoody is so clever. He told me to sketch some of the ruins as they are now then he helped me draw what they might have looked like when they were built thousands of years ago. It was like magic. Then we went to an underground chamber which had carvings on the walls. They were so beautiful, sir. I was copying them when those horrid policemen came and just dragged us out.'

'Please stop calling me sir. Why don't you call me Uncle Gryffyn?'

'But you are a sir, aren't you? I heard Miss Trevethan telling that Captain Karim that you are Sir something-or-other Trevethan.'

'Yes, I'm Sir Gryffyn Trevethan, although I think Sir something-or-other Trevethan is a far better name. But I only use the Sir when I want to impress somebody so please just call me Uncle Gryffyn or even Uncle Gryff?'

'Well, if you're going to be Uncle Gryff, that makes me Effie's cousin, so I think she can call me Beattie instead of Miss Trevethan.' She sat down next to me and grinned widely. 'Is that all right, Effie? That we're sort-of-cousins?'

I nodded. A sort-of-cousin was the nearest family I had ever had. 'What did you say Beattie was short for, Miss, I mean Beattie?'

'Beatrice. Do you remember Pa, when I was about six, I came running to you and Mama very proud of myself because I had realised that my initials were B. T.? That made the name Beattie even more special, so I thought anyway.'

It took me a while to get it but when I did, I laughed. 'That's real clever that is.'

'I need to do some shopping for our trip. Do you want to come with me, Effie?'

'Make sure Omar is with you at all times; I don't want either of you to be unaccompanied for even one second.'

'Yes, sir.' She gave a little salute, which made me laugh but I could see Uncle Gryffyn didn't think it was funny.

'I don't care about you, Beattie, but I don't want young Effie to come to any harm.' He raised his paper again so I couldn't see if he was serious or not. Shopping in Cairo was no different to shopping in an East End street market except that the men shouting their wares spoke a different language and there were a lot more flies. Beattie bought some stuff for the bathroom, a small gift for her aunt and some coloured bangles for me. They jangled as I walked, and I loved them.

We were back in time for lunch then Beattie spent the rest of the day packing and preparing for our trip to Luxor the next day and left me to amuse myself. I took a book out of the library and sat in the garden totally engrossed until Uncle Gryffyn came and sat with me. He had a typed report that he started to read but it can't have been all that interesting because after a few minutes he put it down and asked me what I was reading.

'It's by Howard Carter about the discovery of the tomb of Tutankhamun.' I showed him the cover.

'You are very interested in Ancient Egypt, Effie. Why's that? It's a strange thing for a young English girl to be so fascinated by. Beattie told me about you being told you looked like Nefertiti; is that the reason?'

I meant to nod but my head had other ideas and shook instead. Could I tell him? Uncle Gryffyn looked at me with spaniel-brown eyes and waited. I'd never told a soul before; not the nuns, not Ma and Pa Foster, not any of the other children, not anybody. I was frightened that if I told him he'd laugh at me. But he had such a kind face and maybe he could help me find her.

'My mother's an Egyptian princess.' There, I'd said it. He raised his eyebrows but didn't laugh. 'Well, I think she is.'

He leaned forward in his seat as if to hear me better. 'What makes you think that?'

'The way I look and the way she left me. I was in one of them Moses baskets and covered in a lovely blanket and there was a ten pound note in an envelope. That's a lot of money, isn't it? Only someone really rich would be able to leave that much.'

'Why do you think she left you with the nuns?'

'It's obvious, isn't it? She was a princess, and she wasn't married. The man, my father, was probably of a lower class. She was made to give me up and forced to return back to Egypt. I was wondering ....'

He took one of my hands and stroked the back of it, which was very nice. 'You're wondering whether she's here in Cairo.'

A laugh exploded out of me. 'How did you know? Do you think she is? Could you help me find her?'

He continued to stroke the back of my hand but didn't say anything for quite a while. I could tell he was thinking. Maybe of ways he could try and find her.

'How old are you. Effie?'

'Ten years and eight months. Why?'

'So you were born in 1925.'

'They're not sure when exactly but they thought I was about three months old when I was left so they made up a date of the fifteenth of May for by birthday and yes, I was born in 1925.'

'Had you ever thought that it might have been your father who was Egyptian or foreign, anyway?'

I shook my head slightly; I'd never given much thought to my father. 'You mean he might have been an Egyptian prince?'

He pursed his lips and looked as if he'd just eaten a lemon or as if his mouth was full of words that tasted horrid, but he couldn't bring himself to spit them out. The silence went on and on and I began to feel uncomfortable. 'Do you know any Egyptian Princesses or Princes?' He nodded but continued to chew on his words. 'Did any of them go to England eleven years ago?' He looked me in the eye and shook his head. 'You can't know all of them, though? Mightn't there have been one that went but you didn't know?'

'Eleven years ago, I was responsible for the security of all high-class people, including royalty. Travel of such people out of Egypt to England was very rare, almost unheard of.'

I felt my stomach churn in panic but then I thought of something that calmed me. 'Maybe they'd been in England for ages. Then you wouldn't know about them. Maybe they never went back after ... after leaving me. Perhaps there's an Egyptian princess you don't know about.'

'Maybe.' He sounded doubtful. 'Maybe she, or he, wasn't Egyptian but Indian. That would explain your darker skin and black hair. India has a lot of princes and princesses, and I don't know them at all.'

'But I've read all about Egypt; I don't know a thing about India. I don't want to be an Indian, I want to be Egyptian!' My voice had risen to a wail; one part of my brain worrying that my new uncle would think I was being childish and the other part

148

realising that I had always been childish, and that Billy had been right. 'Was Billy right?' Uncle looked confused. 'Billy, one of Ma and Pa's other fosterings. He says my Ma was a whore and my Pa a greasy furriner off one of them tankers. Is he right?' I was screaming by now. 'Is he?'

Uncle Gryffyn put his arms around me and held me tightly to his chest. 'Oh, Effie. I don't know who your parents were but I'm sure they loved you and wanted you to be well looked after. There are many reasons why they couldn't keep you, but you weren't just abandoned, were you? They left you where they knew you'd be cared for and they left a substantial amount of money, far more than a sailor or ... a working girl could have afforded. She may well have been a princess, he may well have been a prince; all I'm saying is that they probably weren't Egyptian. Look at me, Effie.'

I looked into his warm, brown eyes until the tears blurred my vision and I put my head on his shoulder and wept.

I sat at the dressing table and stared crossly at the girl in the mirror. 'You knew all along our mother wasn't an Egyptian princess, didn't you|?' The girl in the mirror looked embarrassed and nodded. 'Why didn't you say something? Why let me dream for all those years?' The girl in the mirror just shrugged. 'Were you just being kind?' She nodded. 'I don't want her to be Indian, do you?' She shook her head violently. 'Do you think Uncle Gryffyn's right that she might have been an Egyptian but just not a princess?' She grinned and nodded but almost immediately she looked down and shook her head. 'Look at me.' The girl in the mirror slowly raised her eyes to mine. 'Do you think Billy's right?' She stared into my eyes for a long time, gave a sad smile and nodded. 'Are you going to cry?' She gave a defiant shake. 'No, me neither.'

Chapter 21

Beattie

I had to wake Effie at five o'clock to give us enough time to catch the Train de Luxe, which left the railway at six o'clock. It was still dark, sun rise wasn't until a quarter to seven, but Effie woke after just one shake and got washed and dressed quickly. She had been very quiet the evening before. After Daddy had taken me aside and explained why, he'd looked at me anxiously. 'Was I wrong, Beattie? Should I have just let her continue believing that her mother was an Egyptian princess?' Then he'd chuckled. 'She was mortified when I suggested one of her parents might be Indian. She said she'd read all about Egypt, not India. Did I do wrong, Beattie?' I had tried to reassure him, but I don't think I succeeded.

This morning, though, she was full of energy and raced up and down the stairs, in and out of rooms, too excited to just stand and wait patiently in the hallway. Daddy had agreed the previous evening that it wasn't necessary for Omar to accompany us as well as Marcus, so it was only Marcus who waited patiently in the hallway. He seemed far too wide awake for that time in the morning, and he grinned when I nodded at the clock and pulled a face.

'We could have gone on the sleeper, Beattie; that wouldn't have been such an early start for you.'

'I thought of that, but Effie wouldn't have seen anything of the journey. We might come back that way, though I think it arrives in Cairo at some ungodly hour so that would be just as bad. Well, all the cases are in the car, so I think we're ready to go.'

My father had got up to see us off and was standing in his dressing gown and slippers, prepared, I'm sure, to go straight back to bed once we'd left. 'Have a good journey and a good time in Luxor, one and all. Effie, I want to see lots of sketches when you come back. Beattie, write every day and telephone me if you need to. Marcus, take care of them.'

I went to him and hugged him. 'I'll give your love to Aunt Edith, shall I?' He merely grunted. Marcus shook his hand and said something to him that I couldn't hear, but he glanced at me and Effie, so I guessed he was promising to make sure nothing happened to us. Effie hurtled across the hallway and flung herself at him, almost knocking him over. 'Why don't you come with us? Will you be safe? What if something happens to you? How will we know?'

'Nobody will hurt me, don't you worry. I'm invincible, didn't you know? And anyway, I have the whole of the police force to look after me. You have a lovely time, Effie dear. Now let me go; you need to leave or you'll miss the train.' When Effie released him, I could see his eyes shining and his mouth curved in a smile.

Even at that time in the morning Ramses station was thronging with people and the noise was overwhelming: dogs barked, children screamed, babies cried, doors banged, whistles blew, and trains puffed and steamed like angry dragons. Lateef used his stick to knock a pathway through the crowd and we all docilely followed, our cases balanced precariously on a trolley pushed by a toothless skeleton covered in wrinkled, dark brown leather.

Whilst Lateef made sure our cases were put in the goods van, the rest of us clambered aboard the shuddering beast and a liveried boy led us to our compartment. He stamped our tickets and quickly pocketed a gold fifty piastre coin Marcus slipped him, guaranteeing we would be well looked after during the journey. We were in first class, of course, so the seats were plush, red velvet with plenty of leg room and a useful wooden table to put books and refreshments on. Effie and I sat next to a window and Marcus sat next to Effie, meaning that I could surreptitiously look at him without being too obvious.

151

The last door banged, the whistle blew, and the train tensed itself ready to start the thirteen-hour journey down to Luxor. As soon as we began to move Effie put her head against the glass and stared avidly as we left the bustling station and moved faster and faster through Cairo, its suburbs and out into the desert. It was still dark and once we were out of the city there wasn't much to see so she was able to concentrate on the rather splendid cooked breakfast that our boy brought us. As the sun rose the small villages, the occasional ruined pyramid and temple, the Nile and the endless desert all became visible. I'd seen the view enough times to find it rather dull but today I enjoyed looking at it through Effie's eyes as she absorbed the scenery, making the odd note and drawing in her sketchbook, the one of mine that Daddy had given her. Captain Karim still hadn't handed her back the one she'd dropped at El Lisht.

I woke with a start to find that I wasn't the only one who had been lulled by the clickety clack of the wheels over the rails. Marcus had his eyes closed and was snoring rather endearingly and Effie was slumped against him, her mouth slightly open. She really was a pretty girl. Her face was oval shaped, framed by her shiny, straight, black hair, cut into a medium-length bob. I knew her eyes, when they were open, were as dark a brown as you could get without them being black. Her skin was the colour of milky tea, darker than a typical English girl's but not as dark as a true Egyptian, or indeed, Indian. I hoped she'd put some weight on during our stay with my aunt; she really did look like a half-starved street urchin. I wondered whether her foster parents fed her properly, whether they were kind to her, whether they made her feel loved. She hadn't said anything to indicate that they didn't, but she was one of, how many was it, five or six? Were we doing her a kindness by taking her under our wing and making her feel special? What would happen when she went back to her Ma and Pa Foster and being just another foster child amongst many. It was unlikely that anyone would adopt her now; what would happen to her when she was too old to be fostered? Would she thank or curse us for our kindness, for showing her what a real family life could have been like?

'Penny for them.' Marcus was awake. I was about to tell him when Effie stirred and then bolted upright, her eyes and mouth wide open. She looked around her in a panic, then relaxed as she realised where she was.

'Gawd, I thought I was trapped in a packing case and was being shipped off to India.' She shook her head, like a spaniel shaking off water. 'Are we there yet?'

Marcus and I laughed then he got a pack of playing cards out of his pocket. 'No, we won't be there until this evening. I've got some cards here if you want to play a game of snap?' We played six games; both Marcus and I are competitive and gave no quarter, but Effie beat us at every game. She was a very poor winner.

We had just started a seventh game when our boy popped his head round the door and told us that luncheon was being server in the restaurant car if we would kindly follow him? It seemed a long time since we'd had breakfast and we all followed him eagerly down the corridors of two coaches, swaying side to side as the train trundled along. The dining car was very luxurious and was easily on a par with the best restaurants in Cairo, if not in London. Effie hung back at the entrance. Most of the tables were already taken and she seemed nervous to walk past the diners who looked at us out of idle curiosity then got back to their talking or eating or both.

I took her hand and pulled her gently along, past the table of four military men well in their cups; past the elderly couple who were both reading as they ate having probably run out of conversation years ago; past the young couple who weren't talking either, intent on staring into each other's eyes; past the family with two sulky teenagers, both of whom looked bored to

153

tears. Effie quickly slipped into the seat at our table, knocking some of the cutlery onto the floor. She blushed in embarrassment and stammered a 'Sorry,' but our boy was there in a flash with clean cutlery and a basket of warm rolls that soon pacified her. I handed her the menu.

'Why isn't everything in English? This is in French, isn't it? Why do the Arabs speak French when they're not speaking Egyptian?'

I let Marcus explain. 'The French ran Egypt for many years before the English and they insisted that everyone spoke French. When the English came along, they decided not to change anything. Do you know what you'd like to eat?' He read out the dishes, translating them into English and her eyes lit up when he said, 'Fish and chips.'

'Can I have that? We used to have fish and chips every Saturday for tea.'

'It won't be quite the same as you're used to because the fish won't be battered but I'm sure it will be very tasty.'

Effie looked dubiously at the delicate sole that lay on the plate before her but having devoured the pommes frites she took a tentative taste of the fish, ready, I could tell, to pull a face and say it was horrid. She looked surprised when she realised how tasty it was and it was soon just a memory. Marcus and I finished our meal with cheese and biscuits but we both wished we'd ordered the ice-cream and chocolate sauce that Effie took great pleasure in slowly eating before our jealous eyes.

After another short doze, numerous games of snap all won by Effie, some desultory reading and far too many cakes mid-afternoon, we steamed into Luxor at seven o'clock in the evening. It was dark once again, the sun having set an hour and a half earlier. Whilst we waited for our trunks to be unloaded, I looked around the station, which was a simple, single-story building, nowhere near as grand as the one in Cairo. Although

I'd been vague about who would be coming, I had been precise about the time of our arrival, but I couldn't see anyone who seemed particularly interested in us. I was just about to say to Marcus that it looked like we might have to hire transport when a voice boomed along the platform.

'Hey there, Beatrice, Marcus! Over here!'

I looked to where the sound came from, along with everyone else in the near vicinity, to see my aunt waving her stick dangerously in the air to get our attention, and the eye of anyone who dared to go within three feet of her in any direction.

'God bless her, she doesn't change.' Marcus grinned and waved back. 'Has Beattie told you about her mad old Aunt, Effie? She's a real character but she has a heart of gold. You'll like her, I know you will.' He strode down the platform and when he reached her, he bowed and kissed the back of her hand. Even though we were still some distance away I could hear her roar of laughter as she pretended to slap his face then gave him a hug as if he was a long-lost son come home from the war. She was almost as tall as Marcus and wiry, whereas my mother, her sister, had been petite and voluptuous. Today Aunt Edith was kitted out in a cream safari suit as wrinkled as if she'd been wearing it for a week, which was not that unlikely. I'd never seen Aunt Edith in a dress or any attire that would have been acceptable at Shepheard's or at the tennis club. She rarely wore a hat; she considered her thick mop of ginger hair, her gift to me, sufficient protection against the Egyptian sun, which had retaliated over the years by bleaching it almost white.

Effie was reluctant to follow me, and I had to pull her along. 'There's nothing to worry about. She's a little eccentric perhaps but she's one of the kindest people in the whole world. She knows an awful lot about the temples of Luxor and Karnak, and she practically lives at the Valley of the Kings.' This did

155

the trick and Effie kept up with me as I almost ran across the platform. Aunt Edith's embrace was firm and reassuring and the strain of the previous days fell away; I felt safe. Having released me she turned to Effie.

'And who's this young lady? Not your love child is it, Marcus?' She roared with laughter, whilst Marcus blushed, I cringed, and Effie looked confused.

'Aunt Edith, please. This is Effie. She's just come over from England and she's in need of some looking after. It's a long story, which I'll tell you later on but for now can we please just go home so we can get changed and have something to eat?' I was surprised to realise that although I had eaten a lot and had hardly moved a muscle all day, I was still hungry.

Aunt Edith held her hand out to Effie. 'Well, my dear, you are very welcome, whoever you are, and if you need looking after then you've come to the right place.' Effie stared at the hand then tentatively shook it, managing a weak and insincere smile.

'Come along now, your carriage awaits.'

I'd hoped for the Rolls Royce, but our carriage turned out to be a cart pulled by two donkeys. Our luggage had already been loaded and Marcus, Effie and I clambered into the back and sat on the wooden benches that lined the two long sides. Aunt Edith took the reins, clicked her tongue and the donkeys dragged us from the station through the streets of Luxor, along the corniche road that ran parallel to the Nile and past the five-star hotels and expensive apartments built especially for the rich tourists.

As we neared the edge of town, where my aunt's house was located, she turned and spoke to Effie. 'Do you know that Luxor used to be called Thebes, which was the capital of ancient Egypt at one time? And that the name Luxor is derived from the Arabic El-Qusûr, which means "the castles"?' Effie did, of course; Aunt Edith didn't yet know that Effie was a keen

Egyptologist. 'The name refers to the castles or temples of ancient times, of course, but the man who built the house where I live called it *Château de Sable* or 'Castle of Sand', although I know Beatrice always calls it the 'Sand Castle'. The man was murdered in his bed by a discontented servant. Slit his throat from ear to ear. Apparently, he was a very cruel man and treated his servants appallingly. And his camels. So, he deserved what he got in my opinion.'

'You won the 'Sand Castle' in a card game, didn't you, Aunt? I remember you telling me that when I was a child. Is it true?'

'Ah, what is truth? Do you know, Effie?' She twisted round and winked at Effie, who looked panic stricken and turned to me for guidance. I just shrugged; I doubt there was an answer a nearly eleven-year-old could give.

Chapter 22

Effie

It was too dark to see much when we arrived, but I could see enough to know that the 'Castle of Sand' wasn't a giant sandcastle as I'd imagined it to be. Instead, it was a two-storey, stone building that didn't have a regular shape as far as I could tell. Lights blazed out of the downstairs windows, throwing paths of gold over the veranda then spilled onto the front garden, which seemed to be nothing but sand. Maybe that's where the name came from.

Beattie's aunt told us to go on in whilst she gave orders to two boys in what seemed to be fluent Arabic; one started to unload the cases and the other led the donkeys away. Beattie and Marcus walked into the house quite confidently; I suppose they had been there lots of times before and felt quite at home. I, on the other hand, was nervous about going in; although Beattie's aunt had said I was very welcome I wondered whether she in fact felt annoyed at being lumbered with a child, especially one like me. I made a silent promise that I'd be on my best behaviour at all times; only talk when spoken to; eat everything put in front of me; be as quiet as a mouse and not drink anything so that there would be no danger of me wetting the bed. Just the very thought of that happening made my palms sweat but the rest of me go cold all over.

The front door led into a large hallway that had a pale pink marble floor and was in the shape of a something-agon, with a pink marble staircase curving up the middle. It had five, no six walls – what was that, a sixagon? Each wall had a door, sometimes in the middle, sometimes not, and each door had a design painted onto it. I stopped and looked at one; it was of a pharaoh seated on a throne, shaded by a huge, feathered fan, slaves kneeling at his feet holding up baskets of grain and fruits. I forgot my promise to only talk when spoken to. 'Is this

158

a copy of something real, Marcus?' He stood by my side and studied it. 'Yes, it is. Each door has a different painting, do you see? This one is taken from a painting on the wall in one of the side rooms in the Temple of Karnak, as is that one over there. Whereas this one,' he walked over to a door on the other side of the hall, 'is a copy of a scene painted in one of the antechambers in Tutankhamun's tomb.'

'They're rather splendid, aren't they? Not as good as the original, of course.' Beattie's aunt bellowed across the hall then strode over to where we were standing and spoke more normally. 'I had these painted, oh, some ten years ago by a local man, who claimed to have been one of the team with Carter when he discovered Tut's tomb. He may well have been, but he died soon after he finished; maybe another victim of the so-called curse.' She looked quite serious, but I could see Marcus and Beattie smiling behind her back. She suddenly clapped her hands, which made me jump. 'Now, I'm sure you all want to freshen up then have something to eat. Beatrice, you're in your usual room, Marcus you can have the Anubis Room and Effie, you can have the Isis Room. Beatrice, you can show them where to go. I'll go and make sure those lazy good for nothing boys of mine are getting dinner ready. Off you go now and be back down in an hour.'

I felt relieved when Beattie's aunt left; she made me feel nervous. Beattie must have noticed my look of relief. 'You'll soon get used to her, Effie. Her bark is worse than her bite. She only has men and boy servants and whatever she says, she adores them, and they adore her. Come on, the bedrooms are up here.' Marcus and I followed Beattie up the stairs, which led on to a landing with more painted doors. As I got closer, I realised that the paintings were of different Egyptian gods. Marcus stopped at the door with the head of the jackal painted on it. I was glad it wasn't my room; I wouldn't have been comfortable sleeping in a room named after Anubis, the god of the dead. My room, of course, had Isis, the mother goddess, with her headdress of cow horns holding a sun disk.

Beattie pointed out the bathroom door and ushered me into my room. 'Get washed and changed and I'll knock on your door in an hour. Will you be alright?'

I nodded and shut the door behind her. The room was quite small, though still larger than the one I shared with the other girls at Ma and Pa Fosters. I felt a short-lived pang when I thought of them. Uncle Gryffyn said he'd contact them and tell them that I was being well looked after and not to worry about me. To be honest, I didn't miss them; up 'til now I was enjoying myself too much. I just had to get used to the fact that it wasn't likely that I had any Egyptian blood running through my veins. The walls of the room were rough and painted white, decorated with small paintings of Isis in her many guises and the only other colour came from the carpet, with its gorgeous gold, reds, greens and blues. The room was simply furnished with a huge bed, a wooden ottoman carved with hieroglyphics, a chest of drawers and a wardrobe with a long mirror on the outside of one of the doors. I peered at the girl in the mirror and saw that she was rather grubby and dishevelled looking. Someone had put my case on the bed; it took me just a few minutes to find a home for everything. I changed into a clean dress and put on a cardigan, it having become chillier as the sun had gone off elsewhere.

I grabbed my wash bag and went to the bathroom, which unsurprisingly had Anuket, the goddess of the Nile painted on its door. It wasn't quite as luxurious as the one in Beattie's home, but it was still a real pleasure to do all the things one has to do in such a place. Although Ma and Pa Foster had an indoor toilet, we kids were encouraged to use the privy at the bottom of the garden and I now appreciated not having to rush in the pouring rain to piss as quickly as possible, with eyes closed so as not to see the spiders hiding in the corners waiting to catch and devour careless passers-by. I would have loved a bath but was frightened of using too much water and taking too much time, so I just ran a basinful of steaming hot water. When I washed my face, I was surprised at how dirty the water was considering that I'd been inside all day.

When I returned to my room, I saw from the clock on the chest of drawers that I still had half an hour remaining of the hour allocated to us, so I sat on the bed, my back against plumped up pillows and started the diary Beattie had suggested I write.

'Wakey, wakey, Effie.'

I'd slipped to the side and was lying on my diary, which I was surprised to see was as empty as it had been when I'd opened it.

'I must have dozed off, just for a minute or so.'

Beattie grinned. 'You were fast asleep half an hour ago when I called for you. I let you sleep a bit longer, but you really need to get up now if you want dinner. Unless you're too tired to eat?'

'Too tired to eat? Never!' I leapt off the bed and was about to rush downstairs to the dining room when I remembered where I was and who was downstairs. 'Beattie, are you sure your aunt is alright with me staying? I don't want to be any trouble.'

'She is absolutely fine, dear, don't you worry. I've told her a little bit about how you got here and how you're interested in Egyptology, and she is very keen to show you round Luxor and Karnak. Just brush your hair, it's sticking out.'

The girl in the mirror did indeed look a bit untidy and a bit scared. I smiled at her shyly to try and make her feel better; she smiled back and made me feel a bit better too.

Beattie had got changed into a pale green dress that suited her colouring and had a lovely cream silk scarf around her shoulders. Billy, also ginger, always insisted on wearing red or orange jumpers that clashed horribly with his hair. Beattie led the way to a room downstairs where Marcus and Beattie's aunt were already sitting, chatting away and drinking sherry. I knew it was sherry because they had those funny-shaped glasses – named after some sort of boat for some reason – just like Ma and Pa Foster used when they had their Christmas drink of Harvey's Bristol Cream. Marcus got up when we entered and asked me what I wanted to drink. I forgot I had promised myself not to drink and asked for a glass of lemonade. He handed Beattie a glass full of sherry.

Beattie's aunt pushed herself out of the sofa, finished her sherry in one long gulp then held her hand out to me. 'Come on, my dear, I'll take you into the dining room. I hope you're hungry. Abdul slaughtered two kids specially.'

'Kids? You eat children?' It came out as a squeak.

'No, dear, Aunt Edith meant baby goats.'

'Baby goats?' Still a squeak.

'It's very similar to lamb. You eat lamb don't you and they're baby sheep.' I nodded but I was lying because I didn't like to admit that I didn't think I ever had; we usually ate fish, corned beef hash, a rabbit or mutton stew and a chicken on a Sunday.

'Here we are, you come and sit next to me, Effie, so we can have a nice chat.' That was the last thing I wanted but Beattie gave me an encouraging smile and the table was small enough so that I was actually close to everyone. It was a very strange room with carpets hanging on the walls and the ceiling was covered in pleated silk and shaped like the roof of a tent. Beattie's aunt saw me looking around. 'I have tried to make this room a bit like the inside of a Bedouin tent. Really we should be sitting cross-legged on the floor; maybe we will tomorrow. What do you think?' I thought she was crazy, but I smiled and nodded as if sitting on the floor to eat my dinner was something I did all the time. A door opened and an Arab

162

came in carrying four laden plates. 'Ah, here comes Abdul with the first course.' I was determined to eat whatever was put before me, expecting it to be unfamiliar in looks and taste, but it was just a plate of vegetables in a clear sauce. 'They're all things grown along the Nile. Here, have some bread.' I took a chunk from the basket that Beattie's aunt offered me and put it on my side plate. Did they say prayers here? I didn't dare start to eat until someone else did. 'Get stuck in, Effie. We don't stand on ceremony here.'

I recognised most of the vegetables and soon cleaned the plate, using the bread to mop up the juices as I saw the others do. 'Beatrice's told me about your rather unconventional manner of getting into Egypt, Effie, and your derring-do escape from that awful orphanage. You're a very resilient and resourceful young lady and should be very proud of yourself.' I didn't understand some of the words she used but I gathered that she was praising me, and I felt my cheeks flush in pleasure. 'She also told me about your interest in Egyptology.' She looked at me intently and stroked my hair with her wrinkly hand. 'You look a little like an Egyptian.'

I didn't know what to say and I looked at Beattie begging her to say something.

'Effie grew up in an orphanage, Aunt. She doesn't know who her parents were but one of them could certainly be Egyptian.'

I didn't like this conversation and didn't want to discuss the possible nationality of my parents yet again. Luckily Abdul came in then with the next course, which was some sort of meat stew with rice and tomatoes. Was this the goat that had been specially slaughtered? I had to admit that it did smell good. Everyone else was tucking in so I took the smallest piece of meat and popped it in my mouth. I didn't think I'd like it, but it actually tasted very nice and before I knew it my plate was clean, and I was nodding my head at the offer of more.

163

The grown-ups were drinking wine and I noticed Beattie's cheeks were pink and her eyes bright. Was she drunk? I hoped not. Pa Foster always came back from the pub on a Saturday night a bit worse for wear, as Ma Foster used to say; he always had very red cheeks and a tendency to cry and tell anyone who was still up that he loved them. Beattie had been very quiet during the meal letting her aunt and Marcus do most of the talking. She suddenly put down her glass, which she had just emptied and said, rather loudly, 'Why have you and Daddy fallen out, Aunt? You're both such lovely people and yet you can't bear the sight or sound of each other. Why is that?'

Marcus looked a little shocked and embarrassed, but Beattie's aunt looked angry and then sad. 'I haven't fallen out with your father.'

'Oh, come on. I remember we all used to come here to see you and you would visit us and you'd all get on splendidly. And then all of a sudden it changed, and Daddy can't even bear to hear your name. I'm not a child, Aunt, tell me what happened.'

Marcus took her hand. 'I don't think this is the right time or place, Beattie. You've had a long day and must be tired. Why don't we all go to bed?'

'Don't patronise me, Marcus. I have a right to know why the two people I love most in the world hate each other so much.'

'I don't hate your father, Beatrice. I just ...'

'Just what?' Beattie glared at her aunt, and I wished I was in bed, fast asleep. 'Just what?' Beattie's aunt sighed and shook her head. She bit her lip, glanced at me, and gave a brief nod. 'Perhaps it is time for you to know the truth, but Marcus is right, dear, now is not the right time or place.'

Chapter 23

Beattie

I lay unable to move; someone was holding me down on the ground. My mouth was dry, and my eyelids seemed to be stuck closed. I couldn't think why anyone would be preventing me from getting up. Was it the Blue Shirts or the Eye of Horus gang? Where was I? I opened one eye then closed it again as the light seared into my eyeball. I had seen enough, though, to recognise my bedroom at Aunt Edith's. The pieces slowly fell into place. I remembered the train journey from Cairo to Luxor, the donkey ride from the station to the 'Sand Castle', changing my clothes, having dinner. The last thing I remembered was shouting at my aunt and her quiet response that it was time for her to tell me the truth but not then or there. Something had happened between my father and aunt and today I would know the reason.

I started to get up but quickly lay down again and waited for the banging inside my head to stop. Was I ill? I carefully raised my hand to my forehead, surprised that it was cool and not at all feverish. I went over the previous day again and remembered sitting in the lounge chatting to Aunt Edith and Marcus. I'd had a glass of sherry, just to be sociable. I wasn't a great drinker and although I liked sherry, I found it rather strong; one glass was more than enough. I remember going to fetch Effie and deciding to leave her to sleep a bit longer. Marcus had handed me a replenished glass when I had come back into the lounge. That was two glasses. And hadn't Marcus handed me yet another glass when I returned with Effie? Three glasses of sherry? And then a glass of wine with the meal. My God, I'd been drunk! And what I was now experiencing was a hangover.

I felt my cheeks burn, not with fever but with embarrassment and shame. What would Effie think of me?

165

Aunt Edith? Marcus? Marcus! It was all his fault; it was he who had given me the three glasses of sherry and filled up my wine glass. My stomach churned at the very thought of all that alcohol swirling inside. I needed to get up to apologise to my aunt. I slowly opened my eyes again and managed to keep them open, avoiding the light that was filtering through the shutters. I knew from Grace, who was a practised drinker, that a hangover experienced by an amateur – such as me – was often accompanied by nausea but apart from a headache I felt no desire to empty the contents of my stomach.

It took me ten long minutes to inch myself into a sitting position on the side of the bed, my progress accompanied by the beating of a drum inside my head. I rested there for a while and slaked my thirst with a glass of water then another glass with a packet of Kaputine powder dissolved in it. If their promise was to be believed, my headache would be gone within ten minutes.

I was horrified to see that it was ten o'clock; half the morning had gone. My head had indeed eased and by the time I got washed and dressed into some slacks and a long-sleeved blouse I felt almost normal again. My footsteps echoed on the marble floor as I walked down the stairs and along the corridor to the dining room and I knew that there would be no one there. Their place settings had been cleared, leaving just mine looking all alone and accusing. I realised that I was hungry and was wondering whether to go to the kitchen to find something to eat when Abdul came in bearing a platter of cooked eggs and meats, a basket of bread rolls and a pot of tea.

I knew Abdul didn't speak French or English, so I didn't bother trying to ask him where everyone was, but my question was answered when he handed me a folded piece of paper. I recognised Aunt Edith's bold scrawl: 'Decided to leave you to sleep. We have gone to the temple. Join us if you can. E xx'

I wondered which temple, Luxor or Karnak? Luxor was the nearest, so I decided to try there first. I put on a wide-brimmed straw hat, added extra protection with a parasol and changed my flimsy sandals for some sturdy shoes. I strolled down the street towards the entrance to the site of the ruined temple of Luxor. There were quite a few tourists milling around, probably all staying at the luxurious Winter Palace. Many were being led around by an Arab guide and all had their copy of Baedeker's. I knew my aunt usually tried to avoid the tourists, apart from when she was haranguing them, but she might be in the more popular areas today if she was showing Effie around. I wandered under the colossal statue of a sitting Ramses II, who eyed me, and all who ventured near, with indifference. I peered into the small sanctuaries and vestibules that lined the walls and round the thick columns, carved with the story of whichever pharaoh had predominated at the time.

The floor was covered in stones that made walking difficult and at one point I stumbled and fell to my knees. Before I could scramble back to my feet, I felt strong hands grip my arms and lift me up. I turned to say thank you, but he kept hold of me and started to drag me back the way I had come. I opened my mouth to scream but the man stopped and put his head close to mine. I smelt his spice-laden breath, hot against my ear. 'Don't make a sound, Miss Trevethan. You come quietly and your aunt, Miss Goodley, won't get hurt, nor Mr Dunwoody, nor the little miss.' How on earth did he know our names and why was I being targeted? I sensed rather than saw that the man was not alone, and I knew that even if I managed to release myself from him others would quickly take over. That didn't stop me from struggling, though.

'Yoo hoo, Beatrice! We're over here!'

Everyone – me, my captor, the tourists – all turned to where Aunt Edith, resplendent in the garb of a Bedouin, appeared from behind a pillar and strode towards me, waving a paintbrush. The man muttered something in Arabic, a curse no doubt, and was suddenly gone, although I could still feel the pressure of his grasp. My legs gave way beneath me and I found myself kneeling on the floor again. My aunt rushed over and knelt by my side. 'Are you all right, dear? Is it the heat?' She obviously hadn't seen anything untoward. All I could do was shake my head. I tried to speak but I could only sob. 'What on earth is the matter, Beatrice? Are you hurt?'

Then someone else squatted beside me and put his arms around me. 'What's happened?'

I took two deep breaths to calm myself. 'He was trying to kidnap me. He said if I didn't go quietly, he'd hurt my aunt, you, and Effie. Oh, Marcus, they're here.'

Marcus leapt to his feet and spun slowly in a circle, scanning the people in the courtyard. He turned a second time then shook his head. 'They've gone, whoever they were. Can you get up? Did they hurt you?'

'No, I'm alright, just a bit shaken.'

'Is this that gang that drove you out of Cairo? They've followed you here? Why would they want to kidnap you?' Aunt Edith's voice trembled, and her face had paled to a greyish brown.

'Let's take her home and we can talk there. God, I'm so sorry, Beattie. I promised your father I would look after you and instead you were almost taken from under my nose. Here, hold on to me. Do you think you can manage to walk back?'

I was quite capable of walking, but I relished Marcus's concern and I clung on to him allowing him to take my weight. I had only gone a few steps when I stopped and looked around frantically. The panic rose from the pit of my stomach and was expelled out of my mouth as a screech. 'Effie! Where's Effie? They know who she is. Have they taken her?'

Aunt Edith turned without saying anything and marched back across the courtyard and disappeared behind a pillar.

168

Marcus and I stood like two more statues. My aunt reappeared holding a large bag that I knew held all her sketching paraphernalia in one hand, and Effie's arm in the other. I released the breath I had been holding and noisily refilled my lungs. 'Oh, thank God.'

As Effie got closer her expression of puzzlement turned to worry. 'Are you alright, Beattie? Has something happened?'

'I'm alright, my dear. I was ... I was approached by a man who wanted me to go with him. He was probably a Blue Shirt or in the Eye of Horus gang.' I didn't want to frighten her by telling her that he knew all their names and that I'd been worried that they'd taken her. 'We're just going home to have some lunch.'

Effie looked nervously around her and began to say something, but she was pulled away by Aunt Edith, who turned and glared at Marcus. 'Hold on to my niece and don't let her go, not even for one second.' I felt Marcus's fingers grip my upper arm tightly, where it was already bruised, but I didn't say anything; I didn't want him to stop holding me. He put his head close to mine and I smelt his comforting aroma of peppermint, soap and sweat. 'I'm never going to let you out of my sight again, Beattie. Christ, to try and kidnap you in broad daylight. I'm going to tell your father that he needs to send down more men to protect you. I can't do it alone.'

As soon as we returned to the 'Sand Castle', Marcus left me sitting on the sofa with Effie and my aunt in close attendance and went off to the telephone office in the town to make a call to my father. When he came back, he looked relieved. 'I managed to get thorough. Your father is arranging for some men to come down, hopefully on the overnight train, in which case they should be here tomorrow morning, otherwise it will be by the evening at the latest. Until then, we must all stay indoors. Edith, can you tell your boys to be extra vigilant and to come and tell one of us immediately if they see someone they don't recognise?' Aunt Edith nodded and left the room to give them the message. 'I'm sorry, Effie, but our outing has been ruined once again by these people. We'll finish our tour of the temples and go over the Nile to visit the Valley of the Kings once we have our protection.'

Effie gave a nervous smile. 'That's alright. Aunt Edith is going to help turn my sketches of the relief work on the columns into proper paintings.'

Aunt Edith had returned by now and patted Effie on the head. 'That's my girl. We can sit in the garden at the back. We'll be perfectly safe there.'

I hadn't been up for long, but I felt a wave of tiredness wash over me. I slumped back and closed my eyes, wanting to slip into a dreamland where I wasn't being chased by men who were determined to drag me away from the people I loved.

I woke to find myself lying on the sofa, an embroidered cushion under my head, a sequin sticking into my cheek. Aunt Edith was sitting in an armchair, looking pensive. There was no sign of Marcus or Effie. 'How long have I been asleep? You didn't have to stay with me.'

'Marcus is showing Effie my collection of artefacts. I thought I'd just sit quietly with you. The attempt to kidnap you has been a shock for us all. I know I won't relax until the men your father is sending are here.'

'I'm so sorry, Aunt. Perhaps I shouldn't have come but I thought we'd be safe here.'

'And so you should be. What concerns me is how they knew you were at the temple. Either they followed you from Cairo, which is bad enough, but even worse if someone in Cairo found out you were here and contacted these men and told them what to do. Both scenarios involve good organisation and preparation.'

These were my own worries, made worse by being spoken out loud. 'Why me, Aunt?' It wasn't cold but I shivered. Aunt

Edith pulled a shawl off the back of her chair, came over and wrapped it round my shoulders. She stayed sitting next to me, her bony arm around me. A memory suddenly flashed into my head. I was fourteen and sitting on this same settee; Aunt Edith was by my side with her arm around me. I was sobbing, great gasping sobs that wracked my whole body. I had pushed my aunt away and spluttered that I wanted my Mummy even though I knew that she couldn't come, that she would never come, ever again.

'It's been ten or so years since she died. My father brought me down from Cairo but didn't tell me why we were coming; it was you who broke the news to me. I was sitting right here when you told me. Do you remember? I was angry with you; I blamed you for a while.'

'Your father has never stopped blaming me.'

I turned to look at her. 'Do you mean that Daddy blames you for Mama's death? But why? You didn't kill her. Did you?'

She gave a grim smile. 'No, Beatrice, I didn't kill her, but I ...' She shook her head vigorously. Then she nodded, took her arm from around me and placed her hands neatly on her knees. I noticed a brown age spot on the back of her hand and realised that she was getting old. 'I suppose now is as good a time as any. Are you sure you want to know what happened Beatrice? It's not a happy story.'

'Any story that ends in the death of a mother can't possibly be a happy one. But I need to know what happened, Aunt, please just tell me.'

'First of all, you need to know that your mother always loved you and your father. But she hated to be alone. Do you remember when you were thirteen your father started spending a lot of time visiting and assessing all the small villages? He was away for weeks, even months, at a time.'

I nodded. 'Yes, I remember.'

My aunt looked into the distance, where the past lay crouching. 'Your mother filled her time with doing good works in the day and socialising in the evenings. You have to realise, Beatrice, that your mother ... your mother needed to feel loved.'

I felt a pang of guilt. Surely Mama had known that I'd loved her? Should I have told her more often? 'But she was loved by both me and Daddy.'

'I know, dear, but at that time your father wasn't there to show his love. People thought Evelyn was assured but she wasn't, she lacked confidence and felt very insecure.' Aunt Edith stopped talking and looked down at her hands that were curled into fists.

I suddenly realised what my fourteen-year-old self never could have. 'She took a lover.' I said it as a matter of fact.

My aunt gave the smallest of nods. 'Not so much taking a lover as falling in love.'

I was confused; how did having a lover explain her death and Daddy's antipathy towards Aunt Edith? 'Who was he?'

'Someone quite high up in the police. She met him at a charity event. She used to write me long letters and tell me all about him; about how they had both fallen in love at first sight. I only ever saw pictures of him, but I could see he was a handsome fellow. Your mother used to say he was her Egyptian god.'

Someone took my intestines and screwed them into a tight ball. 'He was an Egyptian?' Another small nod. My brow creased into a puzzled frown. I had so many questions but didn't want to bombard my aunt with them. 'Why did she come to Luxor? Was he here as well?'

My aunt took a deep breath and blurted out, 'She came here to have the baby.'

The tick of the clock on the table echoed around the room, filling the silence that had fallen.

'Was it her lover's child?' My aunt opened her eyes, and I could see the truth in them. 'But why did she die?' A thought occurred to me, so awful it knocked the breath out of me and flung me to the back of the sofa. 'She didn't ... she didn't kill herself, did she? Oh Aunt, please don't tell me she killed herself?'

'No, no, no, she didn't. It was a difficult birth, and she lost a lot of blood. The doctors couldn't save her.'

My whole body was shuddering as I imagined my poor mother bleeding so much she died. 'Did she suffer?'

My aunt was silent for so long I didn't think she was going to answer. 'At first but once the baby was born, she lost consciousness and never really came around again. I was with her the whole time. I held her in my arms,' she stopped, tears streaming down her cheeks, 'I held her in my arms as she took her last breath. I couldn't save her, Beatrice, I couldn't save my little sister.'

Chapter 24

Effie

I didn't mean to eavesdrop. Marcus had been showing me some statues that were dotted about the back garden, stolen, he suspected, from the Valley of the Kings by the man who had built the giant sandcastle and had been murdered in his bed. I needed to go to the toilet and was on my way to the bathroom when I heard sobbing coming from the lounge. The door was ajar and through the gap I could see Aunt Edith and Beattie facing me sitting side by side on the settee. Beattie was hugging her aunt, who was crying and saying over and over again, 'I couldn't save her, Beatrice, I couldn't save her.'

I should have carried on walking, but I didn't; I was too interested in what was going on and I forgot the reason I had come indoors in the first place. Eventually the sobbing stopped, and the two women separated themselves. It was Beattie who spoke next, her voice trembling. 'If you've never met the man, I assume he wasn't here when she was giving birth to his child?'

Aunt Edith shook her head. 'The plan was that he'd stay in Cairo until after the birth, then he'd come down here and they'd leave together to start a new life.'

Who on earth were they talking about? Beattie's response soon answered my question. 'A new life? She was going to start a new life without me? With an Egyptian?'

'No, no, no, dear. She wasn't leaving you. No, it was your father she was leaving. She was going to fetch you after the birth, I promise you.'

There was a long silence and I tried not to break it with a sneeze that threatened.

'I remember she said she needed to get away but left me in Cairo because she didn't want me to miss school. It was only meant to be for a few weeks, that's what she said. But it was months. She must have known it would be months. She left me in Cairo with just old Mrs Bartholomew to look after me because she didn't want anyone to know she was having a child. An illegitimate child.' She suddenly put her hand to her chest and seemed to struggle to breathe. Was she having a heart attack? Should I go in to help? But she didn't collapse so I stayed where I was.

Aunt Edith looked down, as if too embarrassed to look at Beattie. 'She was so torn, Beatrice. She desperately wanted you with her, but she couldn't take you away from school for so long. She'd had two miscarriages since you were born, and she and your father had agreed not to have any more children. She couldn't stay in Cairo and pretend that it was your father's child and anyway, as soon as the baby was born it would be obvious if it took after the real father.' Aunt Edith took a deep, shuddering breath. 'Your mother was all alone and so very frightened. It had been agreed that the other man would not visit her here, so I was the only one she had. I couldn't turn her away, Beatrice. She was my sister and she needed me.' There was a few minutes silence, broken only by Beattie's quiet sobs. I wanted to go in and hug her better but resisted the temptation.

Beattie wiped her eyes and raised her face to look at her aunt. 'Did you contact her lover when she died?'

'No. I sent a telegraph to your father immediately and then one to the other one a few days later. I told him she'd died but that the baby had lived. I didn't really expect him to come and claim the child, and I was not wrong.'

Beattie's hand moved from her chest to her mouth and even from where I was standing I could see the tears spill from her eyes. 'Poor, poor Papa. What did you tell him?'

'I told him the truth. That's why he's never forgiven me. I told him that I gave his wife, my sister, a place to hide whilst she gave birth to another man's child and that I was going to help her run away. As far as he's concerned, I did everything I could to ruin his life and did nothing to save his wife's.'

I noticed Beattie had pulled away from her aunt and I knew it was time I left. As I was creeping away, I heard Beattie's next question, 'What happened to the baby?' and the reply, 'Your father didn't want anything to do with it. It was shipped off to England.' As I climbed the stairs to the bathroom, I thought I heard someone call my name,   but I couldn't stop; my need had become desperate.

As I sat on the pan, Aunt Edith's words swirled around me. 'It was shipped off to England.' It? Why call the baby it? Surely they must have known whether it was a boy or a girl? Even when I'd finished my business I continued sitting, trying to remember when Beattie had said her mother had died. Then it came to me; it was ten or so years ago when she was fourteen. I was ten years and eight months old; that could be considered to be ten years or so, couldn't it?

The realisation didn't come slowly and tentatively but in a blinding flash of absolute certainty.

I was that baby.

I was the result of an affair between Beattie's mother, a high-society Lady and an Egyptian man high-up in the police. Not a princess or prince, but near enough.

My heart did a somersault as another realisation hit me. Beattie and I had the same mother.

We were half-sisters.

Whilst I washed my hands the girl in the mirror couldn't stop grinning. Her cheeks were flushed and her eyes wide with delight. 'We have a sister. A sister. Sister. Sister. Sister.' I couldn't speak any more; the girl in the mirror was bent over with laughter.

'We should tell Beattie. She'll be so happy.' The first worm of doubt wriggled at the nape of my neck. 'Won't she?' The girl in the mirror nodded fervently. 'Yes, of course she will. I knew one of my parents was Egyptian; I just knew it. Do you think God arranged it so that I came here and that it was Beattie who found me and took me home?' The girl in the mirror tilted her head, pondering, then nodded her head. 'Yes, God obviously wants me to find my family. It must have been Him who showed me that picture of Nefertiti because that's where it all started, isn't it?' The girl in the mirror grinned and then wiped the tears from her eyes. 'Don't cry. Are they tears of happiness? I've read about them but never had them.'

The girl in the mirror suddenly frowned and bit her bottom lip. 'What's the matter? Are you worried that Uncle Gryffyn will send you packing when he finds out who I am?' She looked back at me worriedly and gave the slightest of nods. 'It's a possibility I suppose, but we seem to get on really well; I think he likes me. He wouldn't turn me out on the streets, would he?' The girl in the mirror continued to look worried and shrugged her shoulders. 'Beattie, our sister Beattie, wouldn't let that happen. Come on, let's go and tell her our news.'

When I went back downstairs, I found the lounge to be empty. I went outside to see but there was only Marcus waiting for me. 'You were a long time. I thought you'd fallen down the toilet and been flushed into the Nile.' I giggled more than the joke deserved. I really liked Marcus; if he married Beattie then he would be a sort of brother to me. How wonderful! From having nobody this morning I now had a sister, a brother, Aunt Edith would be a real Aunt and Uncle Gryffyn would be a sort-of-father, rather than a sort-of-uncle.

I hugged my secret to myself; I was dying to tell someone, but it had to be Beattie first. Marcus and I continued walking round the garden. He told me all about the statues, but I found it difficult to concentrate and didn't remember anything that he told me. It's a good job there was no test afterwards otherwise I would have failed miserably. When we had finished the tour, we sat in the shade of a tree. There was a slight breeze causing something to rattle. Marcus noticed me looking around to see what was making the sound. 'It's this tree. They call it the chatterbox tree or the women's tongue tree because it sounds like women chattering. It's the seeds inside those long pods that are making the noise.' I plucked one of the pods off the tree and shook it, then split the pod open with my nail and held out the seeds in the palm of my hand. 'If I plant one will it grow into a chatterbox tree?'

'I expect so. Let's go and ask Aunt Edith, shall we? Perhaps you can take them home with you and see if they grow in your garden.' I couldn't help smiling to myself. He thought I would be planting them in Ma and Pa Foster's back garden. I clutched the seeds tightly in my hand and tried to visualise the layout of the Trevethan's garden; they grew into big trees, so I'd have to be careful where I planted them.

We went in search of Aunt Edith, eventually finding her in the kitchen. She looked pale and her eyes were red; I knew it was from crying. Marcus didn't seem to notice. She managed a smile when she saw us. 'Hello you two. I'm afraid I've been a terrible hostess and I'm only just sorting out lunch.'

'Can I help, Aunt?' The pain in my stomach wasn't just from excitement at my discovery, it was also hunger.

'No thank you, dear. One of the boys will bring it. Shall we eat outside?' She didn't wait for an answer and walked briskly out of the kitchen and into the garden. There was a veranda along the back with a plant with purple flowers growing over the top so that it was nicely shaded underneath. We had only just sat down when a young Arab boy brought trays and trays of food, which he placed rather noisily on the table before Aunt Edith spoke sternly to him, after which he was a lot quieter. Aunt Edith told us to start but both Marcus and I hung back. I was waiting for Beattie, and I expect Marcus was too.

Aunt Edith noticed our hesitancy. 'Beatrice is in her room. I've sent a tray up. She's had rather a shock.'

Marcus looked flustered and ran his fingers through his hair, making it stick up. 'I feel so responsible, Aunt. I'm meant to be looking after her. Her father told me specifically to take care of her and then she almost gets kidnapped.'

'It's not that that's upset her, Marcus.'

Marcus looked puzzled for a moment then his face cleared. 'You've told her the reason you and her father aren't speaking?'

Aunt Edith nodded. 'I'm going to tell you as well; I think you need to know so you can help her come to terms with it. Effie, I believe you know some if not all of it? It was you listening by the door, wasn't it?'

My face flared and I almost choked on a piece of cheese. 'I didn't mean to listen. I was passing and I heard crying. I didn't hear very much, honestly.'

Aunt Edith didn't look convinced. 'Well, I think you should know the full story as well.' She took a sip of lemonade followed by a deep breath. 'Evelyn, my younger sister and Beatrice's mother, sought refuge here in 1925 to give birth to a child.' Marcus opened his mouth to say something but shut it when Aunt Edith raised a finger to silence him. 'The father was not Beatrice's father. She had fallen in love with an Egyptian and was going to run away with him and start a new life. She intended to take Beatrice with them. She died giving birth. Her lover, I think his name was Commandant Karim, never responded to my messages. When Gryffyn came I told him the truth. He was understandably distraught and hurt beyond words at his wife's deceit. He wouldn't have anything to do with the baby and told me it was my responsibility.' She hung her head for a moment then raised it again, her face grey and the skin stretched tight across her cheek bones. 'I should have cared for it, it was my sister's child, after all, but I was stricken with grief and guilt and so I had it shipped off to England to be adopted. Gryffyn took Beatrice home and has been a model father to her ever since. He thought that I should have told him what was happening and done everything in my power to stop them rather than aid and abet them. But she was my sister, Marcus, and I would have done anything for her. He's never spoken me from that day to this.'

Something she had said worried me, but I couldn't think what it was. I wanted to shout out, 'I'm that baby! I'm your niece. I'm Beattie's sister.' But I didn't because I wanted to tell Beattie first.

Marcus gave a big sigh. 'How upset was Beattie? She'd always held a torch for her mother. To find out she had feet of clay must have been devastating.'

'She didn't say very much, to be honest. She went very quiet; asked a few questions then went up to her room.'

Marcus went to stand up, but Aunt Edith flapped a bony hand at him. 'Leave her, Marcus. She will need you to help her through this but not now. Let her rest and sort things out in her head. I just hope she doesn't blame me as well, which is one of the reasons I never told her before; I couldn't bear to lose her. I took a risk today, but I decided she was old enough to make her own mind up about who was at fault.'

We finished eating in silence; any topic of conversation would somehow have been insensitive. It occurred to me that maybe Beattie wouldn't be all that thrilled to find out I was her sister. I was, after all, the cause of her beloved mother's death. If she was going to blame anyone, it might be me.

Chapter 25

Beattie

I needed to get away from her. I needed to think.

I went to my bedroom and lay on the bed but couldn't be still. I leapt off again and started pacing; ten paces from the bottom of the bed to the wall, about turn, ten paces back. Repeat. My bare feet on the wooden boards slapped the beat for my mantra of 'She's lying to me. She's lying to me.' Halfway across about the tenth crossing I heard a tap at the door then the sound of a tray being placed on the floor. That would be lunch, but I had no appetite and was about to start pacing again when I glimpsed myself in the dressing table mirror. I was shocked at who I saw. She looked crazed; her hair, never sleek at the best of times, stuck out in all directions as if trying to get away from her head; her eyes were wide and wild-looking, her nostrils flared and her mouth set in a thin line; her cheeks were bright red; her chest was heaving as if she'd run a race and her fists were clenched, ready to punch, who?

I watched myself as my breathing slowed down, the blood drained from my face and my shoulders slumped. Of course Aunt Edith wasn't lying. What possible reason did she have? But if she was telling the truth, what did that actually mean? I realised that my pacing had made my calves ache and sweat to trickle between my breasts, something that would have horrified my teachers at finishing school, who refused to acknowledge that girls did anything so vulgar as to sweat. I couldn't bear to sit at my dressing table and look at myself in the mirror, so I sat in the rocking chair, looking out over the back garden. There was a gentle breeze that made the curtains dance and the seeds in the pods of the nearby chatterbox tree to rattle. I could hear the murmur of voices, but they were too far away to distinguish who was speaking or what they were saying. I rubbed at a bit of dirt on the knee of my slacks, a reminder of the kidnap attempt just a few hours earlier; it seemed a lifetime ago and almost inconsequential compared to what I was now having to cope with.

I had worshipped Mama in life and in death. She had been, in my eyes, a perfect wife and mother; she was beautiful, kind, gentle, loving, caring and generous, in fact every maternal and feminine adjective that existed. Was I wrong? Was she none of these things? How could a perfect wife and mother allow herself to fall in love with another man, to have sex with him, to carry his child, to plan to desert her husband and steal his daughter away from him, to make a new life for herself with her lover? How could she ever have thought that she would succeed without causing a lot of pain to a lot of people?

I got up from the rocking chair and lay on my bed, propped up with two thick pillows and studied the framed photograph I always had by my bedside wherever I was. It was a studio photograph of Mama, Daddy and me, a year before her death. My mother was seated, looking elegant in a white dress that both covered and revealed her shapely figure. I was sitting on a low stool and looked exactly what I was: a lanky, awkward, embarrassed thirteen-year-old girl, not sure what to do with her arms and legs. My hair was still long and in two plaits that nearly touched my bottom; my rebellious cutting of my tresses was not to happen for another year. My father was standing behind his wife, his hands on her shoulders, looking very dapper in his dark suit and exuding an air of familial pride. We were all smiling at something stupid the photographer had said; we looked the epitome of a happy family. Aunt Edith had said that Mama met this other man when Daddy had been on his tour assessing the villages. I remember he'd suggested having our photograph taken on one of the rare occasions when he'd come home for a break. I peered closely at the print. Was my mother smiling at the photographer's joke or was she smiling at the thought of her husband being cuckolded? Were her eyes bright because she was happy to be with her family or because she was looking forward to her next tryst with her lover? Was she happy that my father was home or was she impatient for him to be gone again? Did she wish I'd never been born so that she didn't have to bother about me? There were no answers in her smiling face.

I'd always had this bedroom whenever I stayed here. Looking at myself with long hair in the photograph reminded me of when I had cut it all off. It wasn't here but back home in Cairo, but I had been sitting at my dressing table. I went and sat at the dressing table here and the younger me looked back from the mirror. She was angry; her cheeks were bright red and stained where hot, salty tears had run down her rounded cheeks. Her hair was loose and unruly. Her mouth was set in a petulant sulk and her shimmering green eyes, glared defiantly.

I couldn't remember why I'd been so cross, but I do remember taking the pair of kitchen scissors and calmly cutting off all the wavy bits, finishing up with a short, irregular, boyish bob. I'd known that she would be horrified; she'd always been so proud of my hair and we'd both enjoyed the night-time ritual of her brushing it one hundred times. She would stand behind me and we'd chat about mundane things as we both mentally counted as she swept her grandmother's silver-backed brush through my tangles. I picked that same brush up and ran it through my locks, still short but better shaped than when I had done it myself. I supposed that I'd cut it to spite Mama, but I couldn't for the life of me remember why.

As I tried to recall what life had been like back then, little vignettes flashed into my mind of scenes I had kept buried for over ten years: me shouting at my mother, crying that I wanted my Daddy and she slapping my face and saying he wasn't there, he was never there; my loneliness when she went to stay with Aunt Edith for what turned out to be forever; my anger whenever I read her letters telling me to be a good girl and how much she missed me and that we'd be together soon. In one letter she said she hoped I was still brushing my hair one hundred times and then I remembered that it was after reading that letter that I'd cut off my locks. Mama had never seen the result.

I stopped remembering the distant past and recalled Aunt Edith just telling me that my mother had had two miscarriages after I was born and that she and Daddy had both agreed not to try for any more babies. At twenty-four I still had little experience of pregnancy but even I knew that there were ways and means to avoid conceiving. So why had she allowed herself to get pregnant by this other man? Why did she risk another miscarriage? I groaned out loud and shook my head violently to dislodge all the questions that would now never get answered. It was pointless to try and understand what Mama had been thinking or feeling. I just had to accept that she hadn't been perfect and that I would never understand what had driven her into the arms of another man or why she didn't see that there would never have been a fairy tale ending, even if she had lived.

What I did understand was Daddy's antipathy towards Aunt Edith and his refusal to have anything to do with the baby. How humiliated and hurt he must have felt when he found out that his beloved wife had refused to have more children with him, but had happily had one with another man, and an Egyptian man at that. For a brief moment I thought it would have been quite nice to have a baby in the house, but it would have been a constant reminder of his wife's infidelity and deceit, and it wouldn't have had a mother or a father's love. No, adoption was the right thing to do.

I gave no thought to my mother's lover.

I'd been in my room all afternoon; dusk had fallen, and the air was cooler, and I had a sudden desire to walk outside to clear my head. I picked up a shawl and put it around my shoulders. I stepped over the luncheon tray that was still outside my door and realised that I was actually quite hungry. I'd be ready for the evening meal. I thought I'd better tell the others that I was going outside and, guided by the sound of voices, I stuck my head round the door to the lounge. Aunt Edith and Marcus were sitting in the settee and Effie was curled up on the floor, playing with a kitten. They all looked up at the sound of the door opening. Marcus started to get up, but I waved him down.

'I'm just going for a stroll. I need some fresh air. I won't be long.'

'Do you want me to come with you?' Normally I would have jumped at the chance of walking out with Marcus.

'Not this evening. I just want to be alone for a while longer.' I was pleased at the look of disappointment on his face. 'We'll speak later, I promise. I'll just walk around the garden, and I'll be back in plenty of time for dinner. I'm starving. Don't worry about me, I'm quite alright.'

I smiled at Aunt Edith to show her I wasn't angry with her anymore. Effie gave me a huge grin and I blew a kiss at her, although as she was sitting at Marcus's feet, he might have thought it was for him.

Chapter 26

Effie

We all sat looking at the space where Beattie had just stood as if none of us could quite believe she wasn't still there. I desperately wanted to go after her and tell her who I was, who she was, but she had been so definite about wanting to be alone that I was forced to stay sitting expending all my pent-up energy on tickling the stripy kitten that had apparently wandered into the house a few days ago and was now quite at home here. Aunt Edith eventually broke the silence. 'She seemed quite calm and collected. A lot better than I thought she'd be.'

Marcus was perched on the edge of the seat, his whole body tense. 'She shouldn't be out there alone. I know she didn't want company, but we mustn't forget what happened this morning. Should I go to her?'

The kitten was on its back, enjoying having its tummy tickled, when it unexpectedly rolled over and bit me on my hand with its sharp little teeth before running under the armchair opposite. I yelled at the sudden pain and sucked at the droplets of blood. As if my cry had woken him from a trance Marcus stood up and strode across the room and out of the door, leaving behind nothing but a draught.

I looked anxiously at Aunt Edith, but she just smiled. 'The sooner they both admit they love each other the better for everyone. Do you want to be useful and pour three sherries, dear?' Glad of something to do I got to my feet and went over to the drinks cabinet, sidestepping a little stripy paw that shot out from under the armchair and tried to claw me. I removed the stopper from the crystal decanter and had to use two hands to lift it up. Like the genie released from the lamp, the sweet smell of the sherry wafted upwards tickling my nostrils and turning my stomach. I held the decanter poised to pour for seconds before replacing it carefully back onto the silver filigree tray. I don't know how, but I knew they wouldn't be sipping aperitifs that evening. Something was wrong. I stood motionless, listening, but I could only hear my own breathing and the pounding of my heart. I couldn't see her, but I could sense Aunt Edith watching me. She must have felt something as well because she didn't ask why I was just standing there. We both kept perfectly still waiting to be told that our fears had become reality.

It was almost a relief when the door was thrown open and Marcus came lurching into the room. His hair was in total disarray, his face was weeping perspiration, and he was panting as if he had run the one-hundred-yard sprint in record time. He was clutching a shawl to his chest. Beattie's shawl.

'She's gone. Oh God, Edith, they've taken her. I've gone all round the garden but she's not there. I found her shawl,' he hugged it close to him. 'It was caught on a bush. I went as far as the road but there were too many cars and carts; she could've been in any of them. Oh God!' He took a deep breath and made an effort to control himself. 'We need to tell the police.' The blood visibly drained from his face. 'And her father.'

Aunt Edith had stood up as soon as Marcus had entered the room. She now quietly took control. 'I'll send Freddy to the police station to get someone here immediately. Go now, Marcus, and telephone Gryffyn.' She looked at the clock that was ticking indifferently on the table. 'Unfortunately he's missed the sleeper train but he could drive down and be here by mid-morning tomorrow if he drives like the wind.' She was walking towards the door as she spoke and before she opened it she turned to me, as if only just remembering I was there. 'You stay here, Effie. There's nothing you can do. Pray, if you believe in that sort of thing.'

Then I was alone. All the time I had been listening to them I had felt my heart slowly turn to stone and my blood freeze in my veins. My sister. Why had they taken my sister? They wouldn't hurt her, would they? All the other times they'd left the Eye of Horus as a sign. Had they left one this time and Marcus hadn't found it? I needed something to do. Despite Aunt Edith telling me to stay put, I went outside and looked for anything that would identify the kidnappers. It was dark outside but there was sufficient light spilling from the windows to light up the sandy path that ran around the house. I walked slowly along the front, one side and back, without seeing anything unexpected.

About halfway down the side nearest the road I noticed that the sand was churned up a lot more than anywhere else and there was a bush with sharp spikes nearby that could well have been what snagged Beattie's shawl. If this was where she'd been ambushed it was not far to the road and a getaway car. Beattie was a tall girl and I imagined she would have been quite heavy and unwieldy to carry if she had been struggling. What if they'd knocked her out first? I had a sudden image of her curled up in the boot of a car, blood pouring from a wound on the back of her head, her eyes wide open with fear. I began to gasp for breath as I imagined her struggling to breathe. Could she die from lack of air? She'd be no use to them dead, would she?

The possibilities, none of them good, suddenly hit me like a punch in the stomach and I bent over and threw up, the liquid being quickly absorbed into the sand, leaving bits that immediately attracted the ants. The evening air was cooling down but not enough to explain my shivering. The fact that there was no piece of paper with the Eye of Horus drawn on it unsettled me more than if there had been one. Had they not expected to kidnap Beattie this evening so didn't have one on them? Had they just forgotten? Was it not the Eye of Horus gang that had taken her? Something tickled my brain; a memory that refused to wake up. What had happened today that was important, but I couldn't remember? My unanswerable questions were interrupted by a worried voice calling from round the corner. 'Effie? Are you out here?' Then quieter, to herself, 'Please be out here.'

I felt a pang of guilt at having left the house without telling anyone. 'I'm here, Aunt Edith. I'm sorry, I should have told you. I wanted to see if they had left any signs.'

Aunt Edith was standing by the front door, silhouetted against the bright lights behind her. She gave a strained smile when she saw me. I was surprised to see tears spring to her eyes and even more surprised when she took me in her arms and hugged me. I could feel her ribs against mine and her bony spine when I returned the hug. 'I was worried that .... well, I was just worried. We don't want to lose you as well. Come inside so we can lock the doors and windows.' Was I terribly heartless for feeling pleased that she was anxious about me?

As soon as we were both inside, she shut the door and turned the key. 'Marcus is with the police now. There are two of them. He's giving them the details of everything that has happened in Cairo and here. They seem quite bright, but it'll be better when Gryffyn's men are here, they should be able to communicate much better than we can.' She took my hand and led me down the hallway and into the dining room. 'I know eating is the last thing on our mind, but we must keep our strength up. It's just a simple meal of chicken and rice. Eat what you can, dear; there's nothing else we can do at the moment.'

I still had the taste of sick in my mouth and my insides were tangled into such a tight ball that I didn't think I'd be able to swallow, but I did and before I knew it my plate was empty. Aunt Edith had only eaten a few forkfuls. She nodded encouragingly when I was offered second helpings, so I accepted. I was tucking in when Marcus came into the room, looking like an old man; his shoulders were down, his skin an unhealthy grey colour and there were lines on his face which I'm sure weren't there this morning. He slumped into his chair and brushed away the plate of food that was offered to him. Both Aunt Edith and I said, 'You've got to eat.'

'I can't. It would choke me.'

Aunt Edith pushed her plate away and I felt guilty at having finished not one but two platefuls. Would they think I didn't care about Beattie? If only they knew that I was a closer relative than either of them. 'Tell us what the police said.'

'Not much at all. They just both made notes and nodded or shook their head in unison as appropriate. They did say something interesting, though.' He paused to take a sip of wine that had been poured without me even noticing. 'The older one, who I assume is the most senior, said that they'd had no demonstrations against the British in Luxor recently and he knew of no gangs who left pieces of paper with the Eye of Horus drawn on them. He wondered whether they'd come down from Cairo. It seems a lot of effort when they could have snatched plenty of others in the city. Why come all this way just to kidnap one girl?'

I found myself shrugging along with Aunt Edith, who said, 'Let's hope they contact us soon and tell us their demands. Then at least we know where we stand.'

'What could they want, Aunt?' My voice sounded shrill and panicky; a fair reflection of how I felt.

'Money, I hope; that should be no problem. If they want the British out of Egypt, that would be more problematic, and I can't see how they would hope to achieve that by kidnapping just one daughter. Maybe ...' she looked at Marcus in horror. 'Maybe other sons and daughters are being kidnapped even as we speak.'

Marcus put his head in his hands and gave a big sigh. 'I feel so powerless, Edith. I feel I should be out there searching for her, but I don't know where to start. She could be anywhere:

locked in a room or on a boat; still in a car being taken goodness knows where.'

'Somewhere in the Valley of the Kings,' Aunt Edith added.

'Or the Valley of the Queens,' I chipped in.

The number of places where they could hide Beattie was too many to even think about. How on earth was anyone going to find her? The food I'd just eaten started to churn in my stomach and I knew I was going to be sick. I put my hand to my mouth and ran out of the room, knocking into one of the boys, who dropped a tray of fruit he was carrying, up the stairs and into the bathroom, making the toilet just in time. Two platefuls of chicken and rice is a lot of sick and by the time I had finished emptying it I was exhausted. I sat on the floor with my head on the toilet seat and cried and cried, a little for myself but mostly for Beattie.

My vision was blurred, and I didn't see Aunt Edith until she was by my side, gently pulling me onto my feet. She handed me a wet flannel to wash my face and a glass of water to wash out my mouth. 'It's a terrible thing that has happened, Effie, I can't pretend that it isn't. But we must all be brave for Beatrice's sake and be ready to do whatever we need to do to get her released. Marcus says the police are making enquiries to see if anyone saw anything and if anyone knows who might have taken her. Beatrice's father will be driving down and will be here sometime in the morning. He'll know what to do, I'm sure.'

'But what if they try and contact him in Cairo and he doesn't get the message and they kill her? Oh, Aunt Edith! What if they kill her? She's my ... she's my sister.'

'They won't kill her, Effie, they won't. I know you two have grown very close but at the moment all we can do is wait. I know it's hard.'

I was pleased she hadn't realised that I had meant Beattie and I were really sisters because at the mention of her father it occurred to me that he wouldn't be pleased to know I was the child who had caused his wife's death. He might want me out of the house; maybe he'd send me back to the orphanage. No, I wouldn't tell anyone, not until Beattie was safely home. I drew comfort from Aunt Edith's arm around me and I thought she might need a little too, so I put my arms around her and gave her a squeeze and said, 'Thank you.'

'Thank you for what?'

'Thank you for worrying that I might have been kidnapped as well. Thank you for being so kind and letting me stay here.' She gave a snort which might have been a laugh or a sob, or maybe both.

'Do you want to come down for a bit or go to your room?'

'I won't sleep but I think I'll go to my room.'

'I've made sure all the doors and windows are locked but even so, don't leave your room, Effie, until I come and get you in the morning. I'll send up a plate of sandwiches; you might get hungry during the night.' Aunt Edith came into the bedroom with me, checked that the windows were securely closed and looked around to make sure there was no one hiding behind the chair or under the bed. 'Try and get some sleep, dear, tomorrow's going to be a long day.'

I sat at the dressing table but couldn't bear to see the pale, haggard looking girl on the other side of the mirror. She couldn't even raise a smile but looked at me with tearful eyes. She was no comfort to me and I none to her. I lay on the top of the bed, fully dressed but switched off the light. In the darkness I relived everything that had happened that day. I remembered eating breakfast with just Marcus and Aunt Edith because Beattie was still in bed; I remembered admiring Aunt Edith's outfit and her telling me it was based on what Bedouin men wore; I remembered helping Aunt Edith carry her paint paraphernalia and a parasol to the Temple and setting up behind a pillar. Aunt Edith sat on a shooting-stick and sketched the colonnade, ignoring the people who wandered into and out of view. I looked at the detail etched into just one pillar and copied the hieroglyphics into my sketch pad whilst Marcus tried to translate them. I remembered Aunt Edith seeing Beattie and waving at her, before getting up and going towards her, quickly followed by Marcus. I tried to think what had happened next but the image in my head wouldn't shift until my heart started to beat faster and I felt a stab of fear as I remembered looking around me.

I remembered who I'd seen.

Chapter 27

Beattie

The realisation that I was inside a coffin dawned on me slowly.

I came to with a conviction that my head had been split open. There was an excruciating pounding at the back of my skull that pinned my head down so that I couldn't move without sending an agonising shard of pain into my brain. It took me a while to become aware that I was lying on bare wood rather than my cotton-sheeted mattress. But there was something loosely covering my face; I could feel it fall and rise as I breathed in and out. It smelt musty. I lifted my hand to see what it was and let out a yelp as it hit something hard barely a few inches above my prone body. I raised my hand again slowly and my fingertips felt rough wood. I followed it carefully to my left until it almost immediately came to a corner and the same thing to my right. I was in a wooden box; a coffin!

Was I dead? Was the covering over my face my shroud?

But I couldn't be dead; the dead don't feel pain; the dead don't feel sick; the dead don't feel claustrophobic; the dead don't feel panic-stricken. I instinctively tried to sit up but hit my head, shifting the pain from the back to the front of my skull. I pushed my arms against the sides but they didn't shift. Then I screamed and screamed but the cries seemed to hover inside the box and then tumble uselessly down and the cloth kept getting into my mouth, making me splutter. This was no good; I needed to calm down; I needed to remember; I needed to think.

I lay with my arms straight down by my sides, unclenched my fists and slowed down my breathing, inhaling for five seconds, exhaling for five seconds. In, out, in, out. It was only then that I was conscious of another sound other than my own heart and breath; it was a deep, regular mechanical noise that sounded familiar and yet I couldn't identify it. I wanted to know what was covering my face. I inched my fingers over my body; I felt only my clothes until I came to my neck and face, which was covered in rough hessian. I explored the cloth and realised that my head was covered in a sack. It wasn't physically suffocating me, but it was mentally. I gingerly lifted it over my head that had now subsided to a more bearable throb, and I took in deep, unrestrained breaths with relief. It was a small victory.

A hessian sack pulled over my head. I remembered now. I'd spent the afternoon coming to terms with my mother's flaws and frailty and early evening I'd popped into the sitting room to tell the others I was alright and just wanted to take a walk outside on my own. I'd strolled almost all around the house, enjoying the cooling evening air and savouring the almost intoxicating scent of the jasmine. I was deciding whether to go back inside or to make another circuit when two shadows peeled away from the bushes and encircled me. Before I could even open my mouth to scream a hand had been clamped over my mouth and nose, preventing me from both shouting and breathing. I'd started to thrash my arms and legs, but someone else's arms were quickly wrapped around my upper body pinning my limbs to my sides. And then the sack was put over my head, I'd felt a prick and after that nothing until now.

I'd been kidnapped, that was perfectly evident. Based on the past few days it was either the Blue Shirts or the Eye of Horus gang; my gut feeling was that it was the latter. I couldn't think what they hoped to gain; I doubted the British Government would agree to withdraw from Egypt just because my life was threatened. My father might, in fact I'm sure he would, but these people wouldn't be satisfied until every British administrator and military man was on his own home soil. Maybe I wasn't the only person being kidnapped. Maybe there were tens or even hundreds of daughters, sons and wives being abducted at this very moment. I doubted it though; that would have taken an enormous amount of co-ordination. From what I had seen so far, the protesters were driven by passion not planning and resorted to short-term violence rather than a long-term strategy.

I screamed, more out of frustration than a belief that anyone would hear me. I stopped when my throat became sore and my mouth dry. I cursed for giving myself a dreadful thirst that I had no way of quenching. Where was I or rather, where was the box? I could feel gaps in the wooden planks that encased me, but no light filtered through, so we must be inside somewhere dark. I had the impression, based on the constant vibration that I could feel, that we were moving. So, we were inside something that was moving and somewhere dark that was long enough to hold a box the length and width of a coffin. It couldn't be a car, that wasn't big enough. Whatever it was made a constant noise and even as I thought the words 'clickety clack' I realised I must be on a train, probably in the goods wagon. They were taking me back to Cairo.

I imagined myself as a bird, an egret would be appropriate, flying high in the sky, looking down on the train trundling along the rails that ran parallel to the sparkling Nile. Depending on the time of day the passengers would be eating, reading, chatting, playing cards, sleeping or just watching the scenery as it flashed past. I focussed on the goods wagon at the back of the train and peered through a murky window into the interior, where there were trunks and suitcases, bags of mail, bicycles, prams and a coffin. With my magical bird's eye, I looked through the lid to see myself, lying flat on my back, my arms by my side, my eyes open wide. Even as I watched, the flesh fell off my body and within seconds all that was left of me was a skeleton that soon crumbled to dust. Damn my imagination! I was gripped with panic and a sense of being suffocated and spent a few useless minutes screaming and lashing out, to be left even thirstier, my head hurting again, and splinters in my elbows and knees.

I needed to stop wasting my energy; I would need it to escape. I controlled my breathing and tried to think positive thoughts. At least I was alive. If they'd wanted to kill me, they'd have done it in Luxor; they wouldn't have bothered to take me all the way to Cairo just to kill me there. So they must want me alive. What would they do when we arrived at the station? Did they expect me to still be drugged? Would that be an opportunity to get someone's attention? I almost laughed as I imagined people's reaction when screaming was heard coming from a coffin. Perhaps the kidnappers would just drop the box and run away? Then when someone removed the lid, I'd calmly ask to be helped out and taken to the British Embassy, where I'd fall into Daddy's arms, and everything would be alright. This was, of course, assuming they didn't check my state before removing me from the carriage. I don't suppose it would take them long to give me another disabling injection.

It was no good. I couldn't make plans. I just needed to wait and see what they were going to do and then try and get away. I had no idea how long I'd been on the train or how long we were from Cairo. I had a moment's panic when I questioned whether there was enough air for me to breathe but then remembered the gaps in the box and I knew the goods wagon itself would not be airtight. I didn't want to miss any opportunity to escape and I was determined to stay awake but the rhythm of the wheels on the rails soon lulled me to sleep and just as I was dropping off I wondered whether everyone at the 'Sand Castle' had missed me and whether they realised I'd been kidnapped and if so, would they spend all their efforts searching fruitlessly in Luxor.

I awoke instantly. I may have been asleep for minutes or hours; I had no way of knowing. I listened. It was silent. I could

197

hear no clickety clack and I could feel no vibration. We had stopped. We couldn't have stopped at a station because all I could hear was the creaking of the carriage; even at night stations are noisy places. Then I heard the door being opened and the sound as one, no two, people clambered into the wagon, grunting with the effort. I decided not to scream but to pretend to be still in a drugged sleep, so I closed my eyes and lay motionless. Damn! I remembered too late that I had removed the sack and there was no way I could replace it now. Maybe they wouldn't notice. As each nail was torn out of the lid, I felt more and more nervous, and I had to force myself to keep perfectly still when the lid was thrown off. I was worried that the light might make me squint involuntarily but there was little difference in the brightness; I assumed either the sunlight didn't reach where the box had been placed or it was still dark outside. I was desperate to open my eyes and see who my kidnappers were, but I was also desperate not to be given another injection, so I remained supposedly unconscious. I could tell by their hushed voices that there were two Arab men. How I wished I had made more of an effort and learned the wretched language.

Suddenly the world tilted as I was roughly lifted out of the box and thrown over someone's shoulder like a sack of coal. I had to bite my tongue to stop myself crying out. I risked opening my eyes very slightly; all I could see was the floor of the carriage and then, once he'd climbed down, sand illuminated by the light of the torch held by the second man. We walked away from the train, away from any help there might have been. I knew there would be nothing gained and maybe a lot to lose if I shouted out now. The terrain was rough, but the man strode purposefully onwards with me banging my chin against his back. I was no lightweight despite the fact I had missed the evening meal, but the man didn't seem to find me a heavy load and I got the impression he was tall and well built. I heard the train start to move and I wondered how they'd managed to make it stop in what was evidently the middle of nowhere; I hoped they hadn't hurt anyone in the process.

I could see from the bouncing torchlight that we were walking along a rough track, and I wondered where we were going – perhaps to a village? Maybe there would be a chance there to get someone's attention. A short time later, however, we stopped and out of the corner of my eye all I could see was the tyres of a car. I hoped I would be bundled onto the back seat where I could at least sit upright but when the boot was opened, I knew that I was going to be a horizontal rather than a vertical passenger. The man dropped me unceremoniously into the cavity and I couldn't stop myself from yelping as my left elbow, hip and knee hit the hard floor. It was obvious that I was awake, so I decided to try and make a run for it and got as far as getting onto my elbow before I felt a sharp prick in my thigh. The torch was focussed on me, so the two men were hidden in darkness, apart from two hands that came towards me and shoved me back down before closing the boot of the car. It was pitch black and smelt of petrol and I suddenly became terrified and started screaming but my screams quickly became whimpers as the drug they'd injected into me spread warmly through my body, numbing my pain and shutting down my brain.

Chapter 28

Effie

I banged on Marcus's bedroom door shouting, 'I know who I saw, I know who I saw!' There was no answer. I wasn't sure what time it was, perhaps he hadn't come up to bed yet and was still in the sitting room. I raced downstairs and threw open the door, startling Aunt Edith and Marcus, who were sitting side by side on the settee. They both looked at me with mouths open as I shouted again, 'I know who I saw!'

Aunt Edith got up and came over to me, a look a concern on her face. 'What on earth is the matter, child? Why are you shouting? Who did you see? Was he in your room?'

'No, no, you don't understand. When we were painting, I saw someone but then I forgot about him but now I remembered.'

'You're making no sense, Effie. Come and sit down and start from the beginning.'

I allowed myself to be led to the armchair opposite the settee and I waited impatiently for Aunt Edith to settle back down next to Marcus, who, I couldn't help but notice, looked awful. When they were both looking at me expectantly, I started my explanation again. 'This morning, when we were at the temple painting behind that pillar and when you'd both gone because you'd seen Beattie, I sensed someone watching me. You know how the hairs on the back of your neck stand up? Well, that's what mine did and when I turned around there was the man looking straight at me. I knew I recognised him, but I couldn't think from where and then you came for me Aunt Edith and I forgot about him because then I was worried about Beattie.'

'But what man, Effie?' Marcus looked puzzled and I wanted to smooth the lines from his face that had grown since Beattie had been taken.

'You remember the really tall policeman that dragged me from the crypt at El Lisht and wouldn't let me pick up my sketch book? Well, it was him.'

'How can you be sure? There must be lots of tall Arab men. Why would a policeman from Cairo be in Luxor?'

'It was definitely him, Marcus. He smiled, no, leered at me and his golden tooth glinted. It was him, I'm absolutely sure of it.'

It was Aunt Edith's turn to look puzzled. 'Even if it was him, it doesn't mean anything, surely? He might well have been on holiday. Lots of people from Cairo come to Luxor for their holidays. Was he in his police uniform?'

I closed my eyes to try and remember what he was wearing. 'No. He was in the usual Arab gear.'

'There you are then; he must have been on holiday. It's just a coincidence that you happen to know him. He can't have anything to do with Beatrice's disappearance.'

I shook my head in frustration. 'It's not a coincidence. There's something not right about it. Marcus, did you see the man who tried to grab Beattie this morning?' He shook his head. 'I bet you anything on earth that he was one of the other policemen that were with Captain Karim at El Lisht.'

Aunt Edith's head jolted up. 'Who did you say?'

'Captain Karim. He's a policeman in Cairo,' Marcus explained. 'We've got to know him because of all the things that have been happening. He and some men were at El Lisht when we went the other day. He asked us to leave because they were on some sort of stake-out; looking for drug runners he said. Why, do you know him?

'How old is he?'

Marcus shrugged his shoulders. 'I don't know, about my age perhaps?'

Aunt Edith shook her head. 'I don't know him but the man who was Evelyn's lover was called Karim. Commandant

Karim. It's quite a common name. It must just be a coincidence.'

I shouted 'No! I can't explain it, but I've never trusted Captain Karim and I don't believe for one minute that he and those men were looking for drugs. They were up to something fishy and didn't want us around.'

Marcus suddenly seemed to deflate, and his shoulders sagged, and his head drooped. 'Whatever they were doing they've not got anything to do with Beattie being taken. That policemen being here, if it was him, must just be a coincidence, Effie. The police don't go round kidnapping people. Look, we can't do anything tonight. We need to see what Mr Trevethan and his men will do. He may already have been sent a message. Oh God! I feel so useless. I should be out there looking for her but .... I know, I know.' He pushed away Aunt Edith's arm. 'I'd just be wasting my time. I have no idea where to look. Oh, my poor, poor Beattie. If they hurt one hair on her head, I swear to God I'll kill every single one of them.' His voice had got louder and angrier so that by the end he was shouting. One of Aunt Edith's boys popped his head round the door but withdrew when he saw we weren't under attack.

Aunt Edith put a restraining hand back on Marcus's arm. 'We must all try and be calm, Marcus, dear. Getting angry won't help Beatrice. There's nothing we can do and hard though it is we must just let the police do whatever they are doing and see what Gryffyn wants us to do when he arrives tomorrow. Effie, you need to go back to bed. I'm coming up as well. Marcus, you need to rest; you'll need all your energy.'

Marcus slumped back on the settee and seemed to age by ten years in front of my eyes. 'I'll stay here for a bit longer. I won't sleep. I want to be awake if they send a message or the police find anything. You two go and I'll see you tomorrow.' He got up, went over to the drinks table and poured himself an orangey coloured liquid into a glass tumbler. He downed it in one, coughed then poured another. I could see that Aunt Edith was dying to tell him off, but she just pursed her lips, took my hand and walked me out of the room.

She stopped outside my bedroom door, gave me a hug and kissed me on my forehead. 'This is all so horrid, but you are being very brave. We'll get Beatrice back, just you see.'

'Aunt Edith, I just know that that policeman I saw has something to do with it.' I just wish I could explain the feeling of certainty in my stomach.

'We'll tell the police and Gryffyn tomorrow. They may be able to do some checking. Try and get some sleep, dear.' She kissed me again and then left to go to her bedroom. I went into my own room, but I felt restless and started to pace up and down. I cast my mind back to when we had been dragged out of the crypt at El Lisht and frog-marched to where Captain Karim was waiting with Beattie. It had been the tall man who had had hold of me, and I still had the bruises on my upper arms where he had gripped me too hard. It was him who had refused to let me pick up my sketch book. I had to admit, though, that it was a giant step from being rough and rude to being a kidnapper. I skipped to this morning and wondered why the tall man had been standing just looking at me. Someone else had tried to take Beattie so what was the tall man doing? Was he meant to grab me as well? Or was he just there in case there was trouble? Was the other man a policeman as well? Aunt Edith was right, why would the police want to kidnap Beattie?

I sat at the dressing table and looked glumly at the girl in the mirror, who looked as miserable as I felt. 'I wish ... I wish ...' But there was just too much I wished for and the girl in the mirror was no fairy godmother who would wave a wand and make my wishes come true. We looked dejectedly at each other and then the girl in the mirror got up and went to bed, so I did too.

I don't know how I did but I slept and was woken by the sound of voices from downstairs. It was still dark but when I peeped out of the window, I could see a pale strip in the sky so it must have been nearly dawn. I realised the men sent by Uncle Gryffyn must have arrived. I was determined to tell them about my theory that policemen were somehow involved so I went downstairs, still in my pyjamas, meeting Aunt Edith at the top of the stairs; she had been disturbed by the noise as well. We followed the sounds to the dining room, where the two men and Marcus were seated around the dining table.

I recognised Lateef and Omar with pleasure and remembered the gun Omar had had in the car the other day. I wondered whether both men were carrying guns, but it was hard to tell what they might be wearing under their loose robes. Marcus stopped talking when he saw us standing in the doorway. 'I thought it best to explain everything to them in Arabic to make sure they understand what's been happening.'

Both men had stood up when we entered, and they both now bowed to Aunt Edith and Omar gave me a sad smile. 'I'm sorry to see you again so soon, Miss Effie.'

Marcus took charge. 'Sit down everyone and I'll finish telling these two what has been happening.' Aunt Edith didn't seem to mind being told to sit down in her own house. By the dark smudges under his eye, it was obvious that Marcus hadn't slept but he had changed his clothes and shaved so he looked smart and ready for action. He finished explaining the events and then turned to Aunt Edith and asked her if there was anything she wanted to add. She shook her head but then looked at me. 'Did you tell them about the man Effie saw? The one she's convinced is a policeman working for Captain Karim?' When Marcus nodded, she continued, 'It should be easy enough to check who he is and why he is in Luxor. We'll get Gryffyn to call Captain Karim and he should be able to tell us his name.'

I blurted out, 'I don't trust Captain Karim. Could Uncle Gryffyn check on him as well?' No one answered me. Lateef and Omar had said nothing, just listened but now Omar spoke to Marcus. When he'd finished, Marcus told us that Omar would stay here to help protect us and Lateef would make himself known to the local police and offer his services to help make enquiries and question people. Lateef said something, to which the others all nodded and then he turned and left the room. We heard him walk across the hallway, his sandals making a slapping noise on the marble, the opening and closing of the front door and then silence as the sand swallowed his footsteps.

Aunt Edith suddenly sat bolt upright and started to get up. 'I'll organise breakfast. Are you hungry, Omar?'

Omar nodded. 'Yes, thank you, Miss Goodley. Breakfast would be most welcome but first I would like to walk through and around the house. Mr Dunwoody, would you show me?' The two men went out and Aunt Edith went to organise breakfast, leaving me alone to sit, wait and worry.

Chapter 29

Beattie

I was being dragged along the ground by a runaway camel, my left foot stuck in the stirrup. He was going as fast as a racehorse and my body was being shredded to pieces by the sharp stones embedded in the sand. Suddenly I felt nothing under me; we were flying! No, not flying, falling. The camel and I did an ungainly waltz together as we tumbled over a precipice until we hit the bottom. Funnily enough I could still feel pain in the whole of my body although I could see that I was shattered into pieces. My one open eye slowly focussed on the sand my head rested on and I watched in fascination as a line of giant ants marched right in front of me. I expected to hear the stamping of their feet, like soldiers' hobnail boots on a parade ground, but they drilled past silently. I slowly scanned to left and right, as far as my eye would swivel, expecting to see bits of the camel and myself scattered around but all I could see was ants, sand and boulders. My mouth felt dry and gritty; I must have swallowed some of the sand when I landed on it.

A man's distant laugh broke the silence. A laugh?

I somehow knew that my camel ride and plunge over the precipice had been a dream but that the laugh was real. I wasn't broken into little bits after all, but I was indeed lying on the sandy ground and I hurt all over, thought I didn't know why. There was more laughter and then two men's voices, talking in Arabic. The veil of forgetfulness suddenly lifted, and I remembered that I'd been kidnapped. I'd been in a coffin on a train and then thrown into the back of a car. They'd injected me for at least a second time with a drug that put me instantly asleep and now they'd dumped me here, wherever here was. I tried to lift my head up, but the pain was too great and I merely whimpered. I heard a metallic sound then someone knelt down behind me and shook me hard, grinding the stones into the parts of my body that touched the ground. He said something I didn't understand. I tried to speak but my mouth was so dry the words went no further than the back of my throat.

I wanted to move but whatever drug they'd given me had sapped all my strength and I could do nothing other than wriggle my fingers and toes. The man must have seen the movement because he grunted then called to another man, who came and helped him lift me unceremoniously into a sitting position then they dragged me so that I was propped against a rough wall. Something hard dug into my spine, but I didn't even have the energy to shift myself away. One man got up and walked away but the other stayed squatting by my side staring at me. I managed to turn my head to look at him and I was surprised to find that he looked familiar, but my brain was still too foggy to do anything other than just make a note of the fact. He gently stroked my cheek with one calloused finger, then slid it down to my throat and made a slicing gesture from ear to ear. He grinned, got up and started to walk away.

I remembered that in the box in the train I had convinced myself that they weren't going to kill me but now I was certain they would. I didn't want to die by having my throat cut; I didn't want to die at all. Abject terror ran through my veins and my body reacted to the poison by shivering uncontrollably and my bladder by emptying itself. I was too petrified to feel embarrassed but watching the liquid soak into the sand reminded me how thirsty I was. I tried to say 'water' to the man who was in the process of padlocking an iron grille, but it came out as a croak. He heard me though and looked at me. He noticed the dampness of my crotch and his lip turned up in disgust. I croaked again and tried to lick my lips with a tongue as dry as a desiccated leaf. He called out and waited by the gate, opening it so the other man could put a canteen of water and a plate of food on the floor, then proceeded to lock it. They both walked out of sight, and I sat cursing them for putting the water out of reach. I wasn't tied up, but I might as well have been and all I could do was to wait impatiently for my body to become functional again. I tortured myself by imagining drinking a glass of ice-cold lemonade, sitting in our garden with Daddy and Marcus. The glass was opaque with condensation and the ice cubes knocked against my teeth as the cool liquid slid down my throat.

Daddy and Marcus must be beside themselves with worry. Had Daddy gone down to Luxor, his antipathy to Aunt Edith superseded by his fear for my safety? The men he was going to send to guard us would have arrived by now. They must all be looking for me. Had they found out I'd been transported from Luxor to ... To where? I had no idea where I was. Even if I could get them a message – and how could I possibly do that – I couldn't tell them where I was, other than somewhere in what looked like a cave. I looked around more carefully and saw that there were carvings and splashes of colour on the walls. My heart sank; I was in an ancient Egyptian ruin somewhere between Luxor and Cairo, but which one?

I tried flexing my legs and found I could now bend my knees and use my elbows to lift myself slightly. I still couldn't manage to get up and walk but I could shuffle along the sand on my bottom. I made slow progress but my desire for a drink of water was so strong that I bore the pain of the stones tearing into the back of my legs and my bottom. About halfway across what seemed to be a huge expanse but was probably only about four yards, my hand rested on something smooth and bendy. I picked it up; it was a sketch pad. As soon as I opened it, I knew whose it was and where I was.

It was the pad that Effie had dropped when the police had dragged her and Marcus out of the burial chamber at El Lisht. Were the two men members of a gang Captain Karim and his team had been looking for? He had said they were looking for drug runners but perhaps they had also turned to kidnapping.

My heart lifted on a wave of hope. If the police were watching the site, they would surely have seen me being carried from the car to the burial chamber. They might at this very minute be planning a rescue. They would want to make sure my release was assured and that there was no risk of me being hurt; they would probably wait until night-time. The expectation of being saved gave me a surge of energy and I managed to haul myself upright and stagger to where the drink and food had been left. I clung onto the grille to steady myself and gave it a shake for good measure but to no avail; I could see that it was hung on sturdy hinges and that the padlock meant business; both of them looked shiny new. I squatted down and put the canteen water to my lips. It was warm and earthy, but it tasted like nectar, and I drank it all without taking a breath. There was only a stale bread roll and a chunk of warm, greasy cheese on the plate, but I was starving, and I gulped it down, barely bothering to chew it. The cell, for that is what it was now, was partly lit by the sunlight that filtered down a tunnel that I guessed led from an opening to the outside world.

There was no sign of the two kidnappers, and I had no desire to see them. I moved away from the grille and found a flat piece of wall to lean against and tried not to think of my predicament but rather of being reunited with everyone. I closed my eyes and felt each of their hugs: Daddy's would be strong and reassuring and he wouldn't want to let me go; Marcus's would be more tentative but oh, so comforting but it would finish too soon; Aunt Edith's would be bony and sharp, and Effie would fling herself at me and squeeze me until I had no breath in my lungs.

The sound of the gate being opened startled me out of my reverie. It was the two men; their grins gone, replaced by a grimness that turned me to stone – until I saw the knife. Then I leapt to my feet and raced towards the open gate, screaming at the top of my voice; no words just primal shrieks born of terror and panic. I didn't get halfway there before one of the men grabbed me and pinned my arms behind my back. I made the most of my legs still being free and lashed out behind me, feeling a moment of satisfaction when my captor gave a grunt when my heel kicked his knee. His pain was nothing, though, to my own when the other man punched me on my cheek.

The man behind me released my arms and stepped away, so there was nothing to stop me falling backwards and crumpling to the floor, where I lay gasping in shock and agony, spitting out blood and a tooth. The sight of that small bit of white bone edged in red filled me with a fury that gave me the energy to lurch to my feet and hurl myself at the man in front of me, kicking, scratching, spitting, biting anything that I came into contact with, accompanied by a high-pitched screech that echoed around the walls of the burial chamber. It was a useless attempt, of course, and it only took the other man to grab my flailing arms and hold the point of the knife to my throat for me to be drained of resistance.

I don't know what it was that triggered the memory, but in that instant, when the man in front of me was glaring at me whilst he wiped the blood from his cheek where I had scratched him, I remembered where I had seen him before. It was here, in El Lisht. He wasn't one of the gang the police had been looking for; he *was* one of the police. He had been the one who had led Marcus from this very burial chamber. He must have seen the recognition in my face because he gave me a mock salute and his mouth curled up with contempt.

'*Asseyez!*' He nodded his head towards a block of stone, one of many that littered the ground.

I had a vivid image of my severed head on its top and I began to whimper. 'Please, please don't kill me. I have money, lots of it.' In my fear I forgot all the French I ever knew. 'Please, why are you doing this?' I felt the warmth as the water I had so recently enjoyed vacated my body and I began to sob hysterically. My legs became boneless and gave way beneath me so that I had to be dragged to my last resting place. I dropped to the ground and began to plead for my life, but the sight of the knife made the words die in my mouth and I only had time to wonder whether I should pray before I succumbed to blessed oblivion.

Chapter 30

Effie

Aunt Edith had said that everything would be alright when Uncle Gryffyn arrived but the sight of his grey, lined face and the look of despair in his eyes just made me feel more frightened. He had driven through the night, stopping only to fill the car with petrol and he looked exhausted. He brushed away Aunt Edith's offer of food and a bed. 'I'll eat and sleep when my daughter's back home.' Even though he had so many other things on his mind he still came over and held me to him. I could hear his heart pounding in his chest, and I don't know why but the sound of it made me cry. 'Now, now, Effie, tears won't help, we need to be strong. You can help by coming with the others and telling me absolutely everything, however small and irrelevant you think it is, that you can remember from the moment you left the house in Cairo to this very minute.' I opened my mouth to tell him about seeing the policeman at the Temple of Luxor but just then Omar came in from his security check of the grounds and everyone moved to the dining room so that we could all sit around the table. Marcus started telling him the sequence of events and I bided my time until he came to tell how Beattie was almost snatched in front of our eyes.

Marcus, with my help, described the journey from Cairo to Luxor; it didn't take long as there wasn't much to say. Neither of us had noticed anything unusual about any of the other passengers and we certainly didn't recognise any of them. He then described the trip to the temple at Luxor yesterday morning. 'We three,' he swept his arm in a circle to include me, Aunt Edith and himself, 'were sitting behind a pillar painting or sketching, waiting for Beattie who we'd let sleep late. You tell the next bit, Edith.'

'I stood up to stretch my legs and walked around to the front of the pillar. Although there were quite a few people, blasted tourists mainly, milling around I thought I saw Beatrice in the distance, and I waved and called out to her. I'd only just started walking towards her when I saw her collapse to the ground. I've thought and thought, Gryffyn, but I honestly don't remember seeing anyone suspicious nearby. I know you blame me ...'

'I don't blame you, Edith, not this time. Then what happened?'

I was about to tell him about who I saw when Marcus took over telling the story. 'I heard Edith call Beattie's name, so I told Effie to stay where she was and went to join them. When I ...'

I was so desperate to interrupt Marcus and tell my part of the story that I shouted, 'That's when I saw him!'

They all looked a bit stunned, but Uncle Gryffyn soon recovered. 'Saw who, Effie?'

'Effie thinks she saw ...'

'Let her tell it in her own way, Marcus. She obviously thinks it's important.'

'It is important, Uncle. I didn't remember who he was at first but when I was left alone, I sensed someone behind me and when I turned there was this man just standing and staring at me. I remembered later that it was the big policeman who had pulled me out of the burial chamber at El Lisht. You know, the one that wouldn't let me pick up my sketch book, so you gave me one that used to belong to Beattie. Do you remember, you promised you'd tell Captain Karim to get it for me? Anyway, one of Aunt Edith's blasted tourists walked in front of me and when I looked again the tall man was gone.'

'He didn't say anything or threaten you in any way?'

I almost wished he had. 'No, but he grinned at me in a horrible way. Uncle, I know it doesn't seem like much, but I have a bad feeling about him. Why was he in Luxor? Why was he in the place where someone tried to snatch Beattie? I just don't believe he was there on holiday. I don't believe it was a coincidence.'

Uncle Gryffyn glanced at Marcus, who shrugged. 'Perhaps you could make a few calls, sir? We don't know his name, but the policeman Effie is referring to works for a Captain Karim in Cairo.'

At the sound of the name Uncle Gryffyn jerked and looked at Aunt Edith, who said, 'It's a common name, a very common name.' There was a moment's silence then she continued. 'We all came straight back here once we realised what had nearly happened at the temple. Marcus called you straight away and Beattie had a rest on the settee. I sat with her.' She paused and bit her lip. 'She wanted to know about her mother. So, I told her.' She sat upright, her back straight and a defiant look on her face. 'She needed to know, Gryffyn. These two know the story as well.' I think she expected Beattie's father to scream and shout but all he did was give a small sigh and a little nod.

'How did she react?'

'She was angry, sad, bewildered, disappointed – all the emotions you would expect her to go through. She spent the afternoon in her room thinking it all through, she said, then early evening she came down and popped her head through the door and ...' Aunt Edith's voice deepened and trembled; she waved a hand at Marcus for him to continue.

'She said she was just going for a walk and wanted to be alone. A few minutes later I went to look for her but all I found was her shawl caught on a bush. I ran to the road but there was so much traffic and pedestrians I couldn't see her. I'll never forgive myself for letting her go by herself.' Aunt Edith patted his hand but didn't try and ease his guilt. If he had insisted on going with her, she wouldn't have been kidnapped and she'd be here now, and everything would be normal, so he was right to feel guilty.

'I suspect that if you had been with her, you would have been kidnapped as well, or put out of action, maybe permanently. These people were obviously determined to get her, one way or another.' Uncle Gryffyn rubbed his eyes and turned to Aunt Edith. 'Perhaps some coffee?' She got up and went into the kitchen.

'There wasn't a note, Uncle. Wouldn't they have left a note if it was the Eye of Horus gang? Or at least one of their signs? Shouldn't they have sent you a message by now?'

He nodded his head. 'I agree, Effie; I would have thought they'd leave a message of some sort. I wish I knew what they wanted. I've told the office to ring the police here immediately if they receive any communication from the kidnappers. I'm going to ring the bank later to warn them I may need to take all my money out.'

'You can have all mine,' Marcus said.

'And mine.' Aunt Edith said as she came back into the room.

'What if they don't want money?' I felt I had to ask, and my voice rose in panic. 'What if they want you to leave Egypt? All of you. Would you go?' No one said anything. Uncle Gryffyn sipped his coffee then got up, saying he needed to go to the telephone office as he had some calls to make. Marcus got up and suggested to Omar that they make a tour of the building again. I don't know what they hoped to find but I suppose it made them feel useful. Aunt Edith and I were left staring at our knees. 'What would they do, Aunt? Would they go?' It came out as a whisper.

'I really don't know, Effie but they'll find her; they've just got to.'

We sat for what seemed like hours but probably wasn't, until there was the sound of voices from the hallway and then the men came back into the dining room, including Lateef, who had come back from spending time with the police. He spoke in Arabic and Marcus quietly translated for me.

'I went with the policemen to the Temple and interviewed the native guides and hawkers. A couple of them remember a disturbance around Miss Trevethan and one of them said he did happen to see a man in traditional Arab garb approach her. What most of them remember is Miss Goodley because of her dress. She is quite well known to these people it appears.'

Uncle Gryffyn raised his eyebrows and Aunt Edith explained, 'Yesterday, I wore a Bedouin robe. Very cool and practical; I don't know why more women don't wear them. Gryffyn, ask him if anyone remembers seeing a tall man with a gold tooth standing over by where we were painting?' My heart sank when Lateef shook his head. People were going to think I'd made it all up, but I hadn't; it was him, I knew it was.

Just as quickly my heart rose again when Uncle Gryffyn said, 'I can give an update on that.' He spoke in English so I could understand, and this time Marcus translated into Arabaic for Lateef's benefit. 'I've just rung Captain Karim from the Cairo Police. I described the man Effie saw and said it was the same man who had escorted her out of the chamber at El Lisht.'

'He didn't escort me, he dragged me; I still have the bruises!' I held out my arms ringed with dark smudges for them all to see. Aunt Edith tutted and Uncle Gryffyn frowned.

'Captain Karim admitted he was one of his men and said that he was on a few days' leave. He said he didn't know whether he'd gone away but he might well have come to Luxor as he is very interested in the ancient history of his country.' I snorted. The man who had dragged me away had shown no interest in the carvings and painting on the walls of the burial chamber and no understanding of my distress at leaving my sketch pad behind. 'He said he'd try and find out where he'd gone. He was most upset when he heard about Beattie and has offered his help; he said he would ask his informers if they had heard anything, especially from members of the Blue Shirts or the Eye of Horus gangs.'

The offer of help from Captain Karim gave me no comfort nor did the rest of Lateef's report. 'We've visited most of the hotels to see what male guests they have had who left yesterday. If they stayed in a hotel at all I suspect they would have chosen a cheap one, where they just need to show their cash and nothing else. There are a couple of possibilities which the police are chasing down now. They are also going to round up any gangs they are aware of and bring them in for questioning. They won't allow me to sit in on the interviews, of course, but they may let Sir Trevethan do so.'

Lateef took a sip of lemonade that had magically appeared by his side. 'The police say there is little they can do until you hear from the kidnappers.'

Uncle Gryffyn shook his head. 'Thank you, Lateef. Go and get yourself something to eat.' Marcus stood up and paced up and down. 'I can't just sit here, sir. I should be tearing the town apart stone by stone looking for her. Edith, can I borrow your car to drive around? I know I'm unlikely to find her, but I need to be doing something.'

'Oh, Marcus, she could be anywhere. If they've gagged her, she could be in any room in any house. But, of course, you can borrow the car. Omar or Lateef need to drive you, though; you mustn't go alone.'

Uncle Gryffyn indicated for Omar to go with Marcus whilst Lateef went to get something to eat. Aunt Edith and Uncle Gryffyn talked for a bit longer, politely and without bitterness. Beattie's kidnapping seemed to have blown the ten-year-old feud away. I was glad. Uncle Gryffyn put his head in his hands. 'She's done nothing to deserve this, Edith. What if they hurt her? What if they hurt my little girl?'

'Don't despair, Gryffyn. They'll send a message, I'm sure of it; otherwise, what was the point of taking her? Go upstairs and get some sleep. You'll be no good to her or anyone if you're too tired to think straight. Go on, the Ra room is ready for you.' Uncle Gryffyn slowly got to his feet and shuffled like an old man across the room and out of the door. 'Poor man,' Aunt Edith whispered. 'I'd better get one of the boys to make sure he goes to the right room.' She rang a little bell, which was quickly answered by a young boy who looked no older than me. She spoke to him, and I heard him run across the hallway and up the stairs in his bare feet. Aunt Edith came and sat next to me. 'You're holding up very well, Effie. Beatrice would be very proud of you. This waiting is the worst. I feel like Marcus; my heart wants to be out there looking for her, but my head knows there's no point. She really could be anywhere; she might not even be in Luxor.'

'Maybe that's why I can't sense her. I should be able to, shouldn't I?' I paused, still unsure whether to tell her but then decided I would. 'As I'm her sister.'

I don't know how I expected her to react but certainly not just with a polite, 'That's a lovely thing to say, dear,' followed by an invitation to help her organise lunch. She'd obviously not understood that I'd meant being Beattie's real sister; I'd try again when we were next alone together.

The rest of the day passed. I couldn't tell you what I did with my time; all I know is that it passed very slowly. As expected, Marcus didn't find Beattie and Lateef reported that he'd heard from the police that they hadn't learnt anything from any of the criminals they'd interviewed but that they'd gather up some more during the night and they were hopeful they might have a result the next day. None of us seemed to share their optimism and we all went to our rooms early so that we couldn't see each other's miserable faces.

I was the first up. I heard the kitten mewing, so I opened the front door to let it in and saw the box on the step. It was about six inches in all directions and neatly wrapped in brown paper and addressed in bold, black letters to Sir G Trevethan, c/o Miss E Goodley, Le Chateau de Sable, Louxor. I picked it up and shook it, but nothing moved inside. Was it from the kidnappers? Oh, I hoped so! I ran back upstairs and knocked loudly on the door with the glorious sun God Ra painted in gold on it. 'Uncle Gryffyn, there's a parcel here addressed to you. It might be from the kidnappers.' He must already have been up because the door opened almost immediately. I eagerly gave him the box. 'Is it from them? Is it?'

He didn't do what I did and shake it; instead, he carefully unwrapped the paper, revealing a white, lidded box. By this time Marcus and Aunt Edith had joined us and we all leaned forward as he lifted the lid.

I'm not sure which of us screamed, perhaps we all did.

Chapter 31

Beattie

This time I knew exactly where I was when I woke up and it certainly wasn't heaven; it was my own hell on earth. They had laid me on my back on what felt like a thin mattress. Although I knew they couldn't have carried out their threat, I raised a hand to check that my head was still attached to my body. Something was wrong though; I just didn't know what. I raised my head as far as the throbbing allowed and quickly scanned my body. I couldn't see anything wrong.

'Be thankful Malik only tore off a lock of your hair. If he'd had his way he'd have sliced off your nose or one of your breasts.'

I put my hand to my hair and quickly found a place where the hair had been ripped out, leaving a damp, sore bald patch. He was sitting in shadow perched on a stone block. I wasn't surprised he was there; after all, I had expected to see him this evening.

'Captain Karim. You haven't come to rescue me, have you.' A statement, not a question.

'How very perceptive of you.'

I felt calmer than I should have done, bearing in mind I was in the presence of a man who had had me kidnapped and doubtless had plans for me that I didn't want to think about.

'You aren't part of the Blue Shirts or Eye of Horus gang, are you?' I don't know how I knew this, but I did.

'Of course not. It's not allowed for policemen to be members of such groups. I merely took advantage of them; they suited my purpose.'

'You're not allowed to be a member of such groups but you're allowed to kidnap a British citizen?' He didn't bother to answer, merely raised an eyebrow, a gesture I might once have found attractive. 'So what exactly is your purpose?' He watched as I sat up and shuffled to the back of the mattress until I could lean against the wall. I somehow felt more in control being in a semi-upright position, although I was aware it was a false supposition. I repeated my question. 'What is your purpose? Money?'

He laughed as if he really thought I had told a funny joke. 'There are far richer men whose daughter I could kidnap if all I wanted was money.'

I knew the answer but I asked anyway. 'Is it to get the British to leave Egypt?'

'You must think very highly of yourself if you think the British would leave here just because your life is being threatened. You cannot be naive enough to believe that they care one jot about you. They would forfeit every son and daughter before they did what they should have done fifteen years ago. So no, your being here is nothing to do with your country's incursion into my country.'

My calmness was wearing off. 'Then what? What is the point of all this? Why are you doing this?'

'You are far too inquisitive. A woman should not ask questions.' I didn't rise to the bait; I didn't feel up to an argument on a woman's place in society and the home. He looked at me coldly; it surprised me that dark brown eyes could look so devoid of emotion. 'Unfortunately for you, you are the tool by which I will hurt someone else.' He must have seen my puzzled expression. 'Who will be most hurt by your loss?'

My loss? Did he mean to kill me then? My fear expelled itself from my body as a stream of bile. He watched as I used my handkerchief to wipe my mouth and blot the tears from my eyes. Then he got up and brought me a canteen of water. I hesitated. 'Take it. It's not poisoned.' I still hesitated. Why would I believe him? But my thirst and the foul taste in my mouth won the contest and I gulped down a few mouthfuls. 'So, have you worked out who I want to hurt?' I didn't want to say it out loud; somehow that would make it real, would mean that he would be hurt. 'Say it!' He' sat back down and now he leaned forward, his bestial power and cruelty straining to be released.

'My father.' It came out as a whisper, but he heard and gave a grim smile.

'Indeed, the man himself, Sir Gryffyn Trevethan.' He almost spat his name out as if he couldn't bear to hold the words in his mouth for a second longer. 'He'll have received his little present of the lock of your hair by now. Did you know he'd driven through the night down to Luxor? Well, of course you don't. But it meant that we had to send the parcel on the overnight train and this morning it was left on the front doorstep of your Aunt's house. The young girl you call Effie found it and took it inside. I wonder how he reacted when he opened it? What do you think?' He didn't wait for me to answer. 'I expect he's worried and frightened, but his suffering isn't gnawing away at his insides, tearing through his heart, sucking the life from his soul. Not yet, anyway. What shall we send him next? How about a finger? Or a toe? Or perhaps an ear? I tell you what, I'll let you choose.'

I instinctively curled my fingers and toes. 'Why? Why are you doing this? What have I ever done to you to deserve this?'

'Oh, you've done nothing. You just have the misfortune to have the father that you have. '

'But what's he done? He's never met you, has he?'

'I met him for the first time when I came to your house to investigate the Case of the Scorpion.' He said it as if it were a Sherlock Holmes mystery.

I was suddenly filled with anger at his prevaricating. 'Why can't you just tell me why you want my father to suffer? I assume you have a reason? And is it worth what will happen to you when you're caught? Because you will be, you know, and then let's see who suffers.'

Captain Karim seemed amused at my outburst of bravado. 'You think your lover will come to your rescue like a knight on a white charger? No one has any idea where you are, and they never will. Just accept that you're going to be here for quite a while. Make the most of your time. I see you have found the young girl's sketch pad. I'll bring you a pencil and you can write your memoir.'

I wanted to ask how long I'd be here. When would enough be enough, but I was too scared of what the answer would be. I watched as he stood, brushed the creases from his trousers and went over to the grille. He took a key from the pocket at the front of his shirt, unlocked the padlock, went through, relocked the padlock, put the key back into his pocket and walked away, all without saying a word, without looking at me.

I needed to relieve myself. I was strong enough now to get to my feet and shuffle over to a dark corner and squat behind a large stone that had been painted thousands of years ago with a scene of a man walking behind an ox ploughing a field of corn, which was being gathered into sheaves by a gang of women. There were some hieroglyphics carved down the side but, like Arabic, I had never bothered to learn it. There was so much I needed still to learn, to experience. How dare Captain Karim take it all away? What right had he to wipe me out of history before I had even made a mark? My anger and frustration gave me the strength to rush over to the gate and shake it as hard as I could, half hoping that the screws would rattle free from the hinges and the grille fall away at my feet. I would fight anyone who opposed me and run all the way back to Cairo. I screamed and bellowed my frustration and rage as the hinges stayed intact, until my voice became nothing more than a hoarse whisper. My kidnappers must have been close by, but they didn't come; the venting of my wrath was witnessed just by a lizard, which seemed fascinated by my performance for a few minutes but then scuttled off to continue his lizardy life in more peaceful surroundings.

I slumped to the ground and gave into a bout of weeping that did nothing except saturate my handkerchief. Everything that Captain Karim had said was spinning inside my head. If he had only first met my father a few days ago why, oh why, did he want him to suffer? God help me I even wondered why he couldn't just have kidnapped Daddy rather than me? But Captain Karim didn't seem to want to hurt Daddy directly; he wanted him to suffer mentally rather than physically. But why?

There was only one person who could answer that question, but I had no desire to see or speak to him. I remembered he'd said that my father had gone down to Luxor as I thought he would. Everyone was three hundred miles away and had no idea I was no longer in Luxor; even if they guessed I'd been moved they would have no idea to where. No, if I was going to get out of here it would have to be under my own steam. As I was obviously not going to be able to exit via the grille, I decided to explore the chamber. The whole site was a ruin; perhaps there was a gap in the walls or ceiling that I could crawl through. And these stone blocks on the floor, they had to have come from somewhere, perhaps from this very chamber? I felt quite excited at the thought and stood up and started walking slowly along the wall, feeling with my fingers for a hole between the stones or for a waft of air that would indicate a gap to the outside. The only opening I found, though, was when I had circumnavigated the whole place and returned to where I had started from. I was about to inspect the ceiling when I heard footfalls coming down the tunnel. I didn't want them to know I was looking for an escape route, so I sat back down on the mattress and tried to look nonchalant.

'Did your screaming and shouting make you feel better, Miss Trevethan? There is no one to hear apart from me, Malik and Zain and we only had to walk a little bit away before they were nothing but whispers on the breeze. Now, have you decided what I'm going to cut off?'

It was as if someone had given me an electric shock. He was joking, wasn't he? Surely, he was joking! But he sat on the stone block and laid a knife on his knee. The other two men stood behind him, but I didn't see if they were grinning; I only had eyes for the blade which seemed to glow. 'No? I'll decide then and it can be a surprise. Is that alright with you?'

I raised my eyes from the slightly curved blade to his face that was half in shadow. 'Are you serious? Of course, it's not alright! Captain Karim, please don't do this. I don't understand why you want to hurt my father so badly, but surely kidnapping me is enough? He'll be worried stiff already.'

'I thought I'd made myself clear earlier. I want him to wonder every minute of every day where you are, whether you're hurting, whether you're alive. I want every minute of every day to be a torment.' He looked over his shoulder and snapped something to the two men, who walked purposefully towards me. I instinctively struggled to my feet, which just made it easier for them to grab hold of me and drag me across to Captain Karim, who sat like some ancient Egyptian statue, his hands on his knees, his face as stone and his eyes expressionless.

Both men pulled me down to the ground so that I was lying with my cheek on a stone block then Malik or Zain pulled my right hand from under me and laid it next to my head. My hand was palm down and my fingers forced apart. I tried to struggle but the captain's men had me pinned down and I couldn't move any part of me.

'The knife is extremely sharp; this won't hurt Miss Trevethan.'

Before I could scream or beg or pray there was a flash and then mercifully nothing.

Chapter 32

Effie

'It's only hair. It's only hair. It's only hair.' I said it over and over. Uncle Gryffyn had dropped the box and we now all stood staring at the ginger curl that lay discarded on the floor. The hair was still attached to bloody bits of skin. No one moved until I bent to pick it up.

'Don't touch it, Effie. There may be some evidence. Just leave it until the police have inspected it. Oh God, my poor Beattie. She must be so frightened. Marcus, Lateef is in the servants' dormitory round the back. Go and wake him and tell him to go and fetch the police.' Marcus didn't seem to have heard. He stood mesmerised, his eyes fixed on the lock of hair, his mouth moving but making no sound; perhaps he was praying or casting an ancient Egyptian curse on the kidnappers. Uncle Gryffyn put his hand on the younger man's shoulder and raised his voice. 'Marcus, go and fetch Lateef.' Marcus gave a jolt then nodded and left without saying a word.

Aunt Edith was sobbing quietly, wiping her eyes with the sleeve of her dressing gown. She looked like a feeble old woman, especially as she was still in her dressing gown. 'Come on, Aunt Edith, we'll go and make sure they're making breakfast. Come on, come with me.' I took her arm and gently pulled her away. As I passed Uncle Gryffyn he whispered. 'Thank you.'

The kitchen was a hive of activity, and it was obvious we weren't needed; I led her into the sitting room and made her sit down on the settee. She was still weeping, and I found myself doing the same. Aunt Edith put her bony arms around me and rocked me and we both cried until we had no tears left.

'I don't think I believed she'd been taken until I saw her hair. I mean I knew she had but it didn't seem real, somehow. But someone really has taken her and has cut off one of her beautiful curls. They've bothered to put it into a box, wrap it in brown paper, address it to Gryffyn and post it here.' Aunt Edith took in a shuddering breath and held me closer. 'I know I have to be strong, Effie, but it's hard, so very hard. If only we knew what they wanted. I didn't see a message in the box, did you?'

I shook my head, but I doubt anyone would have noticed anything once they'd seen the hair. I tried to think which curl they'd cut off, but I realised with a rising panic that I couldn't remember what Beattie looked like, no matter how her hair curled. I gave a whimper and pulled away from Aunt Edith. 'I can't remember her face! When I think of her she's just got a white oval. I'm her sister; I should be able to remember every freckle.'

I started bawling again whilst Aunt Edith tried to calm me down. 'You're just in shock, dear. We all are.'

'It's so unfair, Aunt Edith, she doesn't even know.'

'Doesn't know what, dear?'

'That she's my sister.'

Aunt Edith pushed me away from her and held me by my shoulders. She looked puzzled. 'You've said you were her sister a few times now.' She took my chin in her hand and looked me in the eye. 'What exactly do you mean?'

'I'm her sister. I'm the baby you sent off to England. I worked it out. They reckon I was a few months old when I was left on the steps of the convent. That was in July, so I was born in May. May. That's when Beattie's mother gave birth isn't it?' She nodded and I'm sure I saw her expression change as she realised the truth in what I was saying. 'And look at me. I used to think that it was my mother who was Egyptian, but it could just have well have been my father. Beattie's mother was my mother and Commandant Karim was my father. It's true. It has to be. We're sisters and ...' my chest heaved, and I felt my heart tear in two, 'and she doesn't know, and we need to find her so I can tell her. She'll be pleased, won't she? Uncle Gryffyn won't

227

hate me, will he? He won't send me away? Oh, Aunt Edith.' My bones turned to blancmange, and I collapsed against her, wailing like a hungry baby.

'Oh, Effie, my poor, sweet, girl. I'm so sorry.'

The door opened and the room filled with men: Uncle Gryffyn, Marcus, Lateef and Omar. Uncle Gryffyn sat down and rubbed his eyes. He'd got dressed, which is more than Aunt Edith or I had done. 'The police are trying to find how the ...' he pursed his lips, 'how the parcel was delivered. It wasn't by anyone from the Post Office; it must have been hand delivered. They've taken the ... they've taken it all away for someone to take a close look at. There may be clues but I don't hold out much hope.'

'Was there a note in the box, Gryffyn? Anything at all to tell us what they want?'

Uncle Gryffyn gave a small nod. 'There was a piece of paper with the Eye of Horus drawn on it. No worded message but I know what they're saying. "We've got her and there's nothing you can do about it, you hopeless, pathetic paper cut-out of a father, who doesn't deserve to have such a beautiful daughter."'

There was a full minute's silence. What could anyone say?

Marcus eventually cleared his throat. 'When we find who delivered the parcel, we can find out who gave it to him. Then when we find him, we find who has Beattie and we save her. We'll find her, sir, and we'll make the bastards pay.' No one blinked an eye at his swearing.

Uncle Gryffyn stood up so quickly he knocked his chair over, but Lateef caught it before it could crash to the floor. 'I'm going to the telephone office. I want to call Captain Karim again. We need to speak to the tall policeman that Effie saw. Even if he's not involved, he may have seen something at the temple without realising the significance. If he's still in Luxor we'll track him down; if he's back in Cairo, Captain Karim can speak to him.'

Marcus stood up as well, without overturning his chair. 'I'll come with you.'

Uncle Gryffyn nodded and told Omar to go with them, leaving Lateef to watch over us.

Aunt Edith looked down at her dressing gown as if only just realising that she was still in her night clothes. 'Goodness, Effie, we should get dressed and then we'll have breakfast. I need to speak to you about ... about what you've just said.' She suddenly smiled. 'Would you like me to make you an Arab outfit? You said the other day you thought mine was splendid. It will give us something to do.'

So that's what we spent the whole day doing.

At evening time, I stood in front of the dressing table and twirled around, showing the girl in the mirror my knee-length, stripy tunic over white, baggy pantaloons. The girl in the mirror laughed at my obvious delight. 'They're cool and comfortable and there's no buttons or bows to do up, just the cord to hold up the trousers.' I stopped spinning and sat down. The girl in the mirror looked at me; her expression serious. She lifted an eyebrow. I shook my head. 'We didn't talk about Beattie being my sister at all. I thought she would, but she just chatted about her childhood in England and why she came to Egypt and stuff like that. She talked a lot about her sister, Evelyn.' I paused as I realised. 'I suppose she was trying to tell me about my mother.' I grinned at the girl in the mirror. 'She was very naughty as a child. I wish ...' The girl in the mirror wiped a tear. 'I wish I'd known her.'

I felt so tired all of a sudden that I crawled into bed, still in my Arab clothes, curled up hugging a pillow to my tummy and fell fast asleep.

If I dreamt, I don't remember what about and I was woken by the sound of cries and raised voices. I jumped out of bed and rushed downstairs. Uncle Gryffyn, dressed in the clothes he had worn the day before, was holding a box in his hand and Omar was holding onto a young Arab boy, who must only have been about eight years old and was struggling and crying. Omar was shouting at the boy and Uncle Gryffyn was shouting at Omar to make sure he didn't let the boy get away and at Lateef to go and get the police. Marcus and Aunt Edith, still in their night clothes, joined me in the hallway and we watched as Lateef left the house, Omar dragged the still crying boy away to lock him in a room and Uncle Gryffyn stood still clutching the box.

'I've been here since midnight and the other two were outside, waiting to see if another box was delivered. That boy came and put the box on the front step at six o'clock. Omar grabbed him and well, here we are.' We all looked at the box, which he was holding in hands that were shaking slightly. 'I'll go and open this by myself, if you don't mind. There's no point in all of us being there.'

'But sir ...'

'No, Marcus. Let me do this. I'll let you know what's inside, but I want to open it alone.' He turned away and went into a room that Aunt Edith used as a study. We three didn't move, didn't speak; just waited. Uncle Gryffyn had closed the door behind him, so we didn't hear the rustle of paper as he tore it off, or the sound of the lid being removed but we did hear his groan. As one we moved towards the door. Marcus opened it and we all walked slowly in. Uncle Gryffyn was sitting, his face as white as a clean sheet of paper. We all crept forward until we could see what was in the box. Marcus cursed; Aunt Edith gasped and moaned; I threw up.

It was part of an ear. Beattie's ear. I knew it was hers because one of the earrings she had been wearing the day she was taken was still clipped on. They were gold with a small tear drop hanging down that contained an opal stone. Pretty. The earring and part of ear were lying on a piece of white paper; I could just see the corner of Horus's eye stained red with Beattie's blood. I swayed as the world shifted and I fell.

When I came to, I was in my bed. The curtains were drawn but the shaft of light that managed to squeeze through the gap was so bright it hurt my eyes and I guessed it was still daytime.

'How are you feeling, dear?' Aunt Edith was sitting on a chair next to my bed. She had a book on her lap, but it was too dim to read.

It took me a few seconds to remember the contents of the box that had been hand delivered to Uncle Gryffyn and the bile rose in my throat again. I clamped my mouth shut tight and struggled to sit up. Aunt Edith helped me upright whilst at the same time holding out a bowl, which soon received the last dregs of what was still in my stomach. She handed me a damp cloth with one hand and a glass of water with the other. I wiped my face and took a sip of water. 'You're a good nurse. I don't need to be in bed, do I? I only fainted.'

'You hit your head on the corner of a table and cut it quite badly. The doctor has bandaged it and recommended that you stay in bed today.' I felt my head and found there was a bandage wrapped all around the top of it. I prodded where I had hit it; it hurt, and I realised that I had a headache.

'But ...' But what? I had nothing to do apart from fret and wait; I could do that anywhere. 'Have they spoken to that young boy?'

Aunt Edith sat upright and nodded her head. 'Yes, there has actually been some progress. The police came and questioned the boy. He was terrified poor thing, but he said he'd been told to deliver the box by his uncle. He was able to give his uncle's name and address, so the police are on their way there now. It's a real step forward.' I relaxed back into my pillow and closed my eyes in relief, just for a second.

When I woke again Aunt Edith was packing all my clothes into a trunk. I watched for a few minutes, too terrified of the answer to ask the question. She must have sensed I was awake because she came over and sat on the edge of the bed.

'Do you think you can get up? Everyone else has gone back to Cairo in the cars but we are going on the overnight train. We need to leave the house in a couple of hours. Do you think you can manage that?'

I shook my head, not in denial but to clear my head that seemed to be filled with sawdust. 'What's happened? Why are we going back to Cairo? Have they found Beattie?'

'No, not yet. But the police found the little boy's uncle, the one who told him to leave the parcel on my doorstep and when they started to question him sang like a canary, as they say in the gangster films.'

I'd never seen a gangster film, but I had no reason not to believe her. 'What did he say? Did he say where Beattie is?'

'He said that he'd had a visit from a man a few days ago who told him that every morning and evening he must go to the railway station and find the head guard on the train from Cairo and see if he had a package addressed to Sir Trevethan. If there was then he must immediately put the package on the doorstep of this house without being seen. So that's what he's been doing. He put the box on the doorstep yesterday morning but this morning he gave it to his nephew.'

'But who is this man? Why was he chosen to collect and deliver the parcels? And who was the man who gave him the instructions in the first place?'

Aunt Edith broke out in a wide smile and patted my arm. 'The man here in Luxor is in the local police and the man who visited him said he was a policeman from Cairo. The uncle described him as being very tall with a gold tooth and he frightened him half to death.'

I gasped and felt a stab of satisfaction that I'd been right. 'Have they found him? Have they arrested him?'

'No. Gryffyn contacted one of the top policemen in Cairo and asked him to make some enquiries.'

'He didn't speak to Captain Karim, did he? I don't trust him, Aunt. I'm sure he's involved.'

'I'm not sure who Gryffyn spoke to, someone higher up the ladder, I think. Anyway, this man rang back after an hour and said that both Captain Karim and a couple of his men, including the tall man with the golden tooth, have been on leave for a few days and weren't expected back until next week. The local police here found the head guard who was on the overnight train last night and questioned him. He said he was given the box at Cairo station by a man in a police uniform. He wasn't our man with the gold tooth, though. So we know the boxes with Beatrice's hair and .... and earring were sent from Cairo, so it is most likely that she is up there rather than down here.' She got up and carried on emptying my clothes from the drawers into the trunk. 'The men couldn't wait, you know how impatient they are, so they decided it would be quicker for them to drive up to Cairo. They were going to leave us here, but I told them absolutely not! There wasn't room for us in the car so I agreed we would travel up tonight. They'll find her, Effie, I know they will.'

I felt both optimistic and pessimistic at the same time. Optimistic because we now knew some of the people involved and which part of the country Beattie was being held, but pessimistic because Cairo is a big place surrounded by the boundless desert. There were an infinite number of places to hide someone.

Chapter 33

Beattie

My ear lobe was itching; a sign it was healing, I supposed. It was yesterday it had happened and when I'd come to from my faint, I had found myself alone. There had been a gauze pad and a bottle of iodine laid out neatly on one of the stone blocks as well as a canteen of water and a bag full of bread rolls, apples, chunks of cheese and slices of cold meat. Of Captain Karim and his two cronies there had been neither sight nor sound. I had shouted but I sensed that there was no one near enough to hear.

Since then, I had dressed my wound, drunk most of the water, eaten most of the food, slept, shouted and explored every inch of my cell and discovered no gaps I could widen and escape through. No one had visited me since yesterday and although I was relieved on the one hand, on the other I was terrified that they'd abandoned me here to slowly starve to death. I'd used some of the iodine to cleanse my fingertips which were cut to shreds from scrabbling at the walls. Afterwards I'd wondered whether I should have left them; it might be preferable to die from a blood infection than from starvation. Thinking of starving made me feel hungry again. Was there any point in saving it for later? The bread was already stale, the apples soft, the cheese and meat beginning to go rancid. I added food poisoning to my list of fatal possibilities.

I'd used the darkest corner of the chamber as my toilet, but the blackness did nothing to smother the smell. I didn't want to die in a hole under the ground that smelled of my own excrement. I burst out laughing as I imagined what I must look like with my soiled clothes; unbrushed hair with a clump pulled out; one earlobe missing and tattered nails. Would Marcus still love me? If he had loved me at all, that is. My laughter turned to sobs and I allowed myself to wallow in self-pity and regret at all the things I would now never experience. I wanted a husband who was funny, kind, charming, good looking and an archaeologist. I wanted sex with this man. I wanted children with this man. To die without having had sex! My despair turned momentarily to anger but it didn't last long; I didn't have the energy.

I lay down to doze, what else was there to do, and that's when I saw it. I had spent most of my time studying the walls and ceiling but hadn't bothered with the floor; I knew there wouldn't be a means of escape down there. There was a bit of newspaper sticking out from under a stone next to the wall by the head of the mattress. It wasn't hidden; I just hadn't looked there. I lifted the stone and saw that it was a page that had been ripped from *The Egyptian Gazette*. Had Captain Karim left it for me? Not for the advertisements, surely, or the piece on a jumble sale at St. Andrew's, or a train crash that had killed fifty men, women and children who had been packed like sardines into a third-class carriage. I looked at the date printed at the top of the page – October 16th, 1925. The paper was more than ten years old. I turned the page over and glanced down each column looking for something that would explain why he'd left the paper for me.

It was the name Karim that caught my eye. It was an obituary.

Ex-Commandant Karim

Two days ago on October 14th Darius Karim, aged sixteen, went in search of his father to tell him to come in for his evening meal. He went to the garage where his father often went to tinker with his car. He found his father hanging from a roof beam. The father, Yusuf Karim, had been a Commandant in the Egyptian Police, based in Cairo. He had left the police five months earlier under a cloud and hadn't worked since. His distraught wife said the police had treated him very badly and he had been very depressed. Members of the police force spoke very highly of Karim but Sir Griffin Trevethan, Karim's ultimate boss, refused an interview. Karim leaves a wife and three children, Darius being the eldest.

I read it three times. Commandant Karim had been Mama's lover; the father of the child whose birth had killed her. The obituary didn't say in so many words, but it was my father who got him thrown out of the police force; a commandant was high up, but Daddy was even higher. Darius was sixteen. I'd been fifteen in October 1925. Captain Karim was my sort of age. Captain Karim was Darius. Captain Karim had found his father, who had committed suicide because of my father. That was why Captain Karim hated my father so much, why he wanted him to suffer. As he had said, he had nothing against me personally; he was just using me as a means to get to my father. I wondered why it had taken so long for Karim to seek vengeance. I had no way of knowing, of course, but perhaps he had only just found out the details of those involved in his father's disgrace. Life cannot have been easy for the Karim family. After the father's dismissal from the police force, they would have had to leave their house and I doubted that Karim senior would have received a pension. After the suicide the family would most likely have been shunned as social outcasts. It occurred to me, though, that if Karim's father had succeeded in running away with my mother, he would have left his wife and three children unsupported and still condemned to be social outcasts.

For a very short second I felt sorry for Karim, but only for a second.

So now I knew why I was here. Knowing didn't make me feel any better and the fact that I hadn't seen him or anyone for a whole day made me think that no one was going to come again. Unless someone came to chop off a bit more of me.

I cursed Karim for not bringing me a pencil as he'd promised; I could have written everything I knew in Effie's sketch book. Poor Effie. What would happen to her? I supposed she would be packed off back to England to the redoubtable Mr and Mrs Foster and their brood of foster children. She'd certainly had some adventures she could tell her children. I chuckled as I remembered how we'd found her in the packing crate, nearer dead than alive. Then her horrible time at the orphanage and her brave escape. She was a good girl and I know my father had been fond of her. Maybe he could adopt her, and she would become his daughter to replace me, the dead one. He had got over the death of his wife eventually, would he get over mine? Or would he suffer a lifetime of torment as Karim so desired? If my body was never found, he would always be wondering where I was and whether I might possibly still be alive. There would be no closure; an open wound that never healed. With any luck Marcus would come to El Lisht again one day and he'd find me, or my bones at least. Then they'd be able to bury me and move on with their lives.

I carefully ripped round the obituary and placed it inside the sketch book. If Marcus found it, he would understand the implications. Dear Marcus, how I loved him. How long would it take for him to forget me? Maybe he'd end up married to Grace. I hoped not; she'd make a terrible wife and he deserved so much better.

I ate all the contents of the paper bag but kept a few mouthfuls of water left in the canteen. My last supper.

Chapter 34

Effie

We both pretended to sleep but neither of us did. The sound of the train wheels on the rails should have lulled me but my brain was too busy thinking about where Beattie might be, who had taken her and why. I was absolutely convinced that Captain Karim was involved.

'Are you awake?' I whispered in case she wasn't.

'Yes. Can't you sleep either?'

'No. Can I put the light on?' She answered by pulling the cord herself and filling the cabin with a soft, yellow glow. 'I was just thinking. What if the fact that Captain Karim has the same surname as Mrs Trevethan's lover isn't a coincidence? What if they're related?'

'Go on. I'm listening.'

I swung my legs over the side of the bed, clambered down the ladder and sat on the edge of Aunt Edith's bed.

'What happened to Commandant Karim? Do you know?'

Aunt Edith sat up, her head nearly touching the bottom of my bed above her. She turned to plump her pillows then sat back and sighed. 'Yes, I know. When Gryffyn found out who his wife's lover was he was beside himself with rage. He had Evelyn's body transported back to Cairo and after the funeral he apparently went to Karim's office and nearly beat him to a pulp. So I heard anyway. Karim was kicked out of the police force in disgrace though I don't think anyone knew the real reason; the rumour was that he was heavily involved in the drug trade. I'm not sure what happened to him after that.'

We had eaten a big evening meal, but I was peckish and I took a biscuit from the plateful that had been left on the tiny table that pulled down from the wall of the cabin. Everything in the cabin was small and either folded up or slid into a hole of

238

just the right size. I handed the plate to Aunt Edith who took one distractedly. I thought as I nibbled.

'So, if Captain Karim is related to Commandant Karim, maybe his son or his nephew, he would have a good reason, in his eyes anyway, to hate Sir Trevethan, wouldn't he? For forcing him out of the police in disgrace.'

Aunt Edith gazed into the distance. 'It's very possible, Effie. Something must have triggered these recent events. Maybe he found some letters, or he was told the truth by his dying mother.'

'Has his mother just died then?'

'I don't know, dear, I'm just thinking of different scenarios that might have led him to kidnap Beatrice.'

'But why hurt Beattie? Why not Uncle Gryffyn?'

'Oh, because Gryffyn is hurting much more now than if he was himself kidnapped. He is suffering mental torture, which is far worse than physical.'

'They'll find her, won't they?'

'Of course they will. They might already have arrested the tall policeman with the golden tooth, who will have told them where Beatrice is being held, and they'll have gone there and found her safe and well and she's now in her own bed.'

'Yes, but ...'

'No buts, Effie.'

I sat on the edge of Aunt Edith's bed for as long as it took me to finish the plate of biscuits. I imagined arriving at the Trevethan's house in Cairo, running up the stairs, flinging open the bedroom door and throwing myself onto Beattie, who would be sitting up in bed, wearing her pretty, lacy nightdress and a wide, happy grin, which grew even wider when I told her that we were sisters. I hugged myself with joyful anticipation then clambered back into my bed, careful not to wake Aunt Edith, who had fallen asleep still sitting up.

The next thing I knew we were approaching Cairo. Aunt Edith was already dressed and washed, and she had laid out my clothes ready. I too was dressed and washed by the time we came to a squealing standstill. I'd forgotten how noisy and busy the railway station was and I was glad to be with Aunt Edith, who had no qualms about swinging her parasol in wide arcs in front of her so that the crowd divided just like the picture I'd seen in Sunday School of Moses parting the Red Sea. When we got to the entrance, I was relieved to see Omar waiting for us. He directed us and the man with our luggage to the car and we were soon on our way.

'Has there been any progress, Omar?'

He shook his head. 'We didn't get back until late last night, Miss Goodley. But Sir Trevethan has gone to the police with Mr Dunwoody and Lateef just now.' I saw him look at me in the mirror and he winked. 'He's going to tell them to bring Captain Karim and the policeman with the gold tooth in for questioning.'

'Wasn't Uncle Gryffyn told they were on leave? What if they can't find them? What if ...'

'No more what ifs, Effie dear. Let's just give the police time to do their job and what we can do is to make sure everything is ready for Beattie to come home.' She took my hand and squeezed it hard; I think for her own comfort rather than mine.

There was no one in the house when we arrived, other than the Arab servants. Aunt Edith spoke quietly to one of them, who nodded and went towards the kitchen. 'I've asked him to make sure there is plenty of cold food left in the dining room for people to eat as and when they feel the need. I'm going to go to my room to refresh myself. I suggest you do the same, Effie. There's nothing we can do at the moment.'

I hadn't slept in the bedroom for all that long before leaving for Luxor, but all the same I enjoyed the feeling of familiarity

240

and the sense of coming home. I unpacked my own trunk and got changed into the Arab clothing Aunt Edith had made for me. I felt much more relaxed than being buttoned up in a dress. I was downstairs before Aunt Edith and as there was no one else around and nothing for me to do I drifted to the dining room and started sampling each of the plates of food that had been brought in. I don't remember what I ate or what it tasted like; I ate mechanically and for the sake of something to do rather than because I was hungry.

Aunt Edith didn't come down until early afternoon. By then I'd paced every inch of downstairs and outside; I'd taken one book after another from the library and read none of them; I'd sat poised with a pencil over a clean sheet of paper and made not a mark. Aunt Edith came and sat in the garden with a book of poetry open on her lap. When I walked passed her on one of my circuits round the garden I noticed it was upside down.

We heard the men come back late afternoon. We both jumped to our feet but stood rooted to the spot; I know I was terrified of what they had to say. Uncle Gryffyn and Marcus came through the French windows, and I could tell by their walk and the way their shoulders drooped that they didn't have any good news. They both slumped down onto the seats, and both gave a deep sigh.

'They managed to locate Constable Hasan, that's the name of your tall policeman with the golden tooth, Effie.'

'But that's good news, isn't it Gryffyn?'

'He's not talking. Not yet, anyway. All he does is grin and shrug his shoulders, apparently. They're going to question him through the night; they won't let him rest. They're hoping to wear him down. I suspect he's very loyal and won't snitch on the rest of the gang easily.'

'Give me five minutes with him and he'll talk.' Marcus sounded fierce but by the look of him he couldn't raise a smile never mind a fist. The two men looked exhausted. I doubted they'd had any proper sleep for ages.

'What about Captain Karim? Have they found him? Aunt Edith and I have a theory about him, don't we?' I looked at her, silently pleading with her to tell them; it would sound much better coming from her than from me.

'We were wondering whether Captain Karim is related to Commandant Karim after all.' Uncle Gryffyn winced at the name. 'If he is then that might explain why he has kidnapped your daughter, Gryffyn. To make you suffer as perhaps he and his family have done since the Commandant's fall from grace.'

Uncle Gryffyn nodded and looked down at his hands that lay curled tightly on his lap. 'I'd thought of that and have been making some enquiries today. You were right all along, Effie. He's not to be trusted and is doubtless the leader of this kidnapping gang. Commandant Karim was indeed his father and...'

'Was?' Aunt Edith interrupted.

Uncle Gryffyn raised his eyes from his lap and stared into the distance. 'Commandant Karim committed suicide a few months after Evelyn died. His son found him. Captain Karim was that son.'

There was a few moments' silence as Aunt Edith and I took in that piece of information. Then I asked, 'But why has he waited so long? And why has he kidnapped Beattie rather than you?'

Uncle Gryffyn continued to look into the air rather than at me. 'Apparently his mother died six months ago. Perhaps she told him what had really happened, and she demanded revenge on her deathbed. We may never know. But Captain Karim knew that the best way to hurt me was to hurt the person I loved most in the world. He certainly got that right.'

'Where is Captain Karim?' It came out as a whisper.

'He hasn't been found yet, Effie. But he will be. Every police station in Egypt has been alerted, as have the airports and ports.' No one said it but we must all have been thinking that he must be found before it was too late; too late for Beattie.

I went to my room as soon as possible after the evening meal. We'd run out of things to say but I found the silence unbearable; I couldn't even get a word out of the girl in the mirror. I lay on top of the bed and pulled at a piece of thread that had worked loose on the coverlet. I was surprised when there was a knock on my door; it was Aunt Edith.

'Have you come to tuck me in and tell me a story?'

'Would you like me to?' One of the things I had always dreamed of was someone who would read to me, tuck me in and kiss me good night. But I wasn't going to admit that to Aunt Edith, so I shook my head. 'I don't think I can bear to just sit around tomorrow. I wondered if you'd like to go and get the sketch book you say you dropped at El Lisht?'

'Shouldn't we stay here? Just in case?'

'Gryffyn agrees nothing is going to happen tomorrow morning, even if they manage to make your policeman talk, which doesn't seem likely.'

'He's not my policeman. I hate him!'

'Hate is a very destructive and exhausting emotion, I find.'

'You surely don't expect me to love him?'

'That is what the Bible would have us do, but no, I don't expect you to love him but don't become so full of hate and bitterness that you leave no room for compassion and tenderness.' She pulled my hand away from the thread I was still picking at. 'So, shall we go to El Lisht tomorrow?'

I nodded. Why not? It would, as Aunt Edith said, be better than sitting around fretting and fuming.

=======

243

We left straight after breakfast, Aunt Edith driving as we didn't want to use one of the men who could be of service to Uncle Gryffyn. I sat in the front next to her and took absolutely no notice of the scenery that we were passing. I felt a little bit guilty leaving the men, but Uncle Gryffyn had tousled my hair before I left and Marcus had wished me luck in finding my sketch book. Neither of them looked as though they'd slept. How much longer could they go on like that before they collapsed?

When I realised the car had stopped, I looked out of the window and didn't recognise a thing. 'I don't think this is where we stopped last time. Or maybe it is. I don't really know.' We got out of the car, put on our sun hats and Aunt Edith raised her parasol. I walked uncertainly to my right then to my left, trying to find something familiar.

Aunt Edith strode towards a ruin that was on a bit of a hill. 'Let's climb to the top of this; you'll have a better view.' I hurried after her and only caught up with her on top of a stone block that had been part of a wall of the building that had once stood here. 'Turn in a circle and see if you can see something you remember.'

I did as she said and turned slowly around. 'We had lunch in the ruins of a building, and I remember Marcus pointing out those two pyramids. They were nearer than they are now and more to our left.' Aunt Edith nodded her approval, scrambled off the stone and walked carefully in the direction that would hopefully lead us to where we had had the picnic. The ground seemed more littered with debris than I remembered, and we both stumbled on a number of occasions. We passed the mouth of a tunnel. 'Maybe this is the entrance to the chamber Marcus and I went into.' I veered towards it and carefully stepped into the darkness, but only a few steps. I couldn't explain but I knew this wasn't the right one. A beam of light suddenly cut through the blackness and moved about, causing shadows to writhe like

244

demons on the walls. Aunt Edith had had the foresight to bring a torch. 'No, this isn't the one.'

We spent a good hour traipsing around, but I just couldn't find our picnic spot. Aunt Edith sat down on a fallen pillar and indicated that I should join her. She handed me a canteen of water that she had brought with her in her enormous shoulder bag. 'I think we'll have to admit defeat, Effie. I'm getting weary and I think we should go back now. Perhaps we can come with Marcus another day, when ... when things are back to normal.' I had to agree. I was feeling tired and also a little bit peckish. Aunt Edith climbed to the top of a pile of rocks, pinpointed where the car was and started walking in that direction. I occasionally peeped into a tunnel or around the broken-down walls of a building but I found neither the chamber nor the picnic site.

The car was like an oven and although the car had a blower, all it did was blast hot air into our faces. As we drove away, I noticed another track a bit further along going off at an angle back into the necropolis. I nearly didn't say anything but as we passed the entrance to the track I said, 'I think that's where Marcus went.' Aunt Edith carried on driving for at least two minutes before stopping and turning around. 'We're here now. Let's just spend ten minutes looking and if you don't recognise anywhere, we'll go home.'

We drove down the track and I knew immediately where we'd parked and when I got out, I knew where to go. I led the way and within just a few minutes we came to the ruins where we had had our lunch. I pointed out where each of us had sat. 'Omar sat over there. Beattie asked him to join us, but he wouldn't. Look, there're the two pyramids.' I stood for a moment, remembering, then started off down the slope. 'And this is the way to the burial chamber.'

I was so keen to get there that I didn't look where I was going and slipped off a stone and turned my ankle. I yelped in pain and sat down heavily onto the ground. Aunt Edith came rushing over and squatted down beside me. 'Oh, you silly girl. Let me feel.' She rubbed her hands up the sides of my ankle and told me to wiggle my toes, which I was able to do with gritted teeth. 'I don't think you've broken it, just sprained it. It's a good job I bought my parasol; you can use it as a walking stick.' She helped me up and although the parasol sunk deeply into the sand, it did support me enough for me to hobble about. 'Let's get back to the car.'

It was then that I heard it. I stood still and listened, holding up my hand to Aunt Edith to stop her and silence her. There it was again. 'Is that singing?' Aunt Edith tilted her head, the better to listen and then nodded. She moved her head from side to side. 'It's coming from over there. You stay here. I'll go and see.' There was no way on this earth I was going to stay there so I followed as quickly as I could and I managed to keep up because she was walking slowly, stopping every few steps to listen. Eventually we came to a tunnel entrance, and we could hear the singing clearly.

Heaven, I'm in Heaven
And my heart beats so that I can hardly speak.
And I seem to dah di dah di dah di daaaah,
When we're out together dancing cheek to cheek.

The voice was rough and out of tune.

But it was unmistakably Beattie's.

I wanted to rush in, but Aunt Edith held up her hand and put her finger to her lips. She didn't say anything, but I nodded my understanding that we needed to be careful that there was no one else in there. She carefully put down her bag on the ground, put her hand into an inside pocket and pulled out a gun.

Chapter 35

Beattie

I was dancing. The great glass sphere that spun above our heads threw out fragments of light that dropped over us like diamonds. Marcus had his arms tight around me and he was nuzzling my ear. They were playing one of my favourite songs and I sang along quietly.

Heaven, I'm in Heaven
And my heart beats so that I can hardly speak.
And I seem to dah di dah di dah di daaaah,
When we're out together dancing cheek to cheek.

Marcus laughed and sang the line I couldn't remember in his wonderful baritone voice.

And I seem to find the happiness I seek,
When we're out together dancing cheek to cheek.

'We're not though, are we?'
'Not what?'
'Dancing cheek to cheek. You're nuzzling my ear.'
I laughed and laughed and laughed; my laughter echoing off the walls. It sounded like the whole world was laughing. Then there was a loud bang and the music and laughter stopped. I was no longer in Marcus's arms but standing alone in the huge ballroom; it was so big I couldn't see the walls. The glass ball was still slowly spinning above my head but now it was shedding drops of blood onto me like confetti. I wanted to brush them off, but my arms wouldn't move, and I realised that I'd turned to stone. I wasn't surprised; it was inevitable really. I'd turned into one of the ancient Egyptian statues that Marcus found so fascinating. Now maybe he'd love me. I laughed as

much as I was able to as a statue, when it occurred to me that I was the exact opposite to Pygmalion. She had been transformed from a statue to a real woman for her besotted creator to adore, whilst I had been transformed from a living woman to a statue.

Could statues still hear? There was something buzzing in my ears. No, not an insect but words. Words trying to get inside my ear drum. I listened hard but they could only hover outside of my head; something was blocking their entrance. They kept trying and eventually a word managed to creep in.

'Beatrice.'

I may only have been a statue, but I recognised my own name. Who was saying my name? There was no one in the room with me. The word didn't sound as if it had come out of Marcus's mouth. It was too high and light, like a feather on the breeze. Was it Mama calling my name? Of course, I wasn't a statue, I was dead! This was heaven and my mother had come to show me the way. But where was she? I should be able to see her, shouldn't I? She'd be in white, shining robes and she'd be so happy to see me. I was overcome by a wave of tiredness. I'd have a little sleep and when I woke up maybe she'd be there.

What on earth was happening? My body was bouncing around but not of my own volition. My skin was burning; perhaps I was in hell. That would be a turn up for the books, wouldn't it? I wondered what I had done to warrant going down rather than up but I suppose any of my misdemeanours could have angered God. Perhaps Mama was down here as well; after all she had had an affair and God wouldn't have thought very highly of that, would he? All the bouncing made me tired so I decided to have another little sleep in the hope that when I woke up it would have stopped.

My hope was realised. My hearing had come back, and I lay trying to work out what the swooshing noise I could hear was. A breeze played on my cheeks, but it was too warm to be refreshing. The swooshing noise changed in tone, but I still couldn't decide what it was. It was beginning to annoy me, and I wished I couldn't hear again. I don't know why I was so tired, perhaps that is what hell is like: constant unidentified noise, shaking and tiredness.

Someone was prodding me. If I'd had the energy I would have pushed them away but as it was all I could do was go back to sleep.

This surely must be Heaven. Hell wouldn't be so white and bright. So bright I had to close my eyes.

'Beattie. Beattie?' Someone was calling my name. I recognised the voice but couldn't think who it was. The light wasn't too bright this time and I was able to open my eyes slightly.

'She's opened her eyes! Nurse!' I quickly closed them again hoping the noise would cease. But there was chattering and pummelling and pricking and it was exhausting, and I just wanted it all to stop.

I watched fascinated as the clear liquid dripped from the upturned bottle into a smaller cylinder then down a tube. I followed the tube until it disappeared into my arm. I knew exactly what it was and where I was. I moved my head slowly to look around the room. Daddy was slumped in a chair, his head thrown back and his mouth open. His face was more lined than I remembered it. He looked pale and thin. I didn't want to wake him, so I just lay there looking at him, remembering why I was here and why he was there. The door opened softly and a big, round, brown face peeped in. She grinned when she saw that I was awake and came in quietly.

'*Je suis content que vous soyez reveille. Pouvez-vous gérer une tasse de thé?*'

I didn't understand everything she said but I recognised *tasse de thé* and realised that a cup of tea was the thing I wanted most in the world. I nodded, pointed at my father, and put up two fingers.

The nurse had returned with the tea, sat me up, made me comfortable and gone away to fetch the doctor before my father stirred. He jerked awake and looked around him confused. His eyes swept passed me, stopped then slowly returned to my face. I smiled at him. 'Hullo Daddy, good sleep?'

He jumped to his feet and came quickly to my side but then didn't know what to do. I had tubes coming out from everywhere and I think he was frightened of pulling some of them out. So he just stood, tears streaming down his face, his mouth opening and closing but uttering no sound until he let out one sob, then another. They must have managed to put some liquid into me because I had enough to make tears to join his wetting the sheet and the floor. We eventually stopped and he dragged his chair so that it was touching the side of the bed and took my hand in his. 'Oh, my darling, darling girl. I am so sorry this has happened to you. It's all my fault. How are you felling? Your hair will grow, and you can't even notice your ear. But how you must have suffered. If I ever get my hands on that man, I swear to God, I'll kill him.'

I laughed, which made him stop gabbling. 'I think I went a little crazy towards the end when I thought I was going to die. In fact, at one point, I was convinced I was dead.' I wriggled my fingers and my toes. 'But I think I feel alright. How did you find me?'

'I didn't I'm so very sorry to say. But I think those who did would prefer to tell you. Are you up to having visitors?'

'Visitors? I'll say if she's up to having more visitors.' He was a huge man with hair redder than mine and a Scottish accent that was as broad now as it had been when he'd left his homeland many years previously. 'Do you know who I am, Miss Trevethan?'

'Of course I do, you're Mr Macintosh, consultant at the Victoria Hospital, where I assume I currently am. You came to dinner only a few weeks ago with your lovely wife called

Fiona, who is far too good for you and apparently you are the worst doctor in Cairo. Or is it the best? I forget now.'

'They didn't steal your rudeness, more's the pity. Let's take a look at you. Gryffyn, if you don't mind?'

My father reluctantly let go of my hand and left the room, but I could see him hovering outside the doors and heard him talking quietly to someone. Mr Macintosh did all the things that doctors do and he gave a grunt of approval as he wrote something on the board hooked over the bottom of the bed. 'Physically you're recovering very well. But Beattie, the mental scars will run very deep and mustn't be underestimated. I'm going to insist you see a psychiatrist when you get out of here.'

'Which will be when, oh he who must be obeyed?'

'A few days more, maybe a week. You went a long time without food and water, and I want to make sure there are no hidden consequences. Your head and ear are healing very well. I understand there was a bottle of iodine left with you?'

'Yes. He obviously wanted me to die a slow death from starvation rather than a quick one from an infection.' Mr Macintosh said something under his breath that I couldn't quite hear but I thought he said, 'Bastard.'

'You can come in now, Gryffyn.'

He came in looking worried. 'Is everything alright? You were a long time.'

'Wheesht, man. You'd not want me to rush, now would you? She's doing very well, although there's nothing I can do for her cheekiness and disrespect of the medical profession. I'll allow visitors this afternoon for ten minutes only. I suggest you go home, Gryffyn, have a bath, get changed and come back after you've had a decent lunch. Your daughter isn't going anywhere and to be honest, man, you're beginning to smell.' I snorted a laugh, Mr Macintosh grinned, and Daddy looked embarrassed.

'Are you sure, Beattie? I won't be long. There's a policeman guarding you day and night, so you are quite safe. Yes, yes, Mac, I'm going. I'll be back after lunch.' He bent to kiss me on both cheeks and my forehead, which made the tears spring to my eyes, but he went without seeing them. I agreed with Mr Macintosh that I would try and eat some thin soup. The morning was spent having it spooned into my mouth, a sponge bath and my sheets and nightdress changed as a result and then a sleep from sheer exhaustion.

When I awoke the room was full of people. I felt quite panic-stricken until I focussed on each one. My father was back in his chair and Aunt Edith was sitting in another one on the other side of the bed. Marcus was standing with his back to the window staring at me and Effie, God bless her, was sitting on the edge of the bed stroking the back of one of my hands. There was a bit of an uproar when they realised I was awake with everyone talking at the same time and everyone trying to touch me.

'*Silence! Rappelez-vous, dix minutes seulement.*' The nurse held up both hands with her fingers and thumbs outstretched in case anyone didn't catch her meaning. Even Effie, who didn't know a word of French, couldn't fail to understand.

'What I really want to know is, who found me and how? Can someone tell me in ten minutes?'

They all looked at each other then Aunt Edith nodded at Effie. 'You tell her, dear.'

Effie took a deep breath. 'Someone else can tell you what happened during the days before we found you, but on the day Aunt Edith suggested we went to El Lisht to look for my sketch book. Do you remember, I dropped it in the burial chamber and the tall policeman with the gold tooth wouldn't let me pick it up?'

'I found it, Effie. It was in the chamber where they put me, so I knew exactly where I was being held.'

252

'We only went because we didn't know what we could do to help. Anyway, Aunt Edith drove and at first, we didn't park in the same place as Marcus had when we all went and I wasn't able to, what's the word?'

'Orient yourself,' Aunt Edith chipped in.

'Yes, I wasn't able to orient myself. So we decided to go home. It makes me go cold and my stomach hurts when I think we could have just gone and never found you. Anyway, we were going home when I recognised the track Marcus had driven down, so we went there and found where we had parked, and I knew where everything was. I found where we'd eaten then I remembered the way to the chamber. I fell and twisted my ankle.' She held up her bandaged limb and I tutted sympathetically. 'Aunt Edith gave me her parasol as a walking stick. Ruined it I did. It was then we heard singing.'

'Do you remember, Beatrice? You were singing that song, *Cheek to Cheek* by Fred Astaire.'

'Was I? Goodness. I wonder why?'

'It's a good job you were, otherwise we'd never have found you 'cos we were going to go back because of my ankle.' She held it up again just to be sure I'd understood. 'Aunt Edith had a gun, Beattie! I was right amazed. Anyway, she went in first in case Captain Karim, you do know it was him that kidnapped you?' I nodded and indicated that she should continue. I wanted to know the end before the ten minutes was up. 'He wasn't there, though. In fact, no one knows where he is. So instead of shooting him, which I'm sure she would have done without blinking an eyelid, she shot the padlock clean off the gate.' I didn't remember the singing, but I remembered the loud bang. 'It was really loud and made us all go a bit deaf, I think. We couldn't get you to hear us and you kept laughing. You were lying on a mattress, and do you know what? Aunt Edith dragged you all the way to the car. It was a bit bumpy, and we were worried we'd hurt you, but you slept most of the way. I

253

wasn't much help, but I carried her bag and tried to remove the larger stones from her path. It took ages, didn't it?'

Aunt Edith nodded. 'Effie was a real soldier. Her ankle must have been hurting but she didn't complain once. We got you to the car eventually. I laid you on the back seat and drove you straight here.'

'That must have been the swooshing sounds I heard. The tyres on the sand then on the road.' There was a moment's pause. 'So it was sheer luck that you went to El Lisht that day but thank God you did.' Everyone nodded in agreement. I was about to ask Daddy to tell me everything that had happened since I was taken but our ten minutes was up, and they were all herded out. As she left, Aunt Edith put a folded piece of paper into my hand and told me to read it later on. Marcus was the last out; he smiled at me, but I don't know whether it was a smile of pity or of love.

Chapter 36

Effie

My world was shattered after a jubilant evening meal celebrating Beattie's return to the land of the living. After I had gone up for the night, Aunt Edith came into my bedroom. I was sitting at the dressing table brushing my hair and grinning at the girl in the mirror, who looked as pleased as punch.

'Effie dear, I need to speak to you. Put the brush down and listen to me.'

She sounded so serious that my stomach crunched up and my heart speeded up. 'Have I done something wrong?'

'No dear, but I need to clear up a misunderstanding. I should have said something days ago, when you first told me, but I don't know, it never seemed an appropriate time.'

'When I said something? What did I say? I don't understand.' She took a deep breath and looked me in the eye, which made me feel very nervous. 'What is it Aunt? What misunderstanding?'

'When you overheard me telling Beatrice about her mother and the child,' she held her hand up to stop me interrupting with more apologies and excuses for my listening to their conversation, 'you heard something that made you think that perhaps you might be that baby?'

She seemed to be waiting for me to answer so I nodded. 'It was because the father was an Egyptian and the mother British and the baby was shipped to England. The dates worked out. I was left at the orphanage in July, and they were sure I was only a couple of months old, which meant that I was born in May. That's why they named me May. It all fitted.'

'I know it did, dear, and I'm so sorry to be the one to dash your hopes.'

Aunt Edith's face made my gut tighten even more and I felt my hands curl into fists. She took another deep breath and said slowly and clearly, 'Evelyn's baby was a boy.'

'A boy?' It came out as a screech. 'Are you sure?' Aunt Edith nodded. She took one of my hands and tried to relax the fingers, but they were clenched too tightly. 'Are you sure?' I said again, in a quieter voice. 'You said the baby was a girl. Didn't you?'

'No, Effie. I think I always referred to the baby as an it, not a he, and certainly never as a she. I found it easier to think of him as an object not a human being. It must have been after you went upstairs that I told Beatrice what became of him.'

'Did he die?' He was nothing to me, but I was interested; after all, he was a cast off, unwanted, just like me.

'No, he didn't die. I'll tell you about him one day, but not now. I'm sorry, my dear, I know you long for a family you can call your own but don't ever forget that we all love you as much as if you were part of our family, perhaps even more so.' She hugged me and patted me awkwardly on the shoulder as if that would compensate for shattering my dreams.

I looked at the girl in the mirror, who looked as devastated as I felt. Her eyes were black circles in a pale face, not white, of course, but a grey colour. 'Billy was right after all. Ma was a whore, and Pa's a greasy furriner off one of them tankers. You're the result of a night's fucking in a dark alley. You're a bastard child. You never had loving parents who weren't able to look after you, they just didn't want you. He probably doesn't even know you exist.' The girl in the mirror blushed at my language but didn't look away. 'You're an embarrassment and don't deserve to have dreams. You need to go home, back to the only family you're ever likely to have.' The girl in the mirror nodded in agreement; the tears streaming down her cheeks. 'Dreams ain't for people like you. You've had an adventure, now go home to Ma and Pa Foster and the other unwanted children.'

I slept badly that night and woke up feeling bruised and the unhappiest I have ever felt. Despite Aunt Edith saying they all loved me, I knew they wouldn't want me here now; I was an unwanted guest and would just be in the way. I felt so stupid thinking that I could be part of their family.

Beattie was still in hospital and would remain there for a week or so, they said. Now I had decided to go home I wanted to go as soon as possible; what was the point in staying any longer? I was nothing but a burden and they'd all be glad to get rid of me so that they could focus on getting Beattie better. I still had a few pennies in my purse but nowhere near enough to buy an aeroplane ticket.

I dressed in one of my Sunday dresses and carefully brushed my hair; I didn't want to look like a scruffy street urchin. As I was going down the stairs Uncle Gryffyn came out of his study. He was humming and he walked as if he had springs on the bottom of his shoes. He looked years younger than he had when Beattie had been missing. He saw me standing on the stairs and gave a grin that made him look as young as Marcus. 'Effie, my dear girl! Did you sleep well? I'm just about to go into the office but Edith's going to get together some things for Beattie; you know, girl's things. Will you help her? We'll meet up for lunch at Shepheard's then all go on to the hospital. Come on, chop chop! Go and have your breakfast.'

How I loved this man. How I wished he was my real uncle. Or my father. I remembered how kind he'd been when we'd sat in the garden, and he'd gently told me how unlikely it was that my mother was an Egyptian princess. Did he know about my silly belief that his dead wife, his deceitful dead wife, was my mother? I hoped not. My mouth was dry, and my question came out as a croak. 'Can I speak to you first?'

His smile slid from his face; he must have realised that there was something wrong. 'Of course. Shall we go into the garden?' He held out his hand and although I didn't feel I should take it, I did because I liked the feel of his big hand encompassing my small one. We sat under the chatterbox tree. There was a lot of conversation going on that morning; there was a lot to talk about. We sat facing each other. He still held one of my hands. 'What's the matter, Effie?'

I couldn't look at him. If I did, I'd cry.

I cried anyway.

He passed me one of his handkerchiefs, which had a G embroidered in the corner and smelled of cigars. When I'd wiped my nose and eyes, I slipped it into my pocket. I suppose you could say I stole it, but I didn't think he'd mind. 'I should go home.'

He put a finger under my chin and lifted my head so that I had to look at him, not at the pattern on the skirt of my dress. 'Yes, you will have to eventually. But not right now. Another few weeks here won't hurt you, will they? Are you worried about missing school? Are you missing your foster family?'

Neither. I nodded but didn't say which. He looked at me for a long time then gave a sad smile. 'I suppose you will have to go back. We'll miss you. We'll call at Cook's this afternoon and see about buying an aeroplane ticket.'

'I'll pay you back. I get pocket money every week. I'll send it to you.'

He stroked my hair and wiped a tear that had crept down my cheek. 'We'll see. Go and get something to eat.' I got up and as I turned to go, he said, 'You're very special, you know. Very special indeed.'

I wasn't hungry but managed to eat some scrambled eggs, bacon, toast and a pear, whose juices dripped onto my dress, adding to the stain of my tears. He'd said I was special. Just the thought of it made my eyes water again. I went upstairs to

258

change. I ignored the girl in the mirror. I didn't want to see or speak to her; we were no comfort to each other.

When I went back down Uncle Gryffyn had obviously told Aunt Edith about me wanting to go home. As soon as she saw me, she came over and hugged me. I didn't think I'd have any tears left but a few escaped. They were absorbed by her colourful, stripy top; they didn't show. 'Is it my fault? Is it because I told you that the baby was a boy and so couldn't have been you?'

I shook my head. I nodded. I shrugged. I mumbled, 'Doesn't matter. Got to go sometime.'

She gave me an extra tight hug then released me. 'Come on. Let's go and get a few things together for Beatrice.' She didn't seem bothered that I would be leaving soon, which made me all the more sure it was the right thing to do. 'Then on the way to Shepheard's we'll pop into the Anglo-Egyptian bookshop and see if we can find a book that Beatrice won't have read.'

'She likes Agatha Christie.'

Aunt Edith beamed at me. 'Excellent. We'll see if they've got a new one in. Otherwise, we'll just buy one that takes our fancy; she's bound not to remember who dunnit.'

'Who done what? And isn't it who did it?' I was surprised at her poor grammar, but she just laughed.

It didn't take us long to put some things into a small case: some clean night dresses, underwear, a shawl, handkerchiefs, bathroom stuff and cosmetics. Uncle Gryffyn had told us we still mustn't go out unescorted because of the gangs that were still demonstrating and because Captain Karim hadn't been caught, so Omar drove us to the bookshop, which was in what Omar said was down-town Cairo. It was a three-storey building and was, unsurprisingly, absolutely crammed with books. Aunt Edith explained that the Arabic language books were kept in the basement and the English language books on the ground floor, whilst upstairs was where writers, artists, clever men and the like met to discuss stuff, books I suppose.

The room we wanted was probably large but seemed small as each wall was lined from floor to ceiling with shelves that were bending under the weight of the books; there must have been millions of them. How on earth were we going to find just one Agatha Christie book? A small Arab man solved our dilemma and on Aunt Agatha's request, led us to a section where the novels were kept. We couldn't see any Agatha Christie, so Aunt Edith selected *Emma* by Jane Austen. She asked me if I'd ever read it and looked surprised when I shook my head. 'You must put it on your Must Read list, Effie. Any book by Jane Austen is excellent but this one is my favourite. I'm sure Beatrice won't mind reading it again.' I didn't like to tell her that I didn't have a Must Read list.

When we got to Shepheard's Uncle Gryffyn was already there, sitting on the veranda and drinking something long and cold. He ordered a jug of lemonade for us and as the two grown-ups chatted, I just watched the people and animals go by. I should have been enjoying the experience of sitting in such a wonderful place with two wonderful people, but I felt dejected and dull. In a few days' time I would be back in London, and all this would be a fading memory. I wish I'd got my sketch book; I could have drawn the street scenes, so I didn't forget them. Was I wrong to have asked to go home? No. They were lovely people and I think they liked me, but they had no duty to take care of me or make me their responsibility. My home was in London. Grey, cold, damp London. A horrid thought occurred to me. Although my dream of having an Egyptian mother was gone, I still wanted to learn as much as I could about Egypt. What if I was banned for life from the British Museum? The very thought made me even more dejected, and I actually groaned.

Aunt Edith and Uncle Gryffyn stopped talking and looked at me. 'Don't look so sad, Effie. Things are never as bad as you think they're going to be. Come on, let's have some lunch then go and see Beattie.' Uncle Gryffyn stood up and held his hand out to me.

'Will Marcus be joining us. Gryffyn?'

'No. He's already there.' And for some reason he laughed.

Chapter 37

Beattie

I was exhausted and it was still only morning. I was just about to do as the nurse ordered and get back to sleep when the door opened, and Marcus took a tentative step inside. He looked around guiltily. 'Can I come in?'

'They've done everything to me they need to for a while. They had me up at God knows what time this morning, it was still dark for crying out loud. I've been bathed, injected, fed and forced to walk down the corridor and then all the way back again. I feel worse now than I did when I first came in here. Have you come to steal me away?'

Marcus blushed. 'No, but ...' He hovered at the bottom of the bed.

'No, but?' He still hovered. I realised that he was wearing his best suit, and his hair was plastered down and not sticking up as I liked it. 'Are you going to an interview or something? You look very .... smart.' He shook his head and kept opening his mouth but didn't say anything. 'Come and sit here and tell me all about it.' He walked to the side of the bed slowly as if it was the last place he wanted to be. 'Oh, for goodness' sake, Marcus, I'm not going to eat you. Whatever is the matter?'

He sat on the side of my bed and tucked my hair behind my ear; the ear which had no lobe. 'You don't need to hide it.'

'Yes, I do.' I shook my head so that my hair fell over my ear again. My hand was lying palm down on the coverlet. Marcus stroked each finger slowly. My toes curled and my heart rate increased. I studied him as he watched his own finger caress each of mine. He really was the most handsome man I knew. It wasn't just his looks I loved, I wasn't that shallow, but they added to his attraction. Why was he so nervous? Had he come to tell me some bad news? He wasn't acting as if any of the family were hurt. It was more as if he was embarrassed

262

about telling me something. Why was he in a suit? The last time he'd worn it was at one of his friend's wedding. Oh my God, was he getting married? To someone else? It was Grace, wasn't it? Was I, after all, nothing more to him than just a friend? I gasped and went to pull my hand away, but he held on to it.

'I'm sorry, was I hurting you?' He looked concerned at the expression on my face, which was, I'm sure, one of shock, disbelief and grief. I managed to shake my head. 'It's a good thing that he didn't cut off one of your fingers.' What? This wasn't what I expected him to say. He gently lifted the ring finger on my left hand. 'Especially this one.'

I suddenly felt annoyed. What was he doing here if he was about to get married to one of my best friends? I managed to snatch my hand away. 'I'm also glad he didn't cut any of my fingers off. Why are you here, Marcus? Have you got something to tell me? Are you getting married?'

He looked puzzled then gave a little laugh. 'Well, I hope to. I'm sorry, I had my speech all planned but I'm making a real mess of it, aren't I?' He fumbled in his pocket and held out his hand. Nestled in his palm was a ring. 'I'm not sure if it will fit.' It was an old ring, ancient in fact. It was a plain gold band, apart from a lapis lazuli stone held in place by the petals of a golden lotus flower. There was something engraved into the stone. I leaned forward to try and make out the pattern and laughed out loud when I realised that it was the eye of Horus.

'Have you stolen it? Where on earth did you get it?'

He grinned and looked like the Marcus I knew and loved. The Marcus who wasn't going to marry Grace. The Marcus who was going to marry me. Wasn't he? He hadn't actually asked yet. 'I found it a couple of years ago. I suppose I did steal it. There was a whole casket of them; I didn't think anyone would notice if I took it. I'm afraid it didn't belong to anyone special. Until now.'

263

'Why did you take it, though?'

'I knew I wanted to give it to you as an ...' he took a deep breath, 'as an engagement ring.'

'You've had it for two years and you've only just asked me? Do you mean to say that I've been fretting and dithering for two years because I didn't know if you even liked me? Oh Marcus!'

He had the decency to look sheepish. He slid it onto my finger. It fitted almost perfectly.

I took it off and handed it back to him.

He looked puzzled then dejected. 'Is your answer "no" then?'

I wasn't in the right position to shake him, so I punched him on his upper arm instead. 'You haven't actually asked me yet.' The blood, which had drained from his face, flooded back. Then he slid off the bed and onto the floor. I heard his knee hit the tiles hard and he winced in pain. I nearly took pity on him and told him to get up, but I had waited so long for this moment, I wanted to make the most of it.

'Beatrice – do you have a middle name?'

'Catherine after my maternal grandmother.'

'Beatrice Catherine Trevethan, will you be a real sport and marry this old duffer and spend the rest of your life going on adventures and digging up treasures?'

'I seem to recall you asking me to marry you when you were about six years old. I can't remember what I answered.'

'It was you who asked me, and I said "certainly not" if I remember correctly. I was a very stupid boy in those days. Will you, then? Will you marry me so that I can get up?'

I pretended to consider. 'Are you in a lot of discomfort down there?'

He nodded.

I pretended to consider some more. 'Oh, all right then. Seeing as you've asked so nicely.'

It took a while to find the ring that had slipped under a crease in the coverlet. He put it back on my finger and we both grinned at each other.

Then a thought occurred to me.

'You're not asking me to marry you because you feel sorry for me, are you? Or in some way responsible for what happened? I don't want that, Marcus. I only want to marry you if ....'

'If what, you goose?'

'If you love me.'

His grin turned into a raucous laugh and tears ran down his cheeks. 'Love you? I've loved you ever since, well, ever since I can remember.'

I felt a surge of relief course through my body. Relief tinged with anger. 'Why the hell didn't you say so sooner?'

'I just didn't think someone as beautiful, funny, clever and talented as you would ever love someone like me. May I kiss you?'

Before he could do the deed Mr Macintosh burst into the room, stopping in his tracks when he saw Marcus. 'Ah, Mr Dunwoody. A bit early for visiting. Out you go. Come back later. I need to make this young lady's life a misery for the next half an hour or so. Go on, shoo.'

Nothing Mr Macintosh did or said stopped me smiling. All those years of uncertainty were forgotten; all I remembered were his eyes as he'd told me he loved me. And his grimace as he'd hauled himself off his knees.

'You need to stay here for a few days more, but you should then be able to go home as long as you promise to take it easy until I say otherwise, eat proper meals, do regular exercise and generally behave as a decorous invalid rather than a wild, ill-mannered tom boy that I know you to be.' Before he left, he kissed me on the cheek and whispered, 'Congratulations. I'm glad someone is finally taking you off that dusty old shelf.'

265

Marcus may have returned but I was fast asleep, waking only when the nurse tapped me on the shoulder when lunch arrived. For a moment I couldn't think why my left hand felt so peculiar but then I remembered. I held it out and, whereas most engaged women admired the glint and size of the diamonds in their engagement ring, I marvelled at the blueness of the lapis lazuli and wondered who had worn it originally and where she was buried. I knew all women wore jewellery in ancient times and it pleased me that the ring may just as well have been the possession of a farmer's daughter as a pharaoh's.

No sooner had I finished my lunch when the family came in, brought up in the rear by Marcus, who had returned to looking charmingly dishevelled. No one said anything about my new status, so I assumed Marcus hadn't told them. There was general chatter and they seemed pleased to hear I would be going home hopefully within the week. Everyone, that is, apart from Effie, who looked more and more glum as the visit progressed. I held out my left hand to take hers in mine. 'What's the matter, Effie? You don't seem to be your usual self.'

Rather than answer my question she burst into an unexpected grin. 'He's gone and done it, then? I told you, didn't I?'

There followed minutes of hugs, laughs and tears. I could tell that Daddy already knew – presumably Marcus had asked for my hand – but that Aunt Edith didn't. I couldn't help but notice that Effie's grin soon disappeared, and she hung back and didn't join in the congratulations. I raised an eyebrow at Aunt Edith, who shook her head slightly and asked me instead whether we had a date in mind. We hadn't, of course, but Marcus, in his new role as my fiancé, realised that the visit had tired me out and said that they'd leave me in peace and be back that evening.

Effie and Aunt Edith were the last to leave and as they started to go through the door I called out, 'Effie, do you have a minute? I won't keep her for long, Aunt Edith.' Aunt Edith gave a small nod and closed the door behind her, leaving Effie standing looking like a schoolgirl caught in the act of doing something naughty. 'I haven't had much of a chance to speak to you recently. Are you alright? Has something happened? You seem so .... so sad.'

Effie shook her head angrily. 'Nah. I've been stupid, that's all. I'm sure your aunt or father will tell you how stupid. I'm right glad you're safe and that Mr Dunwoody came to his senses. I'm ever so grateful to you and your family for looking after me but I have to go home now. I want to go home. It's where I belong.'

She hadn't come any nearer and after her little speech, before I had time to tell her how much I loved her, how much we all loved her, she'd gone.

The note Aunt Edith had left me after yesterday's visit had told me about Effie's belief that she and I were half-sisters. My aunt said she was going to have to tell her the truth that night, which she must have done. Oh, my poor, sweet Effie. I could only imagine how she'd felt thinking she would be part of a family, but I couldn't begin to imagine what she'd felt when told that it was not to be.

Aunt Edith had finished her note by telling me her plan. I wondered how Effie would feel about it. I found out a few days later when she burst into my room like a small dust devil, throwing back the door so hard it crashed into the wall.

'Did you know? Did you?' Gone was the glum expression, the air of dejection. Her eyes were bright, her cheeks flushed, and her grin stretched from ear to ear. 'You knew, didn't you?

'Knew what, dear?' I pretended to look puzzled.

'She never said nothing when we went to Cooks that day when she bought the tickets and it was only this morning, after a telegram arrived that she told me.'

'Told you what dear?' I honestly thought she was going to explode with excitement.

'She told me that she had actually bought return tickets. We're coming back, Beattie. After she's ....'

'After she's, what?'

'After she's sorted out the paperwork.'

'What paperwork, Effie?'

Her face was wet from tears and snot, and she couldn't get the words out. I passed her a handkerchief and she wiped her face, leaving patches of wet and smears of mucus but I don't think I'd ever seen her looking prettier.

'What paperwork, Effie?' I said again.

She swallowed one more time then managed to whisper, 'Adoption papers.'

THE END

ACKNOWLEDGEMENTS

A writer always reads what she should have written, not what she actually has. I'm indebted to Ruth Cooper, who is a strict grammarian, an honest reviewer and a very dear friend. I'm also grateful to my writer friend Margaret Mather, who has an eagle eye for typos and has hopefully found them all. Then to another writer friend, Jacquie Rogers (https://linktr.ee/jacquierogers), for her invaluable feedback on the cover and her suggestions to improve the back cover text (which is much harder to write than the book itself!). Lastly, my thanks go to Mike Linane; the independent publishing house he runs may be small, but he is a man with a big heart and offers a wonderful opportunity for writers just like me. This is the sixth of my books he has published – long may our relationship continue.

ENJOYED *UNDER THE EYE?*

If you enjoyed reading *Under The Eye* could you please leave a review? Write as little or as much as you like, but it will mean so much to me.

KEEP IN TOUCH

Follow me on social media:

Facebook: facebook.com/marilyn.pemberton.391

Blog: writingtokeepsane.wordpress.com

Website: https://marilynpemberton.wixsite.com/author

e-mail: marilyn.pemberton@yahoo.co.uk

Printed in Great Britain
by Amazon

38512681R00158